A MISTY MOURNING

THE BEELER LARGE PRINT MYSTERY SERIES

Edited by Audrey A. Lesko

A MISTY MOURNING

RETT MACPHERSON

BEELER LARGE PRINT
Hampton Falls, New Hampshire, 2001

Library of Congress Cataloging-in-Publication Data

MacPherson, Rett.
   A misty mourning / Rett MacPherson.
     p.   cm.—(The Beeler Large Print mystery series)
   ISBN 1-57490-353-5 (hc : alk. paper)
     O'Shea, Torie (Fictitious character)—Fiction. 2. Inheritance and succession—Fiction. 3. Women genealogists—Fiction. 4. Pregnant women—Fiction. 5. Boardinghouses—Fiction. 6. West Virginia—Fiction. 7. Grandmothers—Fiction. 8. Large type books. I. Title. II. Series.

PS3563.AQ3257 M57 2001
813'.54—dc21   2001025299

Published in Large Print by arrangement with
St. Martin's Press.

BEELER LARGE PRINT
is published by
Thomas T. Beeler, Publisher
Post Office Box 659
Hampton Falls, New Hampshire 03844

Typeset in 16 point Times New Roman type.
Printed on acid-free paper, sewn and bound by
Sheridan Books in Chelsea, Michigan.

This book is dedicated to
my father,
TRUMAN "BUD" ALLEN,
who taught me to question everything.

ACKNOWLEDGMENTS

The author would like to thank the following for all of their invaluable help.

The Alternate Historians: Tom Drennan, Laurell K. Hamilton, Debbie Millitello, Marella Sands, Sharon Shinn (for all of your extra help on this particular book, especially), and Mark Sumner. We'll miss you, Nancy!

My editor Kelley Ragland. My agent Michele Rubin at Writers House, who is positive enough for both of us.

My family: Joe, for never being upset that we don't live on any normal kind of schedule. Rebekah, Elizah, and Dillon for sharing me with a whole other world.

Thank you to Dr. Michael Derosa for keeping Dillon healthy and Dr. Thomas Shaner for delivering him.

Thank you to Jean Erickson for single-handedly multiplying my reading audience by about a hundred!

And thank you to the fantastic group of fans at the University of Missouri bookstore in Columbia, Missouri, for inviting me to their wonderful Murder on Mondays!

A Misty Mourning

ONE

YOU KNOW YOU'RE PREGNANT WHEN THE ONLY TOWEL in the house that will wrap around your ever-enlarging midsection is your husband's Batman beach towel. Taking a shower in general is a fairly precarious task. And forget shaving altogether. I could barely put socks on, much less shave my legs—proof that the state of pregnancy was invented long before personal hygiene.

"I'm taking your beach towel," I said to Rudy as I shoved it into my suitcase.

"That's okay. I don't think I'll be doing much swimming while you're gone," he said. He made an exaggerated sad face. Even the ends of his brown eyes turned downward. "How long did you say you were going to be gone again?"

"Should be a week," I said. "Oh, please. Don't give me that Stan Laurel face."

"But I'll miss you," he said.

"Yeah, right. You're going to miss me getting up fifteen times in the middle of the night? You'll finally get a decent night's sleep," I said. I went over to the closet and pulled out all the maternity clothes I had, which wasn't many, took them off the hangers, and put them into the suitcase on top of Rudy's beach towel.

"Well, at least you're taking your grandmother," he said. He stood with his arms crossed on the opposite side of our bed wearing his plaid sleeping pants and a Samuel Adams beer T-shirt. His hair still stood on end. It was, after all, only six in the morning.

I'm not sure exactly why Rudy thought that if I took my grandmother on my trip to West Virginia no ill

1

would befall me, but he did. Aside from his cinematic exaggeration, he really did look worried about me.

It was June and I was due with our third child in August. I was thirty-one weeks along, and so I had a good two months to go before having to deliver this little O'Shea. While you're pregnant, everybody talks about how big your belly is and, oh, what a big baby you're carrying. Then it comes out and suddenly those same people can't get over how tiny the baby is. It makes no sense, but then, most of the time I think I could give Mother Nature a few lessons on how to run things. Just for the record, stretch marks would be nonexistent.

Now that I thought about it, the fact that I was pregnant was probably why Rudy was being overconcerned about my trip to West Virginia. He's just so darn cute.

"I don't understand why you have to go all the way to West Virginia, Torie," he said. "Why can't this be done over the phone? Or over the Internet?"

We'd just gotten Internet access at home and suddenly Rudy was a computer expert. He talked about things like modems, DNS, HTML, and jpegs. Is it me or do those things sound like exotic communicable diseases? Maybe everything can be done over the Internet, but does it *have* to be?

I'd been fighting technology tooth and nail. That's me, Torie O'Shea, confirmed cavewoman. I have Internet access at my office at the Gaheimer House, because of all the genealogy that I do for the historical society. I have no idea how any of it actually works, mind you. It comes in handy, I'll admit, but I really miss the written letter or a voice on the other end of the line.

"Well, Rudy. I guess maybe this could be done over

2

the computer. But we're dealing with a one-hundred-and-one-year-old woman. There are some people who still do things the old-fashioned way, thank God. At any rate, she requested my presence for the reading of her will and I'm going," I said.

"Why?" he asked. "It's not like she's related to you."

"She was best friends with my grandmother's mother," I said. "That's all I know. Maybe she has something that belonged to my great-grandmother and she wants to make sure that I get it."

He looked at me peculiarly. "Yes, but she's not even dead yet. She's having a reading of her will and she's not dead. If you want my opinion, that is weird." I found it a little bizarre myself, but what would it hurt for me to go? My grandmother hadn't been back to her native West Virginia since 1986. I wanted her to see it again. She was eighty-two now and you just never knew. Besides, I knew this would be a real bonding trip for us.

Rudy carried my suitcase for me down the stairs and into the living room where my grandmother sat waiting. She was early, as usual. Gertrude Crookshank, my grandmother, sat with her cane in one hand and her extremely large black vinyl purse in the other. I knew for a fact that the purse contained a wallet, a photo carrier, and a ton of Kleenex. Why she needed a purse that big for those few items, I'll never know.

Her hair was totally white now, her brown eyes appearing much darker because of it. Her cheekbones were high and wide, and she had absolutely beautiful skin. It was barely wrinkled, which she credited to good genes and Ponds cold cream.

"You ready, Gert?" I asked her. I have always called her Gert or Granny Gert.

3

"As long as I can stop and get some coffee, I'll be fine," she answered.

Rudy carried my suitcase and various other canvas bags, a cooler, and my grandmother's things out to the car while I said good-bye to my daughters. Rachel, who is nine and counting down the days, months, and years until she will be a teenager, was awake and waiting for me to come into the room. On the other hand, Mary, who would be six this fall, was snoring away.

"Don't let Granny get you into trouble," Rachel said to me. Her long straight brownish hair was matted to one side of her head and sticking straight out on the other.

"I won't," I said and kissed her on the forehead. "Try not to fight with your sister."

She rolled her eyes heavenward. "You tell *her* that," she said and pointed to Mary, who was both snoring and drooling at the same time.

It bothered me that my daughters had reached the stage of hating each other. Well, Mary actually adored Rachel; Rachel hated Mary, which made Mary defensive and act like she hated Rachel. I was an only child. I hadn't had this problem.

I sat on Mary's bed and shook her shoulder. "Mare," I said. "Wake up. Mommy's leaving." Now, normally Mary would kick and scream, pull the covers over her head, and demand to sleep just a few more minutes, but she knew I was leaving for a week so she sat straight up in bed. Bob Marley had nothing on this kid; her curly blond hair stuck out like somebody had sent her to bed with wet dreadlocks.

"Be good," I said and kissed her.

Sleepy green eyes tried their darndest to open. Finally, she just gave up, nodded her head up and down, and gave me a big hug. I'd said good-bye to them last night in case they weren't up when I left this morning, but I couldn't actually leave without saying it to them again.

With that, both girls snuggled back into bed—Mary flopped back into bed—and I closed my eyes for a second to burn that vision in my memory.

When I returned to the living room, my mother was there saying good-bye to her mother. My mother, who was wheelchair-bound, was serenely beautiful, with large, dark eyes and a perfectly oval face.

"Be good," my mother said to me. "Don't give your grandmother a hard time."

Wasn't that a variation of what I'd just said to my girls? Funny how that stuff gets recycled.

My mother was marrying the local sheriff, Colin Brooke, at the beginning of August, about two weeks before I was due. I was her matron of honor and still adjusting to the fact that she would be moving out of my house when the nuptials took place.

"Me, give her a hard time?" I asked. "Tell *her* to be good to *me*."

I kissed my mother good-bye and then came Rudy. He wouldn't settle for just a kiss good-bye in the living room. He had to walk me out to the car, help my grandmother get in it, and then kiss me once again.

"I love you," he said.

"I love you, too."

With that, I got in the car and felt that little bubble of excitement in my stomach I always feel when I'm getting ready to make a long trip. As I pulled out of the driveway Rudy yelled, "Hurry home! Call me. Take good care of my son!"

He patted his belly, so that I knew he meant the baby

5

I was carrying. Like I wouldn't know? We didn't know if it was a boy or a girl, but Rudy thought as long as he called it a boy, it would be.

I honked as I pulled away, watching Rudy wave through my rearview mirror.

TWO

LET ME SAY FOR THE RECORD THAT "NINETY-NINE Bottles of Beer on the Wall" is no fun with somebody who can't remember which bottle you're on.

Three fast-food stops, sixteen bathroom breaks, four unfinished conversations, one irritating rendition of "Ninety-nine Bottles of Beer," and twelve hours after I left Rudy standing in the driveway, we pulled up in front of the Panther Run Boardinghouse in central West Virginia. I'll be honest and say that I hadn't thought I was going to make it. My grandmother had this annoying habit of not finishing her sentences until about seven sentences later, once she'd thought of how it was supposed to end, and it was up to me to figure out which sentence went with which ending. Flying would have been much faster, but I have a huge fear of flying, and I'm just certain that in some twisted act of revenge, God will crash the plane while I'm on the toilet. When I do fly, I don't use the toilet. So, not an option in my current state.

Gert and I both looked up at the boardinghouse, nestled into a mountainside as if somehow it was molded into the mountain. To the left and the right of the house were brilliant green pastures that narrowed as the mountains closed in upon the postcard valley. A two-lane road ran in front of the boardinghouse, and the

Gauley River ran in front of that. On the other side of the river were gently sloped mountains plunging into the river.

I loved these mountains. I loved the entire Appalachian range from Alabama to Maine. They were comfortable mountains, like a well-used baseball glove. Soft, smooth, gentle slopes seemed to wedge themselves snugly into the land around them.

The boardinghouse, on the other hand, was not nearly so pleasing to the eye. It was a large two-story building with what looked like an attic in the center above the second story. There was dingy white latticework, about three feet high, all the way around the porch of both floors. The floor of the porch was a slate-blue, as was the trim on all the windows. The building itself was supposed to be white, but the paint was so old that it gave the building an overall grey look. In the center of the building, below the pointed roof, was a white latticework star.

The front steps were cracked and leaned to one side and the screens on the windows and doors were so rusty that you couldn't see through them. The fact that it was early evening and the sun was almost behind the mountain that sat directly behind the boardinghouse added to the overall dingy grey appearance of the building.

"Gee," I said. "Does this look anything like what you remember?"

My grandmother smiled faintly. "Yeah," she said. "Needs some work, but it's the same place."

My grandmother had actually worked at this boardinghouse when it was owned by "the company." Meaning, the Panther Run Coal Company, during the late twenties and early thirties. She was a small girl at

7

the time, but I remember her vivid tales of having to get up at three in the morning to fix the coal miners their breakfasts and pack their pail lunches. Then she had to go on to school after that! If somebody woke my girls up at three in the morning for anything, you'd have certified zombies on your hands.

Gert and I got out of the car and stretched. My back was killing me. It felt like it had a horse sitting on it. It must have been a dead horse, because the pain hadn't let up for about a month now.

I opened the trunk of the car to get the suitcases out just as a high-pitched scream erupted from somewhere within the building. Gert gave a little jump, as did I. The noise got louder and louder until it burst through the front door of the boardinghouse. A teenage girl ran out of the building to the edge of the porch and jumped over the latticework into the yard. About ten seconds later came an older man, probably about seventy, who thrust through the door, down the steps, and around the boardinghouse after her.

Gert gave me a quizzical look. I shrugged.

Just as we made it to the steps with our suitcases, the teenager jumped up into the air and over the latticework on the opposite end of the porch. Unfortunately, her thonged foot became hooked on the lattice railing and she went splat on her stomach onto the porch floor.

The seventy-year-old man came around the boardinghouse now, huffing and puffing. He stopped at the steps, bent over at the knees catching his breath, right in front of us. His glasses came tumbling out of his shirt pocket and fell onto the steps.

"Oh, let me get that," I said and stepped up to help him.

The teenage girl had now come to her feet. She stood

up, tears running down her face. "You can't have it," she said to the older man.

"I'm your grandpa, and you'll do as I say. Now give me that ring!" he demanded.

"No!" she shouted, stomped her foot and reached for her nose. "If I'm your granddaughter without my nose ring, then I'm your granddaughter with my nose ring. I won't take it out! You can't have it."

"The devil's work," the man said. "What will your great-grandma say when she sees it?"

By this point, Gert and I were standing on the steps. I'd given the man his glasses case, which he took as if I was invisible, and I couldn't help but stare at the poor teenage girl. By the amount of tears she had shed, it was obvious that her heart was broken. She wore those wonders of all retro wonders, faded bell-bottom jeans, a tie-dyed shirt, a hemp bracelet and choker, and a big silver nose ring. Her hair was nearly to her butt, bright strawberry-red, with little braids pulled back from her temples.

"Granny has already seen it," she hissed at her grandfather. "What do you care? She'll be dead soon anyway. Isn't that what you said?"

"Excuse me," I interrupted. Both the man and his granddaughter actually looked at me for the first time. "This is the Panther Run Boardinghouse, correct?"

"Yes," the man said. "Who might you be?"

"Oh, I'm Torie O'Shea, and this is my grandmother Gertrude Crookshank—" I didn't get to finish my sentence. The man let out a whoop and a holler, and went over to my grandmother and squeezed the daylights out of her with a big bear hug.

"Lordy, Gertie Crookshank!" he said. He then turned to me. "Of course, she was Gertie Seaborne when I ran with her."

9

My grandmother steadied herself with her cane and studied the man closely. "Well, Lafayette Hart, you old geezer."

"You look as pretty as the day Sam Crookshank ran off into the mountains with you," he said.

"Ran off into the mountains?" I asked. Sam Crookshank was my grandfather, Gert's ex-husband. "Gert, what is he talking about?"

"That Sam," the man went on. "Now he knew what he wanted in a woman. And none of them simpering misses stoked his far, if you know what I mean."

"Far?" I asked.

"Fire," my grandmother said.

"Oh, fire. Of course."

"Gertie Seaborne sure stoked it aplenty," Lafayette said and winked at my grandmother.

"That's nice," I said. It was no surprise to me that the teenage girl had taken this opportune moment to run into the boardinghouse and away from her grandfather. I was wanting to do the same thing.

"Can we go inside?" I asked. "I have a headache."

"Why of course," he said. "Let me get them bags for you. You shouldn't be carrying them heavy bags in your condition."

I really had a headache. The dead horse had moved to my head.

An hour later Gert and I were seated at an elongated table in the dining room with six other people, including Clarissa Hart, the one-hundred-and-one-year-old woman who had invited me to this place.

The food was served in clear cut-glass serving dishes, which sat in the middle of the table on top of ivory-colored doilies. Either that or the doilies were dirty, I wasn't sure which. On my right was my grandmother, and on my left was the teenage fugitive from earlier. The problematic nose ring was still defiantly in place. I'd since learned that her name was Danette Faragher and that she was the daughter of Lafayette's daughter Faith, who was not yet in attendance. It seemed as though Danette had arrived with her grandfather.

To the left of Danette was Lafayette himself. On that end of the table was Maribelle Lewis, Lafayette's sister and Clarissa's only daughter. To her left was Maribelle's husband, Prescott Lewis, and to his left was an unknown boarder. At least, unknown to me. Finally, to the boarder's left and my grandmother's right was Clarissa Hart, seated in her wheelchair at the head of the table.

I'm used to Sylvia, my boss at the historical society, looking so young and spry. Of course, she isn't one hundred and one, but she's only shy of it by about six or seven years. Clarissa Hart looked all of her one hundred and one years. She was hunched over in her wheelchair, with an oxygen tube loosely placed at the bottom of her nose, the hose wrapping around her to the tank hanging off the back of her wheelchair. Her hair was snow-white, her eyes blue under droopy eyelids, and her skin was pink and splotched. Her mouth puckered from years of wearing false teeth, but what amazed me the most was the sheer amount of wrinkles that the woman had. It seemed if you could straighten out the wrinkles on her face, she'd have had enough skin for two people.

But that was on the outside. On the inside she was as sharp as a tack.

"I'm so glad that you could make it, Torie, and bring Gertie back to see us," Clarissa said and aimlessly laid a hand on my grandmother's arm.

11

"It's my pleasure," I said.

"I'll just bet," Prescott Lewis said to me from across the table. He never looked up at me when he said it, so I let it go. He was a large man, late sixties, with a full head of grey-black hair.

"After dinner, come to my room. I have a lot to discuss with you," Clarissa said.

"Of course," I said.

"When is your baby due?" Maribelle asked me.

"The middle of August," I said.

Maribelle smiled, revealing a gold tooth amid a mouth full of stained teeth. She was in her mid-sixties, short, plump, and she had dyed hair that I'm sure was supposed to be some sort of reddish-brown but looked nearly burgundy. Like it was a bottle of wine that had stained her head.

"I remember when I was carrying," she said. "Was the best years of my life."

"Really?" I asked, thinking that the woman was nuts.

"Women are their prettiest when carrying," she said.

I'd have to argue with her when my skin was stretched so far across my stomach that my belly button was turned inside out and purple. But I'll bet she never looked at her belly button when she was pregnant. My nose was starting to swell, too, which had happened with every pregnancy I'd ever had. Oh, yeah. I was a regular Marilyn Monroe.

"There are things I must tell you," Clarissa said, bringing the conversation around to her end of the table again.

"Yeah, like where to spend her inheritance," Prescott piped in.

"Whose?" I asked. Nobody answered me. "Whose inheritance?"

12

My grandmother just shook her head because she didn't know what he was talking about, either.

"How long has it been since you been home, Gertie?" Lafayette asked.

"Since 1986," she answered.

"I had four sons," Maribelle said, as if we were listening to her.

"Only one is worth two hoops in hell," Lafayette said.

"Pass the bread," Danette said to me.

"Tell me, Torie, how long have you been tracing your family tree?" Clarissa asked.

"Oh, since the early eighties," I said, happy to return the conversation to something I thought was harmless.

"Do you have lots of information on your ancestors?" she asked.

"Some lines of the family are easier than others. I have some lines traced back to medieval times, some farther, if you count the royal lines. Others end in the mid-1850s with an ancestor of mine in the poorhouse and pregnant, with no clue as to who the father was. Just depends," I said. "One common thing, though. Except for the French side of the family, my father's mother, almost every line I have came from or through Virginia at some time or other."

"Only people worth anything," Prescott said. The entire meal, he still hadn't looked up from his plate.

"Pass me the pinto beans," the boarder said.

"Torie, this is one of my boarders, Norville Gross," Clarissa said. When she spoke, she stopped and took long deep breaths in between every third word or so. But she never forgot where she was going with her sentence. Wish I could say as much for Gert. If she blinked she got distracted.

13

"Hello," I said. Mr. Gross just nodded his head and tore into his pinto beans.

"I chose you," Clarissa said. "Out of all of Gertie's grandchildren and children, I chose you."

"Why? For what?"

"We'll talk more later. Come to my room as soon as you're finished," she said. With that she pushed a button on her electric wheelchair, backed away from the table, and went down the hall. A clanking noise came from down the hallway, and I jumped at the sound of it.

"It's Granny's elevator," Danette said. "She had it installed before I was born."

"It's one of those kinds with the wrought-iron gate that closes," Lafayette said.

"Oh," I answered.

"Granny likes you," Danette said. "I can tell. She doesn't like too many people."

"Give you the store, she oughta like you," Prescott said.

Okay, I couldn't let this go anymore. "What is he talking about?" I asked.

"Pay him no never mind," Lafayette said.

"Well, obviously he thinks I'm guilty of something, or I've done something," I said. "What do you mean, give me the store? What store?"

"The boardinghouse," Prescott said and finally looked up at me. His eyes were black and fierce little things, set back into his head, with a big Neanderthal brow above them.

"The boardinghouse," I said. "You're joking, right?"

Nobody said anything. Everybody ate their food with new interest, except Prescott, who stared directly at me, and Norville, who seemed oblivious to the conversation.

"Why else would she have asked you here?" Prescott asked.

14

"I'm sure that's not what she asked me here for. I'm the family historian. She wants to tell me something," I said.

"Yeah, well, you're not *our* family," he said.

THREE

I DID AS CLARISSA HART SAID AFTER DINNER AND WENT directly to her room on the second floor of the boardinghouse. In truth, I hated to leave Gert in the company of Prescott Lewis, but she seemed happy to stay and visit with Lafayette and Maribelle, whom she had known as a child.

I hadn't had much of a chance to look around the boardinghouse. We had thrown our suitcases in our room and headed to the dining room for dinner. Now, I didn't want to keep Clarissa waiting because it was heading for nine o'clock, and I knew that she would go to sleep early.

I couldn't help but notice all of the photographs hanging on the wall of the stairway, though. Old photographs hung along the wall in an almost pictorial diary of sorts, although I did not know the cast. There were little photographs, big photographs, some in plain metal frames and others in large, fancy wooden ones. The people in the frames watched me all the way up the stairs until I reached the landing, where the photographs ended and the second floor began.

Clarissa's room was at the very end of the hall on the right. I entered the room and she was already in her bed, which was a hospital bed. She still had the oxygen tube on her face, and she lay on piles of pillows, which made her seem small and weightless.

"I'm so glad you came," she said and held a hand out that beckoned to me.

I walked over beside her bed and felt just a little awkward, because until today, I'd never met the woman. We'd exchanged letters a few times in the past. I'd written to her asking if she had any information or pictures of my great-grandparents. She had obliged with some copies of old photographs and a few old letters. Now, she acted as if she'd known me all my life.

"Do you know I was already old when you were born?" she asked.

Her accent was as strong as her son Lafayette's.

I did the math in my head, and she had been in her late sixties when I was born. Not exactly ancient, but I understood what she meant.

"I didn't think I was gonna live much longer *then,*" she said. "Look at me. Who coulda known?"

"You know, I read about a woman in Texas who was something like a hundred and fifteen," I said and smiled.

"Oh, don't you say that," she said. "Fourteen more years like this?"

I just shrugged. "Why was it so important for me to come to West Virginia?"

"You know that I was best friends with your great-grandmother, Bridie McClanahan? Before she met Mr. Seaborne and got married," she said.

"Yes, of course," I said.

Clarissa took a moment to breathe deeply. "You don't look much like her," she said.

"No," I said. "I look like my father. Except he has black hair."

"Nowadays you can dye your hair any color you want," she said. "Look at Danette. Caribbean Sunset.

16

That's the name of the color she put on it."

"Caribbean Sunset," I said and flashed back to Danette's bright strawberry hair. I would have almost thought it was natural.

"Bridie did me a favor," Clarissa said. "Long, long time ago. And now it's time to return the favor. A debt repaid."

"What sort of favor?" I asked. I must admit that even though I asked the question, I was a little worried about what the answer might be. I waited patiently as she reached up and straightened her oxygen tube.

"I picked you because you care," she said, ignoring my question. "You know about the hills and the people who came here from the highlands. You know about the coal mines and the history. Most people don't know what went on twenty years before their time, and don't care. Just plain ol' don't care. Not you. You're one of the smart ones. You're one of the ones who do care."

All right. I'd agree with her on that, but I wasn't exactly sure where this was going. Not all people were history buffs. They just weren't. No crime there, I suppose. Most of the time, though, when people were history buffs they would go out of their way to learn everything they could about a particular place or time.

"Yes," I said. "I care very much about where my people came from."

"I've waited eighty-three years to repay this debt. I didn't do it before now, because I was afraid," she said.

"Momma?" a voice said from behind me. It startled me a little, and I wondered why I had been so on edge since I'd come here.

I turned around to see a man in his late sixties with slicked-back hair and shiny black shoes. Needless to say, his brown leisure suit was nearly as old as I was. I

17

was probably in first grade when he bought it.

"Momma," he said, with his arms opened wide.

"Edwin?" Clarissa asked. "Is that you?"

"Who else ya think it'd be?" he asked. He walked over to her bed and kissed her on the forehead. He then produced, out of thin air, I might add, a Hershey's candy bar. "For you. Shh, don't tell nobody."

"I'll come back in the morning, Clarissa," I said and let myself out of the room.

On the way to my room, I saw a few other people whom I did not have names for. A crack of thunder shook the boardinghouse and I squealed. Grown woman, here. Just thunder.

As I entered my room, I found my grandmother sitting on the edge of her bed, unpacking her suitcase. Her cane was leaned up against the oak nightstand, which matched all of the other antique furniture in the room. This room even had one of those old dressing tables with the scalloped mirrors. The only lights in the room were two lamps that were covered with old maroon shades.

"Edwin just arrived," I said as I stepped into the room.

"Edwin was always a slick fart," she said. "Never trusted him."

"So what do you think of all of this?" I asked.

"All of what?"

"Nothing," I said with a sigh. "Did you really play with the Hart children?"

"I played with Lafayette a little. I was nine or so when he was . . . By the time the younger two, Edwin and Maribelle, came along . . . We played some. I was baby-sitting age."

"So you baby-sat them?" I asked, trying to make

18

sense of her sentences. It was amazing. Sometimes she could talk for a whole ten minutes with no problems, and then other times her phrases came out unfinished and disjointed.

"Yeah, I was nine when—"

"No, did you baby-sit them, Gert? Edwin and Maribelle?" I asked, trying to keep her on track.

"Yup. I've seen all of their plumbing."

"Gee, that's great, Gert. Just what I wanted to know."

I sat down on the edge of one of the beds and took off my shoes. I was tired. I was going to go to bed and sleep as deep and long as I could. While I had that thought in my head, another crack of thunder exploded, reminding me that I might not sleep as well as I'd hoped.

"I thought we'd go see your aunt Millicent," Gert said. "Tomorrow or the next."

"Sounds good," I said. Aunt Milly—or Millicent—was one of my mother's sisters and the only sibling who had stayed in West Virginia, the others all having moved to Missouri when their mother, Gert, moved back in the fifties.

Without really knowing how it happened, I was in my bed and sound fast asleep within minutes. Not even my grandmother's snoring kept me awake. But, alas, an overfull bladder will do the trick every time. I awoke around two in the morning and had to use the bathroom. Which meant I had to get out of bed and walk down the hall.

I lay there a few more seconds, pondering if it was worth getting out of bed for. Rain crashed against the window in wild surges. I got up and went to the window and looked out. It was pretty cool how the lightning lit up the sky and all of the mountains surrounding this valley were silhouetted against the purple-blue sky.

Then the lightning would die down and all would be pitch-black again.

Once in the bathroom, I did my business and hurried back into my room, stubbing my toe on the overly thick floor runner. It must have been two inches thick. The hallway was pretty creepy, all dark and squeaky, and I really didn't want to stay out there any longer than I had to.

As I got in bed, I did give some thought as to how Clarissa could get her wheelchair up and over the floor runner. Her electric wheelchair must have a really good engine, I decided.

Just as my head hit the pillow, I heard this hair-raising scream that sounded like a woman being attacked. Goose bumps danced along my spine, and I sat straight up in bed. Well, as straight up as I could with a forty-five-inch waist.

"What the heck was that?" I asked aloud. My voice sounded spooked and twelve years old.

"Panther," Gert said in between snores.

"What do you mean, panther?" I asked. "Don't panthers meow or something like that?"

"No. Panthers scream. Like a woman," she said, still without moving. How could she be this calm?

Then I heard it again. I sat in the bed unable to move, except for my eyes, which kept darting around the room expecting to see some rain-soaked crazy woman. The more I listened to it, the more I knew the sound was coming from outside. The scream seemed to get louder or quieter as if it was moving closer to the boardinghouse and then farther away. The fact that it was outside made me feel a little bit better.

"I'm telling you, it's a panther. Go back to sleep."

"Panthers live in the wild," I argued. "In the mountains, in the boonies."

20

"Yes, and you are in the boonies, in the mountains, and this is called Panther Run for a reason. Now go back to sleep before I brain you a good one."

Enough said. Feeling very much like a scolded child, I snuggled back into my big fluffy bed with the covers up around my chin, but I still could not close my eyes. Rain pellets hit so hard against the glass that I thought for certain the windowpanes would break.

I lay like that until the storm moved on and the earliest rays of light caused shadows in my room. I'd heard the panther two more times in the middle of the night, and let me just say that it was the creepiest thing I've ever heard in my life.

At about six in the morning I had to use the bathroom again. I'd had to go for the last hour, but I waited until it became light enough to see where I was walking. As I stepped out into the hallway, I heard a creak. I looked up and down the hallway but didn't see anybody. Between each room, bronze sconces with curved votive cups came out of the walls, and I wondered why they weren't on. I felt inside of one and surmised that all the sconces like this one had no lightbulbs. The plush maroon floor runner was centered down the hallway floor. About three quarters of the way down on the left, the stairs exited into the great room below. A few feet of balcony stretched beyond the stairway until the very end of the hall, where Clarissa's elevator was. Which was the opposite end of the hall where her room was. All of the doors in the hall were shut, except the one I'd just come out of.

I went to the bathroom and then walked back down the hall toward my room. Just as I was about to go into my room, I looked up and saw that the door to Clarissa's room was open about six inches. I stood there a minute waiting

21

for somebody to come out, but nobody did. I glanced up and down the hallway and saw nobody, so I decided to go down and at least check on her.

"Clarissa?" I asked as quietly as I could without it being a whisper.

No answer. I should have turned around and gone back to my room, but I couldn't. I pushed on the already partially open door, and in the dim light of morning I could see Clarissa Hart lying on her throne of pillows, with one of the pillows covering her face.

It took a second for it to register that the old woman who had to use oxygen was lying with a pillow on her face. In all likelihood she would suffocate if I didn't do something.

I rushed into the room and lifted the pillow. "Clarissa?" I said.

A noise at the window made me turn and look. Some sort of white bird flapped its wings and seemed to look into the room through the window right at me. It then made a chirping sound and flew away.

When I turned back around, Norville Gross was standing at the doorway looking at me with an astonished expression. He looked at the pillow in my hand and then at Clarissa, who didn't seem to be breathing. Then ever so slowly he looked back to me.

This could be very bad.

FOUR

"WHAT DID YOU DO TO HER?" HE ASKED.

"I didn't do anything," I said. "I just came in here and found her with a pillow over her face."

"Why'd you come in here in the first place?"

I hate it when people ask you questions that you can't

22

answer without making yourself look bad. If I answered him honestly, it would make me look incredibly nosy. Which I was, but I didn't want to admit it to him. "Her door was open and . . . I heard something," I said. Which I hadn't.

I made a move toward Clarissa to see if she was breathing or if indeed she was as dead as I expected. Norville gave a loud squeal and came partway into the room. "Don't you touch her," he said. His morning shadow was so dark that it was nearly blue in color. Maybe it just looked that color because his skin was a rather unbecoming shade of paste.

"For God's sake," I said. "I want to see if she's breathing. Call 911."

"I'm not leaving you alone with her."

"Don't be ridiculous," I said, realizing that he wasn't going to let this go. I checked for her pulse at her wrist and found nothing. An uneasy feeling settled on me as I set the pillow on the foot of the bed. I looked up at Mr. Gross, whose breathing had become more intense and irregular.

"Well?" he asked.

I went to her dresser and picked up a hand mirror. Carrying it in my sweaty little palms, I couldn't help but wonder if Mr. Gross was so upset because Clarissa was dead, or because he thought I'd killed her. I placed the mirror below her nose and mouth, which was absent of any oxygen tube, and there was nothing. She was dead.

"Mr. Gross, are you going to stand there all morning, or are you going to dial 911? Clarissa is dead," I said.

"No. She can't be dead," he answered. He shook his head in disbelief, and then quickly his expression turned perplexed. "Do you smell something?"

"Like what?" I asked and took a deep breath.

23

"Cologne?"

It was something sweet like a strong air freshener. I nodded my head that I did smell something, but I wasn't sure what.

About that time, sixteen-year-old Danette Faragher walked into the room. She wore nothing but one of her tie-dyed T-shirts that came to just above her knees and, I'm assuming, underwear. She had a tattoo of some sort on her ankle. From where I stood, it looked like a rose or some other kind of flower.

"What's going on?" she asked in a sleepy tone of voice.

"Danette," I said. "Your granny died in her sleep."

Mr. Gross was about to dispute what I'd just said, but the daggers that flew out of my eyes and across the room stopped him. Danette's eyes got real big, and tears perched on her lower lids. Then just like magic, something else replaced the tears. "Oh, gross," she said.

That wasn't exactly the reaction I was expecting, but hey, she was not herself at the moment. She was sixteen. It would be years before she was herself.

"Danette, I need for you to stand guard at the door and not let anybody in," I said.

"Why?" she asked, still staring at Clarissa's body.

"Just do what I say. And I mean, nobody gets in, not even your grandfather, until Mr. Gross and I get back. Is that understood?"

"Yeah," she said.

"Stand out here at the door, because I don't want you to touch anything inside, okay?"

"Okay," she said and did as I asked. She looked a little pale and I felt really bad about leaving her to stand guard, but what other choice did I have?

"Mr. Gross, come with me," I said.

24

He followed me out of the room, down the hall, and downstairs into the great room. The telephone was on the table by the front door. "Stay right there, Mr. Gross. I want you to witness this phone call."

He nodded to me and I dialed 911. When the operator answered and I told her our dilemma, she became very quiet. "Where are you exactly?" she asked.

"We're at Panther Run. The boardinghouse just out of town. Below Quiet Knob," I said.

"On the Gauley River?" she asked.

"Yes."

"Ma'am, have you looked outside this morning?" she asked.

"No," I said. I walked over to the window and looked out across the front porch to water. Nothing but water. Water over the road and nearly into the driveway of the boardinghouse. "Oh, great."

"Flash flood," she said. "From all of the rain last night. It'll go down real fast. Probably a day or two."

"A day or two?" I screeched into the phone. "What am I supposed to do with . . . with . . . the body?"

"Can you put her on ice?"

Oooh. Disgusting. "Uh, I don't think that's possible. Unless maybe they have a cellar?" I said to the operator, but it was a question to Mr. Gross. He shrugged his shoulders to indicate that he did not know. "Even then, I think it will just be cooler, I don't think it would be the same thing as ice."

Oh, I really didn't want to think about this.

"Is there no way you can get a sheriff in here? By boat? A Hummer?" I asked. I'd been through floods before. Hummers are the way to go if the water isn't too high.

"Hummer," she said. "We're not going to call in the

25

National Guard or the army on a flash flood. It's not as if it's going to last a week."

"No, but it's going to last long enough to cause a really disgusting smell in this house," I said. I sighed heavily and tried to get my bearings. "Please, call the sheriff and see if he can get here by boat. I think there might have been foul play involved, but I'm not sure. And I don't want to sound like I'm expecting a miracle here, but her entire family is present. A decomposing Granny would not be a very good thing."

I think I was nearly as hysterical as my voice sounded. The thought of being stuck in this boardinghouse for two days with a decaying body was just more than I wanted to deal with. I wondered where this situation would rank on that stress test I saw in *Cosmopolitan* last week at the doctor's office.

"I'll do my best," she said.

I hung up the phone and looked into the very distressed face of Mr. Gross. A thought occurred to me, and I picked up the phone again. I dialed the number, and it rang about six times before a very groggy Sheriff Colin Brooke answered the phone.

"Hello, Colin?" I asked. He was my future stepfather and I admitted begrudgingly, an all-right guy.

"You are in West Virginia," he said.

"Yes."

"And it is five-fifteen in the morning."

"Yes." I'd forgotten about the time zone difference. He was back home in New Kassel, Missouri.

"What did you do?"

"Nothing," I said.

"Then what's happened? It better be worthy of calling me at five-fifteen in the morning, or I'll wring your neck when you get back to New Kassel. I don't care if

26

you are pregnant," he said.

"You know the old lady that I was coming to visit?" I asked. He acknowledged that he remembered. "Well, she died. In her sleep."

"So?" he asked. "Let me guess . . . you think—"

"No, I have no opinion whatsoever," I said. When in fact I *did* find the pillow on her face. "My problem is . . . there's a flash flood and the water probably won't go down for a day or two. What do I do with the body?"

The sheriff's only response was a long pause on the other end of the line. "Come out with it," he said finally.

He was going to make a good stepfather, because he could almost always tell when I was lying or withholding information. Glad he hadn't been around when I was a teenager.

"All right, when I walked into her room there was a pillow over her face. Colin, tell me what to do. I don't think they can get a sheriff in here until the water goes down," I said. "I . . . I have probably fifteen or twenty people in this place, if you count the hired help. I really don't want people to panic, and yet, I'm about to panic. If she was murdered, I'm not too thrilled about being trapped in this place with a killer."

"Great," he said. A moment passed without either one of us saying anything. Finally, he decided. "Seal off the room."

"What do you mean?" I asked. As he spoke, something in the fireplace caught my attention. I picked the phone up and carried it as far as the cord would reach, which was right up to the fireplace.

"Don't disturb anything. Leave the body as is, and shut the door. Crank the air-conditioning," he said.

"That's it? That's all the advice you have for me?"

Lying in the fireplace was a pile of burned papers.

There hadn't been a fire in the fireplace probably since spring, so whoever had done this had just burned the papers and thrown them in the fireplace and left, thinking they would burn all the way. I knelt down and picked them up as carefully as I could so that they wouldn't crumble.

"If you're certain there was no foul play, then I'd say move the body and put it on ice."

Did everybody think that boardinghouses were equipped with big blocks of ice just waiting to have a dead body piled on it? This was ridiculous. "Well, since we seem to have a shortage of ice, unless you want me to hack Granny up and stuff her in the freezer, I think that one is out."

I happened to remember that Norville Gross was listening to my conversation, and that probably didn't sound too good. I fished all of the papers out of the fireplace and laid them on the hearth. Norville gave me a very perplexed look, with one eyebrow raised.

"They should be able to get a sheriff in there by boat," he said. "Once they realize there's been a murder."

"Okay," I said. "So, clear the room and seal it."

"Yes," he said. "And don't tell your mother."

It irked me slightly that he was telling me what to tell and what not to tell my mother. That had been, up until recently, my job. The sheriff and my mother had a May/December relationship, which was fine by me. My mother robbed the cradle. More power to her. Their relationship did take some getting used to, though. The sheriff had actually arrested me once, when I was being a Good Samaritan, I might add. He and I never really got along, and was my mother sympathetic? No. She decided to marry him.

"I won't have to tell her," I said. "Gert will when she talks to her next."

"What?" he asked.

"Gert will let it slip," I said. "Well, I gotta go. Thanks, Colin."

I hung up the phone, still knelt down at the hearth trying to make sense of the burned pieces of paper. Most of it I could not make out. However, there were a few words that had a familiar ring to me. They were: *of sound body and mind.*

"Mr. Gross," I said. "Could you get me a Baggie or something to put this in?"

"What is it?" he asked.

"I believe it is Clarissa's will."

FIVE

TWO HOURS LATER, EVERYBODY WAS DRESSED AND assembled in the great room of the Panther Run Boardinghouse. I wore the best maternity outfit that I had, which was a blue and white striped dress, with a big white collar and red bow. Why did it seem most maternity clothes were designed to make you look like a sailor? Almost everything else I'd brought along was shorts and shirt sets.

"Okay, let's be calm," I said.

"Who put you in charge?" Prescott Lewis asked me.

His question was legitimate. I had just sort of assumed control of the situation, when in fact I was the biggest suspect there was. I was the one found with the pillow in my hand, no one else. Norville Gross, up to this point, had been gracious enough not to point that out to the others. Of course, it took an hour of talking my fanny off to convince him that he would do more harm than good if he let that piece of information out just yet.

All of the people who had been at dinner the night before were present, plus quite a few new faces. "Please, just be cooperative for right now. Everybody. Please?"

The people in the room quieted down a bit, and so I went on. "If you were not at dinner last night, please introduce yourself and explain how you are related to Mrs. Hart," I said.

Maribelle wailed at the sound of her late mother's name. Prescott rolled his eyes, but an unidentified man was compassionate and handed her a fresh Kleenex.

"Employees first," I said.

"My name's Dexter. Dexter Calloway," a man said. He was about fifty and looked as though he'd lived every year to the limit. He couldn't have spoken any slower if somebody had given him taffy to chew on. "I'm the handyman. Groundskeeper, butler, whatever Mrs. Hart needed me to do."

"I'm Susan Henry. The cook."

"Vanessa Killian. Cleaning lady."

Okay, that took care of the hired help. "Are there any boarders other than Mr. Gross?" I asked.

A tall, slender woman raised her hand. She was about my age, early thirties, had long, straight blond hair to about the middle of her back, and wore tiny framed glasses. "I'm Sherise Tyler," she said. "I'm a journalist."

Oh, that was perfect. I could see people around the room reacting to her announcement moments after she said it. A journalist. They were all worried about the story being written up in the local papers where they had lived and worked their whole lives. That was called gossip. Only, once it was in print, it became fact to most people.

"Faith and Gerrold Faragher," a spunky-looking woman said. She pointed to the man sitting next to her. They were probably in their mid-forties, obvious suburbanites not from this area. "I'm Lafayette's daughter."

And the mother of the ever-rebellious Danette, I thought to myself.

"Craig Lewis," a smooth voice said, and a man held out his hand for me to shake. He had been the bearer of the Kleenex to Maribelle. "I'm Maribelle's son. And this is my wife, Tiffany."

Okay, let's just say that Craig was about forty and Tiffany was . . . well, Tiffany was barely drinking age. She couldn't have been over twenty-two, with long, long legs and bouncy chestnut hair. I didn't think it was my imagination that certain family members turned their noses up and shifted in their seats. She seemed to provoke a reaction from almost everybody there. Oblivious to the reaction she caused, she wrinkled her nose and waved to me.

There was only one other person that I did not know. A round, balding man with a hideous comb-over sat on the edge of the couch clutching a briefcase. It seemed as if nobody else in the room knew who he was, either, because every eye was now focused on him. He looked very uncomfortable in the accusatory silence.

"Sir?" I asked.

"Uh, I . . . uh, I'm Oliver Jett. My friends call me Ollie."

"So who the hell are you?" Lafayette asked.

"I'm Clarissa's lawyer and I came here to read the will. The new one," he said.

I thought about the burned pages that I'd found in the fireplace. Norville Gross thought about them too, because his head snapped around and he looked at me as soon as Mr. Jett made his announcement.

"You've come all this way for nothing," Dexter Calloway said. "As soon as we found out she was dead, I went to her office to get the will to put in a safe place, and it was gone. It was the only copy."

There seemed to be relief in the room. What changes had Clarissa made in her will that had the family so concerned? And who had been bothered enough to go to the great lengths of burning it?

"Does this mean the old will stands?" I asked Mr. Jett the lawyer.

"It would in most cases," he said.

"Why not this one?" I asked.

"Because I have a copy of the new one," Ollie said. "Clarissa downloaded it to me over the Internet three days ago."

You could almost hear the family saying, "Drat! Plan foiled again."

When I'd rebounded from the astonishment of the little old centenarian surfing the Net and transmitting her new will to her lawyer, something occurred to me. "Mr. Calloway," I said.

"Yes?"

"We need to see to it that no more people go in and out of Clarissa's office. Seal it off too until the sheriff arrives," I said.

He nodded his head that he understood.

"I've had about enough of you, Mrs. O'Shea," Prescott said. "Just who put you in charge?"

32

"My granddaughter," Gert said, "knows what she's . . . Her stepfather is a sheriff."

"I don't care if he's an alien," Prescott said. "You think you can just come here from your fancy big city and boss us all around. Well, you can't!"

"Mr. Lewis," Ollie said. "Somebody has to keep things under control, and Mrs. O'Shea is doing a fine job."

"She's just concerned about her inheritance," Prescott said.

"You seemed to be equally concerned about it," I said. "Mr. Lewis, I have no idea what you are talking about. I'm sure that if Clarissa had anything to give to me, it was something that belonged to my great-grandmother. That's all."

"You can act all innocent if you want," he went on. "But we all know better."

I looked around the room, astonished. "Just what do you think is going on here?"

"The boardinghouse," Maribelle said from behind her Kleenex.

"What do you mean?"

"We feel that—"

Maribelle was cut off in mid-sentence by who else? Her husband, Prescott. "She's leaving you the boardinghouse!"

All was quiet a moment and then the quiet was shattered by my laughter. That was the most ridiculous thing I'd ever heard. Why would Clarissa leave me the boardinghouse? And why would they care? It's not as if the place was worth much. The land that it sat on was probably worth something, but not a huge amount.

"Clarissa Hart did not leave me the boardinghouse," I said. "This is the most absurd accusation. There is no reason for her to leave me the boardinghouse. Why would she think I would even want it? She doesn't even know me."

I felt a little uncomfortable with all of the people staring at me as I stood in front of the fireplace where I'd found the burned pages to the will. The *new* will, I reminded myself. Somebody had burned it thinking that the old will would be the one filed in probate since the new one would be nonexistent. And whoever had burned the new will had done so either last night or early this morning. If it was this morning, I would assume that whoever had done so had also put the pillow over her face.

"Now, Prescott," Maribelle cooed. "Maybe Mrs. O'Shea doesn't want the boardinghouse."

"No, I don't want the boardinghouse, and Clarissa didn't leave it to me."

"Why do you keep saying that?" Prescott asked. "Do you really think that we believe you drove all the way from Missourah for a . . . a . . . cake plate or something?"

"We would have driven all the way from Missouri just for the chance to see Clarissa and speak with her. She invited us, we have family here. We had the opportunity to come back here and we did. That's all there is to it," I explained.

"Gertie," Lafayette said. "Talk some sense to your granddaughter."

My grandmother was as confused as I was. She said nothing to me or him, she just looked around the room with a blank stare on her face.

"Do you guys really believe that Clarissa was leaving the boardinghouse to me?" I asked.

"Why else would she invite you to the reading of the will?" Lafayette asked.

"Look, I am telling you that there is no way that Clarissa Hart left me the boardinghouse. Absolutely, positively no way. She had no reason to. It would make no sense. Now, everybody, calm down and relax. I assure you she did not leave the boardinghouse to me."

SIX

CLARISSA HART HAD LEFT ME THE BOARDINGHOUSE.

I felt so stupid. She had left the boardinghouse, the land it sat on, and all of its contents to me. Little old me. What was up with that?

I sat across from Mr. Oliver Jett with Maribelle Lewis, Lafayette Hart, Edwin Hart, and Norville Gross on my side of the great room in the boardinghouse that I now owned. As a matter of fact, if I wanted to get technical, they were sitting on my couch and eating my food. I'd better not go too far with that though, since there was also the matter of my new employees that I would now have to pay.

"I don't understand, Mr. Jett," I said. How can you take a man named Ollie seriously? It's sort of the male equivalent of Buffy. "How can this be? Why would she leave me her boardinghouse?"

"She claimed that it was a 'debt repaid,' " Mr. Jett said.

"A debt?" I asked. "What sort of debt?"

"Yeah, what sort of debt?" Edwin asked.

I was very happy, by the way, that Preston Lewis was not in the room as we discussed this. Mr. Jett had made the spouses leave the room. Preston would have made this uncomfortable situation all the more uncomfortable. But I truly didn't understand what the big deal was about the boardinghouse, anyway. Clarissa Hart owned many other properties, along with insurance policies, money market accounts, and stocks. All of which were worth a lot more than this old boardinghouse, and all of which she had divided up between her three children.

Except for the nice tidy sum of $50,000 dollars. Which she left to Norville Gross. Fifty grand! It takes Rudy almost two years to make that kind of money. I could not imagine having that kind of money just sitting in the bank, much less signing it over to somebody else.

This was very interesting information, though. Just who the heck was Norville Gross? Clarissa had made him out to be just another boarder last night at dinner. I'd say that he was a tad more than that, but I did not know his relationship to her, and he had not volunteered it.

"A debt repaid," I said aloud. "What does it mean?"

"I heard Momma say many times that if there was a person in this world that she owed her life to, it was Bridie McClanahan," Lafayette said.

"My great-grandmother," I said.

"Yes."

"Did she say why?"

"She hinted at a lot of things," Maribelle said. "None of which you could actually pin her down on."

I thought about it a minute and tossed it around in my head. It made absolutely no sense. What could my great-grandmother have done for her that would have inspired this degree of loyalty? My great-grandmother, on my mother's side, had died at the age of twenty-eight in 1926. So whatever it was she had done, she had done it in a relatively short period of time, from about 1916 to 1926. Whatever it was, it had also been extreme enough

36

that Clarissa hadn't forgotten it in the eighty years that followed Bridie's death.

"I don't care about any of this 'debt repaid' nonsense," Edwin said. He turned to Norville Gross. "I wanna know who the hell *you* are."

It was hard to say who was more deathly quiet, Norville Gross or Mr. Jett. They both looked at each other, and then Mr. Jett looked impassively at Edwin. Norville, however, stared at the wall.

"If . . . if Mr. Gross doesn't want to tell you who he is," Mr. Jett said, "he doesn't have to."

"Do you know who he is?" Edwin asked.

"No," Mr. Jett said.

I studied Edwin, and I knew exactly what my grandmother meant by "Edwin was always a slick fart." He had that sort of shiny-suited, used-car-salesman aura about him. He even wore a gold pinkie ring.

I looked up at the wall that Norville was busy studying to see what was so interesting. The fireplace where I had found the burned will was set back into a redbrick wall. The mantel had one of those Home Interiors sculptures of a deer on one end, a mantel clock that was about fifteen minutes slow sitting in the middle, and an ancient, dusty china doll on the other end. Right above the fireplace, on the brick wall, hung a big picture, with a bunch of people in it. From where I sat, it looked like there were twenty people in the picture. On both sides of that big picture were a few other small pictures. I assumed that the nails were driven into the mortar with special mortar nails.

I didn't think there was anything special on the wall. I think Norville Gross was just trying to avoid looking at any of the Hart children. It did not escape my attention that Norville and I were the only two who were not

Clarissa's children who had been left something in her will. We were also the first two who had been in her room after her death.

"I don't think that Mr. Gross is going to answer you," I said.

"Can I be excused?" Norville asked Mr. Jett. Mr. Jett nodded his head, and Norville got up and left the room. I now had everybody's undivided attention, even though I did not necessarily want it.

"Why wouldn't he want people to know who he is?" I asked quickly, in hopes that people would forget that I now owned the boardinghouse.

"Maybe he doesn't want the will to be contested," Mr. Jett said. "So he believes it better to remain quiet."

"Well, we can still contest it," Edwin said.

"I think," I said, ignoring Edwin's last statement, "that it would be better if he just came out with it. This way it makes him appear as though he does have something to hide. Maybe you can speak to him about that, Ollie?"

He checked his comb-over to make sure that it was still plastered in place on top of his head. "Certainly," he said. "I'll try."

It was quiet, suddenly. All three of Clarissa's children—Lafayette, Maribelle, and Edwin—tried very hard to stare at me without obviously staring at me. I shifted uncomfortably in my seat and finally got up and stretched.

"Well," I said. "I don't know what to make of this. I honestly had no idea that this would happen or that my great-grandmother had ever done anything important enough to warrant such devotion from your mother."

"Preston was right," Maribelle said. It wasn't particularly vicious or ugly the way she said it. She was

38

simply stating a fact.

Slowly, they all got up and left the room, leaving Mr. Jett sitting on the couch to ponder the silence in the great room with me. I walked over and looked out the window for the fifteenth time since six o'clock this morning. The water had started to recede, although not fast enough in my opinion. I wanted to be able to leave this place in a hurry if need be.

"You know," I said finally. I walked over to the fireplace and looked up at the large picture that hung on the wall. "I most likely will not keep the boardinghouse. I've no need for it. It doesn't exactly turn a profit, and I'm three states west of here and unable to really take care of it."

"You might want to wait a few months or so before making that sort of rash decision," Mr. Jett said. He picked up his briefcase and put the copy of the will inside. "This is an opportunity that has been handed down to you. Even if you just sell it outright. You have children. It's not worth a fortune, but you could start a college fund for them."

I thought about it a moment as I studied the photograph closely. It was a morbid photograph of a funeral. In the middle of it was a casket, with the lid open and the dead body inside, stiff and pasty-looking. Twenty people surrounded the casket, all looking rather unconcerned. Nobody was partying exactly, but nobody looked all that sad, either, in my opinion.

I'd seen this sort of thing before, especially in Appalachia. One photograph I remember in particular showed the body of Devil Anse Hatfield in his casket. Hatfield of the infamous Hatfields and McCoys.

"Still," I said, looking to Mr. Jett. "I doubt seriously

I'll keep it. I don't feel right about it."

"Contact your lawyer," he said. With that he turned and left the room. It was about two hours before dinnertime and I was starving. I'd just been left a boardinghouse, ten acres, and twenty rooms full of furniture and stuff, and all I could think about was food. Well, that and how much I wished the local sheriff would get here.

SEVEN

IT SOUNDED AS THOUGH DANETTE FARAGHER WAS trying to wake the dead. I walked past her room on the first floor on my way to speak with Sherise Tyler. I thought if anybody knew any good gossip on the place it would be Ms. Tyler, providing, of course, that she was a local journalist. Instead of going on to Ms. Tyler's room, however, I backed up and knocked on Danette's door. She, of course, didn't answer, since she probably couldn't hear me. I knocked louder.

Finally the door opened with an even louder rush of music. Danette looked fairly surprised to see me. She did not invite me in.

"May I come in?" I asked.

Danette shrugged her shoulders and opened the door the rest of the way so I could enter. She flopped on the bed and reached over with one long, incredibly skinny arm and turned off the music. I got the impression that this must have been Danette's room when she came to visit, because there were a few posters on the wall, Limp Bizkit, Korn, and a few other teenage celebrities that I recognized. Not to mention the CD player and a dresser that had quite a few personal items scattered on top. The room look lived in, even if only on a short-term basis.

"You don't have to turn off the music for me," I said. "I happen to like the Offspring."

"Don't think for one minute that you can come in here and pretend to like the in music and that I'll think you're hip and forget that you were the first one in Granny's room. It won't work," she said with more venom than I was ready for.

"Well," I said. "For your information, I'm not the least bit hip, that I know. But I do like the Offspring. I like almost every kind of music there is. I'm a huge Beethoven fan, too, which makes me an old fuddy-duddy. So I assume that makes me a hip old fuddy-duddy? I had no idea that the music I listened to decided my fate on the hip scale. Is that why you listen to it?"

She studied me a moment. Clearly, she was not ready for my retort, as much as I was not ready for her attack in the first place. "What do you want?"

"I simply was going to ask you to turn the music down a little bit, because I know that it drives my grandmother crazy, and I wouldn't doubt it had the same effect on your grandfather," I said. "And then I was also going to try and reassure you that I did not hurt your granny."

She leaned back on the bed and somehow managed to get her legs under her in one of those pretzel positions that only teenagers can make look painless, and that I couldn't even begin to attempt in my present state. "My uncle Prescott said that you came here for the boardinghouse and that you killed Granny to make sure that you got it."

"Why would I have to do that?" I asked. "The new will states that I receive the boardinghouse. The old one does not. So, therefore, if I was after the boardinghouse, I would want to make sure that your granny lived. At least until the will was read."

She thought about that a moment.

"You might inform your uncle Prescott of that."

She said nothing to that, but she looked around the room with big tears welling up in her eyes. "I can't believe somebody would hurt her. She was just a little old lady. She was harmless." Her voice was nearly a whisper from her grief, and suddenly that tough, re-bellious teenager slid away, revealing the true fragile state of most of them. Teenagers' hormones take them on a wild ride that they can't escape until Mother Nature says so: it was kind of like being pregnant, now that I thought about it. No wonder I was so grouchy.

"I don't think Clarissa Hart was as harmless as you think," I said with a smile. "The woman surfed the Net and downloaded her will to her lawyer, a feat that I couldn't accomplish."

"She was so cool," Danette said.

"Yes," I answered. "And I don't have the foggiest idea why somebody would want to hurt an old lady like Clarissa Hart."

I walked toward the door and was just about into the hall when Danette turned the stereo back on. She quickly turned it down to a normal decibel level. "Is that too loud?" she asked.

"No, that's just perfect," I said.

"Shut the door on the way out," she said. "I don't want to be disturbed."

I did as she asked. On to get some gossip.

I reached the room of Sherise Tyler at the end of the hall on the first floor, directly under Clarissa Hart's room. I knocked on the door and barely had my hand

42

back to my side when the door was sucked open. Sherise Tyler looked as though she was expecting somebody and it wasn't me. The disappointment on her face was obvious, and she knew that I'd caught it.

"Mrs. O'Shea," she said from way up in the clouds. This woman was tall, tall, tall. "What brings you to my room?"

"I was hoping that I could have a word with you."

She only stared down at me, as if she was waiting for the real reason.

"Okay, I was hoping that maybe you would share some gossip with me."

With that she smiled and motioned me into her room with a wave of her arm. She walked over and opened the window that faced the river and picked up her cigarettes on the nightstand. "Sorry," she said as she lit the cigarette. "I know you're pregnant and all, but there's a dead body slowly decaying directly above me, and I think that this calls for a cigarette. I'll try and blow it out the window."

"I appreciate that," I said.

She inhaled deeply, causing the end of the cigarette to glow bright red-orange, and then she flipped her long silky blond hair behind her shoulder and smiled. "So, somebody finally offed the old lady."

I tried not to let my surprise register on my face, but I don't think I did a very good job.

"People in this valley have been waiting for Clarissa Hart to die for thirty years," she explained.

"This is good," I said. "I came to you for gossip, and it looks like you have no qualms about talking."

"I can't tell you everything I know, because then I'd have nothing left for my story," she said and blew smoke directly out the window. She held the cigarette so

43

close to the curtains that I just knew at any minute they would go up in flames.

"So, you *are* searching for a story," I said.

"Oh, I'm not searching for anything. I've got my story. I just have to prove it," she said.

"Prove what?" I asked.

"Why should I tell you?"

"Well, partly because if Clarissa was murdered then I'm the number one suspect in a homicide, by the simple fact that I was found in the room with a dead body. I've never been a suspect in a homicide before. I was sort of hoping—"

"Hoping to solve the mystery yourself?" she asked. This time she sucked the smoke up her nostrils, and I wondered if that was worse for her than the initial smoke, since, technically, she would be getting both first- and second-hand smoke. I was enthralled with this, much as I'm enthralled with people who can blow smoke rings. How do they become so talented?

"Well, yes, actually," I answered finally.

"Ask me a question, and I'll try to answer it to the best of my ability," she said.

"Who is Norville Gross?"

"I haven't the foggiest idea," she said. "Obviously somebody important. Or at least important to Clarissa. People come out of the woodwork when there is money to be given or money to be had."

Okay, fair enough answer. "What's the story on Edwin?"

"Oh, dear sweet Edwin. The prodigal son returns. He was actually pronounced dead once. During the Korean War. He came home walking alongside his coffin," she said. "Never married. No children, that he claims, anyway. Knows every shortcut there is to being the richest man in the world."

"So, then why isn't he the richest man in the world? Or is he?"

"Because he is the only one who believes it. He spends money he doesn't have. He files bankruptcy every ten to twelve years, like clockwork. A complete loser."

Pretty much what I thought of him, actually. "What about Ollie?"

"He seems on the up-and-up."

"And the others? Lafayette and Maribelle?"

"Lafayette is a sweetie. Simpleminded, no great education, mind you. But he has a heart of gold and was a decorated soldier in both Korea and Vietnam," she said. She'd finally had enough of the cigarette and put it out in the ashtray on the nightstand. "Maribelle is never what she seems."

"How do you mean?" I asked.

She shrugged. "She tries to come across as this person who is deeply concerned about others. She likes for people to believe that she's this truly sentimental woman, when all she is really concerned with is her money and her station in society."

"How well do you know the family?" I asked.

"Well enough," she said. "But only from a distance. This is the first time they've met me. Although I've met them a time or two."

I decided to let that go, figuring if she was going to tell me, she would have. "What about the staff? Anybody particularly vindictive?"

"Dexter always does what he's told. Faithful. Susan, the cook, is very quiet. I don't have much on her. Vanessa Killian . . ." She hesitated an awfully long time. "She's harmless."

45

"Okay," I said. "I guess that's all I need to know for now."

"Don't you want to know about the boardinghouse? About the place you've inherited?" she asked and stepped away from the window with her arms crossed.

"What about it?" I asked. "It's a boardinghouse. What is there to know?"

"You won't make a good investigator with that kind of attitude," she said. "The where is often as important as the who and the why. This boardinghouse was at one time owned by the company. Do you know what that means? *The company,* back in the first quarter of the century, meant the coal company. Whichever coal company happened to own you and your family. Saying the words *the company* would send chills down some people's spines and contempt would be so heavy they nearly vomited with it."

"So, it was owned by . . . the Panther Run Coal Company, correct?"

"Yes," Sherise said. "And you didn't work for the company. The company owned you."

EIGHT

I WAS ONCE AGAIN LOOKING AT THE PHOTOGRAPH THAT hung on the wall above the fireplace.

A funny thing happened once I stopped looking at the dead guy in the casket and looked at the other people surrounding him. I recognized a woman standing just to the left of the casket. It was Gert's mother, my great-grandmother Bridie McClanahan, who later married and became Bridie Seaborne. She appeared very young in the photograph, in her late teens or early twenties. She

46

stood with one arm draped around the only person in the photograph who truly looked to be grieving. A woman of the same age, but lesser height. My great-grandmother was a hair short of six feet, a genetic trait that was lost to me. I inherited my height from my little short French grandmother on my father's side.

"Who is that?" I asked Gert.

"Who's who?" she asked and got up off the couch. She'd been angrily flipping channels on the television, which was receiving mostly snow since the flash flood occurred. "Can't believe they aren't showing the ball game."

"West Virginia doesn't have a professional baseball team," I said. "They could show the Orioles game. Or . . . the Reds."

My grandmother was a confirmed sports fanatic. When Otis Anderson made his eighty-something-yard run for the Cardiac Cardinals back in the seventies or early eighties, my grandmother jumped up out of her chair and broke her foot on the coffee table, which she had forgotten was sitting there. It was in the same place it always was, but she forgot about it that time. I was the only kid in school whose grandmother broke her foot in anything remotely concerning sports, let alone *watching* a game.

"Well . . . you wouldn't be able to see the picture very well anyway," I said. "Now come over here and tell me who this person is in the picture."

She reared her head back so that she could see out of the bifocal part of her glasses. Then she took them off and blinked her eyes, rubbing the glasses on her shirt.

"Want me to spit on them?" I asked.

She gave me that look. You know, the one that says I'm one heck of a smart-ass and that if I were worth the

47

trouble, she'd hit me a good one. "You think you're funny," she said. "Just wait until you get old."

"I'm getting old waiting for you to tell me who this person is in the picture!"

She put her glasses back on and repeated the process. "I can't see it."

I lifted the picture off the wall, and was immediately attacked by dust and one little bitty furry spider that I flung across the room with such fury that he probably died on impact. I was ashamed when I realized that I had actually squealed at it. When I was sure that there were no more crawly things, I wiped the glass with the extra material on the bottom of my shirt.

Gert took the picture and walked over to the window to get better light. After about twenty seconds she looked up and declared, "That's my mother."

"I know that, Gert. Who is in the coffin?"

"Oh," she said. "Oh, I don't know who that is. Never saw him before."

She examined the photograph again. "That's Clarissa, though. Standing next to Mom."

"It is?" I asked. I walked over and stood next to Gert, examining the photograph over her shoulder. "You recognize anybody else?"

"Sure . . . that's the reverend. That's my uncle Max. Oh, that there is . . . oh, what was that feller's name? Always wore his pants crooked. Can't remember. You know, Max played professional baseball."

She was back to Max. I'd heard this story before.

"Yes, back in 1918 or somewhere around there. For the White Sox."

"And that looks like . . . I don't know. Been too long. Some of these people were workers. For the company."

"How can you tell?"

She shrugged her shoulders. "Well, this picture was taken out back, see, there's the well. And there is the fence that isn't there anymore. So it was taken on the boardinghouse property, and most people that lived here or around here worked for the company. Plus, they look like miners."

I looked at the faces staring back at me across time, and I couldn't tell they were miners. How could she?

"When was this picture taken?"

"Before Mom got married. See . . . her hair's still down to her butt. She cut her hair shortly after she got married."

"So, somewhere between 1916 and 1918."

"Yeah, or it could have been after she was married, before she cut her hair. Although she'd probably be pregnant and she doesn't look it. No later than 1918," Gert answered. She studied the photograph a minute, and then her eyes lit up as if she'd just discovered something. "That man is in a casket!"

"Yup," I said. "I wonder who it could be? It had to be somebody important for the photo to be enlarged this big and hung over the fireplace in such a prominent display."

"People are disturbed," Gert said and made her way back to the couch and the remote control. "No baseball. What kinda state is this?"

"It's your state. You were born and raised here."

She waved her hand at me as if to say shut up.

Dexter Calloway came into the room and stopped, to my grandmother's deep frustration, right in front of the television. "Mrs. O'Shea," he said. "Clarissa said for me to show you the attic."

"What?" I asked. "Clarissa is dead."

"Before you'uns got here, she took me aside and said

that I was to make sure that you saw the attic, there bein' stuff up there that belonged to your great-grandma," he explained. "Since she couldn't show it to you, I was supposed to. Things been so hectic, though, I plumb forgot."

"That's all right, Mr. Calloway—"

"Call me Dexter."

"Dexter. Better late than never."

"The remote control won't work through your blasted leg," Gert said to him.

"Oh, sorry," he said and moved.

"Ignore her," I said. "Can I get up in the attic? In my condition?"

"Sure . . . there's a stairway."

"Okay, let's go."

Dexter Calloway led me directly to Clarissa's bedroom. We stopped in front of it knowing that the dead body of Clarissa Hart was lying in there, exactly as it had been early this morning. The door had masking tape along the seams as more of a deterrent than an actual barrier. If somebody wanted in the room, he could easily remove the tape and go in.

"Why are we here?" I asked.

"The entrance to the attic is in Clarissa's room," he said.

I know I must have looked as though somebody had just clubbed me between the eyes, but I couldn't help it. He knew we weren't supposed to go into Clarissa's room until the sheriff arrived and took her body away. Why would he try and take me up there? It took me a while to formulate words, because I just couldn't believe he would do this.

"Mr. Calloway . . ."

50

"Dexter," he said.

"We can't go in there," I said.

"The entrance to the attic is in her bedroom," he said as if I hadn't heard him.

"Well, we're just going to have to come back after the sheriff has come and taken the body away," I said and tried to lead him back down the hall. Give the man credit for being thoughtful and a good employee but his comprehension score was really low.

Just as I turned to walk down the hallway I stopped. *The entrance to the attic is in Clarissa's bedroom.* I turned and took the few steps back to Dexter, who had not moved away from the door.

"I apologize, Dexter."

"For what?"

"For thinking that you were about as smart as a toad. So, somebody could have escaped into the attic this morning. Is that what you're saying to me?" I asked.

"I'm not saying it," he said.

"Okay," I said. I thought I understood what he meant. He wanted me to be aware of it, but he wasn't going to come out and say it. "Anything else?"

"I was out back picking the last of the strawberries and checking on the tomato plants about mid-mornin' and noticed the window open."

"The attic has a window?"

"Yes," he said. "One on each end. The one toward Quiet Knob was open. Now, it might have been open before, but it's not likely. Since it's summer. Clarissa was a frugal one."

"Did she really tell you to make sure that I saw the attic? Or was that a ploy to get me up here alone?"

Before Dexter could answer my question, the door across the hall from Clarissa's opened and out walked

51

Norville Gross. He looked at us suspiciously because . . . well, because I'm assuming we looked suspicious. We were standing in front of the sealed room that had a dead body inside, talking in hushed tones of voice.

"Afternoon, Mr. Gross," Dexter said and nodded his head as if nothing was amiss.

"What are you two doing out here?" Norville asked.

"Talking," I said. "About the tomato plants."

"Yup, they lookin' mighty healthy," Dexter said.

Norville didn't look much better than he had this morning, and I think the pressure of being cooped up here with all of Clarissa's children was getting to him. They all desperately wanted to know his connection to Clarissa, and he wasn't talking. He also must have known somewhere in the recesses of his mind that they were going to try and contest the will. He stood to lose fifty grand.

"I'm going to go find a rock somewhere on the mountainside and sit until dinner," he said. "It's stuffy in here."

I knew better, since we had the air conditioner set on sixty-two degrees, for Clarissa's sake. It was cool in here for most people, and just right for me. I'm normally cold, but these baby hormones raise my body temperature until I feel like I could warm the moon just by standing in the middle of it. I was liking this sixty-two degrees.

"Well, don't fall off the rock," I said to him and smiled. He looked at me strangely. "It was an attempt at being friendly."

It didn't matter, because he was already making the turn down the stairs. Dexter and I returned to our conversation.

"So is there something in the attic that I am supposed

to see?"

"Yes. I'll show you once they take Clarissa out of here," he said. He reached in his pocket and pulled out a white rabbit's foot key ring and handed it to me. There were probably four or five different keys on it. "It's the keys to the place. It's yours now."

"I don't think so. I mean, aren't there some legalities still to go through before the place is actually mine?" I asked, holding the keys out in front of me as if they were poison to the touch.

"As far as I'm concerned, you're my new boss and this is your place until you decide what you're going to do with it. You have the last say-so on stuff around here," he said. "Your grandma worked for the company, you know. She paid her dues."

"Yes, I know. But I don't know what that has to do with anything."

"You're one of us. Your blood is here. My grandfather died in the big cave-in of seventeen," he said. "All of us got blood in the soil around here. Let me know if I can do anything else for ya."

With that he walked off down the hall, leaving me holding a dead rabbit's foot and wishing that old mountain folk wouldn't speak in riddles.

NINE

IT WAS TIME FOR DINNER, THANK GOODNESS, BECAUSE I'd done all of the snacking I could do without Susan Henry, the cook, kicking me out of the house. Every time I went into the kitchen, she scowled at me. I don't think it was a coincidence, either, that each time she was holding a big knife or a rolling pin.

I took the same seat that I'd had last night at dinner, with Gert to my right. This dinner wasn't nearly so formal; in fact, Danette, Maribelle, and Sherise were the only other people at the table with us. In my house, you eat when it's served, because there may not be anything left over otherwise.

The menu was navy beans, corn bread, a large ham with little pineapple slices stuck on the sides of it, collard greens, green-bean casserole, and fried onions. Dessert was blackberry cobbler or peach pie. In my case, it would probably be blackberry cobbler *and* peach pie, because I really wasn't much of a ham eater. That would be my official excuse for eating two desserts, anyway.

The conversation consisted of the polite type. The weather, what sort of schools we have in Missouri, and remedies for certain ailments. My grandmother also managed to get a few digs in on the fact that West Virginia did not have a professional baseball team.

"We don't need a team of our own," Sherise Tyler said finally. "St. Louis already has Mark McGwire, so what would be the point?"

"And don't you forget it," Gert said.

Sherise smiled at Gert and then winked at me. I smiled back, happy that somebody in this place knew something about St. Louis and baseball, so that my grandmother wouldn't go crazy.

"You know, Yogi Berra was from St. Louis," Gert said.

"Yes, but he didn't play for St. Louis," I said.

"My uncle Max played baseball," she said.

"Yes, but he didn't play for St. Louis, either," I said.

We were all so busy talking that we did not hear the boat approaching the boardinghouse. However, we all jumped when a ferocious hammering at the front door interrupted our conversation. At first, we all just stared at each other.

Then simultaneously we rose and headed for the great room. Maribelle and Gert got stuck in the doorway together, each one thinking the other was going to give way. Neither one backed down and so they just squeezed themselves through it. I think they may have widened the doorway a little bit. I just shook my head.

We reached the great room, but before I could open the door, it burst open. Two deputies entered the room with shotguns in their hands (pointed down, of course), muscles bulging, each one standing well over six feet. A scrawny man about five feet eight stepped in between them, put his hands on his hips and posed for us. It was like something out of a Western.

"Howdy, Sheriff," I said. I couldn't help myself.

"Ma'am," he said and tipped his hat. "Are you the one who made the 911 call?"

"Yes," I said. "The body is upstairs where we found it."

"The body?" he asked, his voice betraying just a slight bit of uneasiness.

"There is usually a body when there's a dead . . . body," I said. "Did you bring something to carry her back in?"

"Yes, we've got a pontoon out here. Water's receding fairly quick," he said. "What's your name?"

"I'm Victory O'Shea," I said. "Call me Torie, though. This is my grandmother, Gertrude Crookshank."

"And your relationship to the deceased?" he asked.

"Long story. Suffice it to say that she knew my grandmother's mother and summoned us here for the reading of her will. Sometime this morning she either

55

accidentally put a pillow over her face or somebody did it for her, and now she is dead."

"Who found her?" he asked.

"I did. With Norville Gross fast on my heels," I said.

"What do you mean?"

"I mean, I walked in and removed the pillow, because I didn't know . . . I thought she could still be alive but knew she wouldn't be much longer if I didn't get the pillow off her face. Norville walked in within half a minute. Danette," I said and pointed to Danette, who was lounging in one of the big brown recliners, "came in about two minutes after that."

"Okay," he said. "Boys, go get the stretcher."

The two very large men relaxed and went back out the door. Dusk was approaching, but it was still light enough outside to see well. The sheriff had a thin mustache and thick, round spectacles that made his eyes look twice as large as they actually were. He had a certain crispness to him, though, which gave the impression that he was efficient and on top of his game. His uniform was spotless and seamed. I knew a sheriff that could take a few pointers from him.

"Sheriff, what is your name?" I asked.

"I'm Sheriff Thomas T. Justice," he said. He reached out and shook my hand. I couldn't help but smile at the fact his last name was Justice and he was a sheriff. Wonder how much ribbing he took over that? "Those are my two best deputies. I've got three others. Small community, you know."

"Oh, I know all about that," I said. "I live in a town of a couple of hundred. We don't even have our own sheriff. We have to borrow the one from the next town."

"Did you seal everything off?"

56

"As best as we could," I said. "We taped up her bedroom, where she was found, and her office."

"Where will you take my mother?" Maribelle asked.

"Ma'am," he said and tipped his hat. "We'll take her to the nearest hospital. Saint Catherine's probably."

"I'm going to go tell my brother, if you'll excuse me," she said.

"How much longer?" the sheriff asked and pointed to my stomach.

"Oh, at least two months," I said, rubbing it absently.

He raised his eyebrows.

"Yes, I know. I always look huge the last trimester. I think it's because I'm so short. The baby doesn't have anywhere to go except out," I said. It was my theory, but I had no idea if it was true.

"Good," he said. "Then you're not going to need an emergency evac or anything, right?"

"No," I said. "We'll be fine right where we are. As long as the water is gone by Friday, because we have to head back home."

"That's almost a week. It'll be gone probably late tomorrow. So, where's home?" he asked.

"Missouri," I said. "South of St. Louis."

"Mark McGwire country," he said.

With that, Sherise Tyler started laughing across the room. She stood by the fireplace, flipping her ashes from her recently lit cigarette into it. "See, told you," she said.

The sheriff looked dutifully lost. I took advantage of the momentary silence to ask a question I'd been wanting to ask for a long time. "Does anybody know who the man is in the casket?" I asked and pointed to the photograph above the fireplace.

"Heard stories," Sheriff Justice said. I hadn't

57

expected *him* to answer.

"None of which are true, I'll bet," Sherise said.

I thought that a rather unusual comeback. "How do you know?"

"Nobody knows who it is. Clarissa would never tell anybody," she said. "Nobody knows who any of those people are."

"Well, one of them is my mother and another one is Clarissa," Gert said before I could stop her.

Sherise looked at me peculiarly. I said, "She's right. My great-grandmother is in the picture next to Clarissa."

"Still," Sherise said, her gaze flicking toward the sheriff. "Nobody knows the man in the casket. It's a fruitless quest."

Who was she trying to convince, anyway? I got the feeling she didn't want anybody to know who the dead man was. First chance I got, I was going to try and find out Sherise's connection to the Harts and this place. She said she already had her story, she just had to prove it. It had something to do with either this place or people who had owned it.

The deputy turned to me then. "So, the first ones in the room were you, the girl," he said and pointed at Danette. "And who else?"

"Norville Gross," I answered.

"Who's he?" he asked. Good question, I thought. Nobody knew who he was or if that was even his real name.

I was about to answer him when one of the deputies came to the door looking pale and worried. "Sheriff, you better come look at this."

We of course all followed out onto the porch as the sheriff went out to see just what it was the deputy was looking all anemic about. There we stood: a gorgeous journalist, Sherise Tyler; my screwy grandmother; a sixteen-year-old pierced version of Janis Joplin; and me, the pregnant lady. The scene just struck me as funny until I saw what the deputies were looking at.

An overturned tree had washed up half in the river and half on the road that was beginning to be visible from the receding water. Lying sprawled over the tree was Norville Gross. Blood pooled just below his neck and all over his shirt, and his eyes were staring off at the top of the mountain.

"Sort of reminds me of the time they found your uncle Jed floating in the Mississippi," Gert said to me. I cussed her silently and smiled at Sheriff Justice as he turned to look at the two of us with an upraised eyebrow. Whoever the brilliant individual was who had thought it would be a good idea to go on a long trip with her grandmother, alone, was an idiot. And I was ignoring the fact that I was that brilliant idiot.

Sherise stepped off the porch, after giving me the questioning eye, to get a closer look. The heels of her shoes sank into the sodden grass as she did so.

"That's Norville Gross," I said to Sheriff justice, hoping he'd forgotten about what my grandmother had just blurted out. My head was a tad swimmy and I thought I'd lose my dinner as the realization sunk in that here was another dead body. And he wasn't as peaceful-looking as Clarissa.

"What do you think happened to him?" Gert asked.

"Looks like a panther got a hold of him, or something," Sheriff Justice answered.

The only phrase spoken after that was a definite expression of disgust from our resident hormone-infested teenager. "Oh, gross."

TEN

I AWOKE THE NEXT MORNING TO FIND MY GRANDMOTHER sitting on the foot of my bed completely dressed, including wearing a hat and holding her purse. At first I thought I was dreaming so I really didn't react. Then I realized that she was sitting on my foot and I couldn't move it, and alas, I knew I was not dreaming.

Groggily, I leaned up on one elbow and rubbed my eyes. I looked over at the travel alarm clock I had packed that was now next to the lamp on the nightstand. It said 7:15 A.M.

"It's about time you woke up," she said.

"What are you doing?"

"I'm sitting here waiting for you to wake up."

"Why?"

"Because it's Sunday and you're taking me out for breakfast and then I want you to take me to church. The one that I went to as a kid," she said.

"There is water covering the road," I said.

"It's gone. Sometime in the middle of the night it receded enough that you can drive on the road now. By noon the river will probably be back within its normal banks," she said. "We'd get this two or three times a year when I lived here."

"Why?" I asked.

"Because the river takes a sharp turn south of here and narrows like a bottleneck. And because just one or two miles north of here the water comes down off the mountain, just gushing," she explained. "It gets all backed up in that bottleneck. Services should start about nine."

60

There was no segue most of the time when she spoke. She just said one thing about one subject and then something else about another subject. It was a good thing that I was used to it.

"Well, I guess I should get dressed," I said. "As soon as you get off my foot."

Gert rushed me around like I was late for school or something so I was completely ready in twenty-five minutes flat. Shower, seven minutes. Makeup, five minutes. Brushing teeth, two minutes. When it came to getting dressed, though, she allowed me a whole ten minutes.

I was a little perturbed, however, because I'd worn my good dress yesterday, not knowing we would be attending church today. My grandmother squirted perfume on it and shook it outside in the breeze and told me it would be fine to wear again, as long as I wore different panty hose. I didn't argue with her.

A little while later we drove over the mountain Gert had referred to when telling me about the flash flooding. We then descended the other side and drove around the base of another mountain. Then the road seemed to part the mountains, and there below us, sprinkled along the valley and the next hill, was the town of Panther Run.

There was one main street with a hanging stoplight and three fairly major cross streets. It was quaint, like a movie set, as if only the fronts of the buildings were painted and perfect and hiding behind them were dirt-poor residents with leaky roofs and yards with no grass.

"That's it. That's the church," she said and pointed to the left on top of the hill. A white church with a pointy steeple sat proudly surrounded by lush green trees, keeping watch over the town below it.

"Okay," I said. "Where do you want to eat?"

"Let's eat at Bucky's. Up here on the right—well, what did they do with Bucky's?"

I looked to where she pointed. "Looks like it's a Denny's," I said.

"What happened to Bucky's?" she asked with genuine sorrow. "Oh, I bet he died."

I couldn't help but laugh because she'd added that last bit as if it was *the* only explanation for what could have happened to Bucky's. The fact that chain restaurants had come in and taken over, making it impossible for the little guy to own his own company, had not occurred to her. Gert could tell me anything I wanted to know about massive earthquakes, massacres in schools, rare and deadly diseases, but she seemed clueless over the quiet catastrophes.

"All right, let's eat at Denny's," she said.

The food was good. Service was good. Conversation was a bit scattered.

Gert inhaled her food, which she swears was caused from thirty-five years of being a waitress and never getting an official lunch break. Whatever the reason, with her I always felt self-conscious about the fact that I was still eating. I guess I was worried it would appear as though I had so much more food than she did that it took me twice as long to eat.

"The sheriff said he should have Clarissa's room and office cleared by this evening," Gert said.

"Good," I said. "Dexter Calloway said that there was some stuff up in the attic that Clarissa wanted me to have. Said that the stuff belonged to your mother."

Gert thought about it a minute. "Wonder what it could be?"

"I don't have a clue," I said. "Gert, why would somebody want to kill Clarissa? I mean, she was a hundred and one years old, like she wasn't going to die soon enough on her own?"

"Seems to me," she said, shaking her head, "that whoever it was wanted to make sure the new will was not read or filed at the courthouse. What other reason could it be?"

"Then that would have to mean it was one of her three children. Other than Norville, who is now out of the picture, and myself, there wasn't anybody else who inherited anything."

"Maybe they were left something in the old will and got left out of the new one," she said.

"Maybe Mr. Jett would let me look at the old will to see who else is listed," I said. I took my last drink of orange juice and sighed. "It just seems so wrong."

"It could be one of her grandchildren," Gert suggested.

"Why?"

"Making sure that their parents got the inheritance so that they would in turn get their inheritance," she said. "And I don't think that was a panther."

It took me a second to realize she had shifted gears and was now talking about Norville Gross. "Why not?" I asked.

"Panther's not going to come that close to people in the day."

"What if he wandered into the woods and stumbled upon the panther?" I said.

"It wouldn't drag him back to the boardinghouse. I might be wrong, but do you think a panther could drag a hundred-and-eighty-pound man back to the house? And if she could or would drag him around, why wouldn't she go farther into the woods with him, instead of back to civilization?"

"Maybe he wasn't dead yet and he crawled back on his own," I said. It was clear that my grandmother had given this a lot of thought.

"Nope," she said. "He wasn't tore up enough for it to be a panther."

I reached into my purse to get out my wallet so I could pay the bill. Her words stopped me. "How would you know?"

" 'Cause, you forget I was born and raised in these mountains," she said. "I've seen what panthers can do. Your great-uncle Martin had a run-in with a panther. Not only did he not live, but there were claw marks and blood everywhere. Teeth marks, too."

My stomach was turning.

"That Norville fellow's face was all in one piece. Panther's gonna go for the head and neck area. As would any wild animal," she said.

"Gee, thanks, Gert. Thanks for the lesson in animal attacks."

"Oh, and the time the bear got a hold of—"

"That's okay. Really. I get the picture."

The waitress came up to us then to see if we wanted refills on coffee or anything. Since I was having to do the no-caffeine, no-chocolate, low-sugar thing, I had no coffee or soda for her to refill. I know my doctor swears that this is the best thing for me and the baby, but I find this grossly unfair. I'm an American, for crying out loud. Take away my caffeine and chocolate, and what's left?

"Where ya'll staying?" the waitress asked.

"The Panther Run Boardinghouse," I said. She must have realized that we either sounded like out-of-towners or acted like them, I wasn't sure which.

"Oh, that old place? What for?"

64

The waitress pronounced *for* as *fer* and I had to smile. My grandmother would slip into her old accent every now and then, but it was just about gone. I always liked it when she'd say things like *poosh* for *push* or *fer* instead of *for.*

Before either one of us could answer her, she spoke again. "Heard you had a painter attack."

I looked lost, so Gert clarified for me. "Panther attack."

"Right after that gulley washer, too," the waitress added.

"Well, we think it was an attack by some sort of wild animal. We're not actually sure if it was a panther," I said.

"Used to be around here, painters were aplenty. They gettin' scarce now," she said.

"I know," Gert said. "I'm from this part of the woods."

"Oh, yeah?" the waitress asked as she picked up our empty plates. "Ain't changed much."

Oh, but it had, I thought, as she walked away. To her maybe it was the same old stagnant small town with the same trappings as every other small town. But it had changed. Bucky's, who or whatever it was, was gone. There was a McDonald's on the corner as we came into town, which I'm sure had been added in the last ten or fifteen years. A chain grocery store was on the right, back at the stoplight. And once upon a time, this had been a coal town. Owned by the coal company. Meaning it had a company store and a company doctor. Oh, it had changed plenty.

Gert and I went to the register and paid the bill. As I waited for my change, I noticed the woman behind the register kept eyeing me. I got that a lot, because I look

65

as if I had a beach ball stuffed under my clothes, and nobody could wait to ask when I was due.

"Think they'll ever find out?" the woman asked.

"Find out what?"

"Now that Mrs. Hart's dead. They say she was the one who knew."

"Knew what?" I was surprised by her line of questioning. It was obvious she had either overhead our conversation with the waitress or the waitress had marched right up here and told her that we were staying at the boardinghouse. I wasn't surprised, however, with how quickly the town knew about Clarissa and the "panther" attack of the night before. I was from a small town. I knew how this worked.

"You know," she said. "Those two miners. You think they'll ever find out what happened to them?"

"We're gonna be late for church," Gert said to me. She all but shooed me out the door. I barely had time to get my change from the woman.

"Gert—"

"Let's just get to church," she said. "Don't give me no trouble or my hand's gonna meet your fanny."

I didn't doubt her. She'd swatted my fanny plenty. I got in the car and drove us to church, wondering all the while what the cashier at Denny's was referring to, and why my grandmother seemed fairly intent on not discussing it.

ELEVEN

GERT AND I SAT IN THE THIRD PEW FROM THE FRONT ON the left-hand side of the church when facing the altar. Shiny hardwood floors reflected everything from the rays of sunlight filtering through the long garden-style windows to my feet, tapping lightly to the sounds of "Swing Low, Sweet Chariot." The walls were plain and brilliant white, and there was no overexhausted ornamentation anywhere within the church walls. The podium was wooden with a cross carved into it, situated just slightly to the left on the altar and a large pine cross hung from the ceiling above the altar. That was it. No other decorations or distractions.

The preacher was a jolly-looking man, with round wire spectacles and a head that was semibald except for the ring of white cotton that started at one temple and wound around the bottom of his head to the other temple. It looked as though somebody had shaved the entire top portion of his head and buffed it until it shined, then glued cotton balls along the bottom portion. As if that weren't enough puffy stuff, his beard was also full and cottony, his pink lips supplying the only color, peering out of the cotton. His voice was raspy, but pleasant, and he shook his jowls when emphasizing a particular word or phrase. He kept his thumbs hooked in his belt, and every now and then he would rub his belly, which could rival my third-trimester belly.

Today's sermon was about the temptations of the flesh. Gluttony, alcohol, and sex seemed to be his primary focus. He talked about taking only what was yours and not borrowing your neighbor's and how it wouldn't hurt for us, as Americans, to give up some of our comforts for those less fortunate in other parts of the world. I agreed with him on all of it, but I couldn't help but wonder how many meals he'd given up for the sake of starving people the world over. It had long been a source of great guilt for me, the things that my family and I had, and yet . . . just over the horizon was always

67

something else that we wanted. Was it that we were never satisfied, or was it that our goals changed? Or was that the same thing?

Also in attendance this morning was Lafayette Hart, seated in the very front pew on our side. Susan Henry, the cook, was seated on the right-hand side halfway back. "Brother Hart," as the pastor kept calling Lafayette, would raise his hand every now and then, and he always led the congregation in singing.

"Brother Hart," the pastor would say, "lead us in song." And Lafayette would stand and begin the song by himself until everybody else recognized the music that he'd chosen and joined in.

"And the sanctity of the physical relationship," the pastor said, "of man and wife . . . is the greatest gift two people can give each other."

I thought about Rudy and was amazed at the overwhelming desire I had to see him. I'd only been gone two nights, and I really and truly missed him. I also thought of the girls and how they were probably sitting on the couch in their pajamas, eating Apple Cinnamon Cheerios and watching Pokémon. Suddenly I wanted to go home.

"But never should you take that sacred act beyond the walls of your marriage," the pastor said. "And consume not the wickedness of alcohol. The spirits. Booze."

It might have been my imagination, but I could have sworn there were a few people squirming in their seats. The pastor slammed his hand down on the podium so hard that the microphone nearly toppled over.

"It is pure evil. The root of everything bad," he said. "Brothers and sisters, when you feel the need to drink, open your Bibles. Turn to God. Brothers and sisters, the alcohol you have in your house—that six-pack of beer.

The half a fifth of whiskey or gin. That bottle of wine you keep saying that you use for cookin' those fancy recipes. Don't be fooled by the devil. You gather up alcoholic evils, and you take them to the river. You take them to the river, and you dump them out! Pour them all into the river, and your sins will be washed away with the tide. You will feel better, and you will be a new person. Brother Hart, lead us in song."

Lafayette Hart stood and without hesitation began singing "Shall We Gather at the River?" The irony was not lost on me nor on half of the congregation as they snickered behind their hands at Lafayette's choice in music. The pastor, however, never faltered and sang along with him.

When the services were over there was a box social luncheon. Gert wanted to stay. I wanted to go home and call my family, but we stayed anyway.

I stood at the end of a table, with a paper plate in hand, waiting for my turn at the potato salad. Gert was already seated and would be finished eating by the time I made it through the line. The pastor stood right behind me talking to Lafayette.

"I am so sorry to hear about your mother," the pastor said to Lafayette.

"Thank you," Lafayette said. "We'd been expectin' it for a time now."

The pastor unexpectedly turned and addressed me. "I'm Pastor Breedlove," he said and stuck his hand out for me to shake.

"Torie O'Shea," I said. My little bundle of joy decided to give a good swift kick at that moment. I gasped because he or she was upside down and kicked me in the ribs, which in turn made me feel as if all of the air had been shoved out of my lungs.

"Looks like you're due about the same time I am," he said, laughing and rubbing his belly.

"You said that, not me," I said. I piled the potato salad on my plate and moved down the line to the baked beans.

"I hear you are the new owner of the boardinghouse," he said, following behind me. "Does that mean you will be moving here?"

"Oh, no," I said. "I could never leave New Kassel. And *will* never leave it."

Again, it did not surprise me that he already knew that I was the so-called heiress of Panther Run. Not one bit. It did seem as though he was fishing for information, however. What the heck, I'd make it easy on him.

"I've not decided exactly what I'm going to do about this situation, Pastor Breedlove. Besides, I'm not entirely sure that the Harts won't contest it," I said and smiled as sweetly as I could at Lafayette. It did not go unnoticed that his potato salad fell into the plate of sliced tomatoes.

"So, tell me, Pastor. What do you know about a man named Norville Gross?" I asked.

"Brother Hart was just asking me the same question not two minutes ago," he said, genuinely. "I don't know."

"Is there a library around here close?" I asked. "So that I don't have to go all the way down to Charleston to the Cultural Center?"

"Yes," he said. "There's one over the hill in the next holler. Quentinton."

"And the county seat?" I asked. "Where is it?"

"Also Quentinton."

"Thank you," I said.

"When is your baby due?" he asked.

"Not soon enough has become my standard answer," I said and smiled. "Seriously, it's due in August."

"That's nice," he said. "So . . . are you from West Virginia?"

"No," I said. By this time I'd made it to the pork steaks. I chose two deviled eggs instead. "My mother was born and raised here. Moved to Missouri in the 1950s. My ancestors go way back in this state."

"How far?"

"Back to when it was Virginia. Back to before it was a state at all. My ancestors were some of the first to spill over the ridge. Did you know that even the Native Americans thought that this land was too hostile to live in all year around?"

"No," he said. "Afraid the only thing I know about the Indians is the Morris Massacre."

"Oh, yes," I said, aware of the story of Mr. Morris and his ill-fated pioneer family. "Well, there's lots more to know about Native Americans than that."

"What are you?" he asked.

"Excuse me?"

"Your nationality?"

"I'm an American, silly." With that I walked away, shoving a deviled egg in my mouth as I went. I sat down across from Gert, and as I had expected, she was already finished eating.

What I hadn't expected was for Pastor Breedlove to follow me to my table, with Lafayette Hart on his heels, and sit down across from me. "We're all Americans," he said. "But what were your ancestors?"

"Little bit of this, little bit of that. Basically, though, my ancestors from this area were Scotch-Irish. Just like everybody else's in this area," I said.

71

"Why the interest in my ancestors, Pastor?"

"Just wonderin' if we were related," he said.

"Go back a few generations, I wouldn't doubt it." And that was a fact. I have a cousin who is my cousin so many times in so many different ways that we are more related to each other than if we were brother and sister.

"This is my grandmother," I said. "Gertrude Crookshank. Originally, Seaborne."

"Seaborne?" he said and nodded at her. "Nice to meet you."

It was quiet a moment until Lafayette finally spoke up. "Gertie's mother was Bridie McClanahan."

Now I doubt seriously that Pastor Breedlove was old enough to remember a woman who had died very young in 1926. But the look on his face said that he at least knew of her. "Bridie Mac," he stated.

"Excuse me?" I asked. "What do you mean, Bridie Mac?"

" 'Lies all those lies, sharp as a tack. Need to keep a secret, tell Bridie Mac,' " he chanted.

I cannot tell you the peculiar feeling that crept down my spine, causing goose bumps to break out along my neck and arms. Was this something he had just made up? If so, why? And if it wasn't something that he had just made up off the top of his head, its implications were quite disturbing.

I was speechless, unable to say a word. I suppose the look on my face relayed everything I was feeling and thinking, because the pastor became very somber and apologetic. "Forgive me," he said.

"What . . . what was that?" I asked. I looked to Gert, who seemed as disturbed as I, but in a different way.

"You know those rhymes that kids on the playground chant when they're a-doin' things like hopscotch?

Somethin' I heard as a kid," he said. "I didn't mean to trouble you."

"Not at all," I said, recovering enough to take a bite of some excellent potato salad. We all ate in silence for a few moments. Two little girls, in their frilly Sunday best, ran around the churchyard chasing each other with chocolate ice-cream cones. I really wanted to talk to my girls.

"So, tell me, Lafayette," I said. "I had a cashier at breakfast ask me something about two miners who either disappeared or had some terrible fate befall them. Do you know what she's referring to?"

Lafayette snapped his plastic fork in two trying to pick up a piece of his pork steak. "Mm, not sure."

"It was said in reference to your mother and the boardinghouse. The woman said that now we may never know what happened to those miners. What was she talking about?" I asked.

Lafayette looked good for his seventy-one years. He normally had healthy coloring, but at the moment he looked a little peaked. He didn't get a chance to answer me, Pastor Breedlove answered for him.

"Oh, she's probably talkin' about those two miners a long time ago that went a-missing and nobody ever saw again. Rumor has it," he said, raising his eyebrows so as to appear mysterious or spooky, "they was last seen in the company of Brother Hart's mother, Clarissa."

I loved the way he just told me all of that without a second thought. It was clear that this was something Lafayette either didn't want me to know or was trying to think of a way to express. Pastor Breedlove saw no danger in it, so he just came out with it. All I could do was nod and say, "You don't say, Pastor Breedlove. You don't say."

TWELVE

"ARE YOU BEING A GOOD GIRL?" I ASKED. I STOOD IN the great room of the boardinghouse, scratching my belly with one hand and holding the phone with the other.

"I've been good, but Rachel is seriously disturved, Mom," Mary answered.

"That's *disturbed,* with a *b,*" I said.

"Whatever," she said. "She likes Brian Filmore, and he's, like, the rudest boy in the whole school. And just because I told him that she liked him, she punched me in the head and now I have a big bruise."

"I've told you before, you're not supposed to do that sort of thing," I said.

"Yeah, but she coulda killed me! She punched me right in the head. What if I get a tumor?" she asked.

"You won't get a tumor from that. You be nice to Rachel," I said. "Put her on the phone."

Mary pulled the phone away from her mouth maybe an inch or two and yelled Rachel's name at the top of her lungs. I jerked the phone away from my ear as the shrillness of her scream went straight to my eardrum.

"Hello?" Rachel said. I could tell that she picked up the other phone instead of taking the one that Mary was holding.

"What are you doing punching Mary in the head?"

"Hi, Mom. How are you?"

"I'm fine," I said. "You're not being good like I asked you to be."

"She told Brian Filmore that I wanted to kiss him and I can't stand him—"

74

"Uh-uh," Mary butted in. "You like him, yes you do."

"All right, Mary, get off the phone," I said. After several moments of protestations she finally did as I asked. "Rachel, you're grounded from swimming for the rest of the week."

"Mom!"

"You don't go around punching people, especially somebody who's half your size," I explained.

"Do you know what Brian Filmore looks like, Mother?" Rachel asked, obviously frustrated with me.

"I don't care if he looks like Chewbacca—"

"Chewbacca is adorable compared to him. He never brushes his teeth," she said.

"Regardless. It wasn't nice of Mary to tell him that, but you just can't go and punch her," I said. "That's not appropriate behavior."

"Fine," she said. I could just see her on the other end of the phone tapping her feet and rolling her eyes heavenward.

What I couldn't figure out was why Rudy hadn't grounded her. I guessed he was waiting for me to lay down the punishment. The more Rachel and Mary began acting like sisters, the more Rudy sort of let me decide the appropriate punishment for things. I'm not sure I appreciated my new responsibility.

"Let me talk to your grandma," I said.

"Hello," my mother said.

"Hey, Mom," I said. "So Rudy's at the ball game?"

"Yeah. He got two free tickets from his boss, and so he took Chuck Velasco," she explained.

"Oh," I said. "Tell him I called."

"You sound down," she said.

"I am," I answered. "I called because I was missing him and the girls really bad, and I get attacked by two quarreling children. Then the man of my dreams is off at the ball game."

"Poor thing," she said in an overly pitying tone of voice.

"Exactly," I said. "I'm feeling very vulnerable."

"You'll get over it," she said. "You always do."

"Gee, thanks, Mom."

"So . . . how's the visit going?"

"Good," I said. "Clarissa died in her sleep, we think, or she may have been suffocated. She left me the boardinghouse plus ten acres and everything in it, and Norville Gross was attacked by a panther, we think, or somebody could have hacked him up. He didn't survive. All in all it's been a fairly exciting vacation."

My mother was quiet on the other end. "You're not joking," she said.

"No. Oh, and you didn't hear any of this from me, because I wasn't supposed to tell you about it."

"Why?"

"Colin told me not to tell you. But you're my mother and I tell you everything."

"I've been really uptight over the wedding. I'm having trouble finding somebody who will make you a maternity maid-of-honor dress," she said. "And they were out of the seafoam-green that I wanted, so I may have to go with peach. I wanted seafoam-green. And the dresses for Rachel and Mary are going to cost twice what I thought."

Every time I think I've forgotten that she's getting married and moving out of my house, she goes and reminds me. "Peach is nice," I said.

"I wanted seafoam-green."

"But peach is nice, Mom."

"Anyway, Colin is worried about me being all

76

upset. He says he can see my blood pressure rising every time something else goes wrong," she said. "I'm sure that's why he didn't want you to tell me all of that."

Great. Now I felt like a heel. I suppose I should have felt like a heel, but she had always been my confidante. "It's nothing," I said. "Gert is holding up just fine and the state is as gorgeous as always."

"Hasn't changed?" she asked.

"No, the mountains are still here, believe it or not."

"Have you seen Milly yet?"

"We're going this afternoon," I said.

"Tell her she better be here in August," my mother said.

"I will. Well, I better get going, Mom. It was good to hear your voice. Tell Rudy I called," I said.

"I will," she said. "Victory—"

"Yes?"

"What do you mean you inherited a boardinghouse, ten acres, and all of its contents?"

THIRTEEN

LATE SUNDAY EVENING MY GRANDMOTHER AND I hopped in the car and drove south along the Gauley River to the town of Ellensdale, where my mother's sister, Millicent, lived. Not only did we go so we could spend the evening with Aunt Milly, but our departure would give the sheriff and his deputies time to do whatever it was they were doing at the boardinghouse. Gathering evidence, I presumed.

"Make a left here," Gert said.

"Where?"

"Here."

I looked to where she was pointing and saw nothing. There was no road. The blacktop that we were on meandered down into the valley, eventually wandering its way through the town of Ellensdale, but off to the left was nothing but tall grass. There was at least an acre of flat land that stretched out before rising into one of the biggest peaks in the area.

"Just turn," she shouted at me.

"Okay," I said. When I had the car crossing the opposite lane I saw the slightest tracks of what could have been a road. I pulled in and followed it across the flat land. Then came the mountain.

"Are you sure we should try this?" I asked. "Maybe we should rent a four-wheel drive. I don't want to get so jostled around that my water breaks."

"I went up mountains bigger than this in a horse-drawn buggy when I was pregnant, and it never made my water break," she declared.

"Yes, but there's always a first time, Granny. And if there's some unusual thing waiting to happen to somebody, it's going to happen to me."

"You worry too much," she said.

"I do not."

"Are you gonna go up that road or not?"

"No," I folded my arms as best I could across my belly.

"Oh, for Pete's sake, as soon as you get around the bend, hers is the first house," she said.

"I was up this road when I was a lot younger with somebody else driving, and I don't remember it being so harmless. Didn't Rudy scrape the whole bottom of his car or something?" It had been fourteen or so years since I'd been to Aunt Millicent's house. Before that, I was a teenager.

"Oh, for Pete's sake," she said again, and opened her car door.

"Where are you going?"

"I'm gonna walk!" She pulled her cane out of the front seat and cussed under her breath when it got caught on the seat belt. "Gosh darn it, anyhow."

"Gert. Gert, get in the car. You can barely walk across the room without getting dizzy, you sure as heck can't climb up this mountain. Now get in!"

"Are you gonna drive up there?"

I tapped my fingers impatiently on the steering wheel. "Yes. Now get in."

She got back in the car, smug as she could be. I wanted to bop her a good one, but what would that solve? I put the car in second gear and headed up the mountain. I only went about eight miles an hour because, I didn't care what she said about horse-drawn buggies, I wasn't taking a chance on prematurely breaking my water.

"You know what the Indians said when they came to the junction of the Gauley River and the New River?" Gert asked.

"No, what?"

"They said, 'Golly! A new river!' Get it? Gauley, golly," she said and slapped herself on the knee.

"Hilarious, Gert. Just hilarious."

Ten minutes later I was still driving as cautiously as ever, very proud of the fact that I had not scraped the underneath part of my car on any ridges or rocks.

"You know," she said. "I did tell Milly that we'd be there this evening."

"Look, Gert. Get off my back over this," I said, slightly more hatefully than I intended. Well, actually I intended for it to be hateful, I just didn't want it to sound like I meant it to be hateful.

Finally, we made it to a clearing on the side of the mountain. It was as if somebody had come along and flattened out about an acre halfway up the mountain. Just enough space for Aunt Millicent to put her house and her chickens.

She lived in a two-story log cabin with a huge screened-in front porch. Her red jeep Cherokee was parked in the front with mud splashed halfway up the doors and all over the tires making them brown instead of black. Two rhododendron bushes stood proudly on each side of her porch, and wind chimes twinkled from the large tree in the front yard.

The chickens ran wild in the yard, and they clucked like mad when we opened the doors of the car. Before I could even get all the way out, Aunt Millicent was out the front door, off the porch, and running across the driveway with her arms wide open. "Momma," she said and hugged Gert.

Gert hugged her back, all the while fighting off the chickens with her cane. Seems they liked the smell of my grandmother's shoes and went about pecking at them.

Aunt Millicent turned to me. "Oh, you're so pregnant!" she said.

"Yup," I said. "I've tried to convince the baby not to get any bigger, but I don't think it's listening."

"It's so good to see you, Torie. The last time I saw you was four years ago when I came out to Missouri to visit everybody," she said. "You-all should move out here."

"No, no," I said. "We like it right where we are."

"Oh, yeah?" she said and took me by the hand to the steps of her front porch. When we got to the top step she turned me around as if presenting me at some fancy ball. Instead, she presented the mountains to me. "Look at that view. No matter how long I've lived here, I have to catch my breath every morning when I look at that."

From her porch I could see forever. Well, almost. A clearing of trees lined up perfectly with her porch and it allowed me to see the valley below. The river snaked through the valley floor, skating over rocks and fallen tree limbs. Above that were the mountains, swelling gently along the river. Beyond that were more mountains, and beyond that more mountains. I come from a fairly flat state, except for the Ozarks in the south. And to get here I had to come through the really flat land of Illinois, Indiana, and Ohio. I knew that these mountains did not go on forever. But as I stood there looking at them ripple all the way to the horizon, you would have been hard-pressed to convince me of that.

"Wow," I said.

"Country roads and misty mornings," she said with a loud sigh. "Let's sit on the porch."

Aunt Millicent was about five feet six and of average build. She was a little top-heavy, but most of my mother's family was. She made her way back down the porch steps to help Gert. Once inside the screened-in porch, Gert sat down next to me, huffing and puffing.

"And you were gonna walk up the mountain," I said.

"Of course not," she said. "I got you movin', though, didn't I?"

Aunt Milly disappeared into her house and came back out with a tray of cookies and crackers and a pitcher of iced tea. She disappeared once again and emerged with three glasses and a pitcher of lemonade.

"I didn't know what anybody wanted to drink, so I made both," she said. "How's your girls? Are they excited about having another sibling?"

"I think for the most part, although Mary insists that it cannot be a boy."

"Ain't much she can do about it, if it is," she said.

We talked for close to two hours, during which time I took a few snapshots of her and Gert with the camera I'd brought along. Then I had Gert take one of me and Aunt Milly. Finally, the conversation made its way to the recent events.

"Clarissa Hart left Torie the boardinghouse," Gert said.

Aunt Millicent nearly dropped her glass of lemonade. "You're joking?"

"No," I said.

Aunt Millicent got up and disappeared into her house yet again. She came out carrying a box of matches and what looked like a photo album. It was starting to get dark out, and so she went about lighting the six huge floor candles around the porch. Instantly the porch was awash in a golden hue. Then she sat down next to me with the album. She opened it up and thumbed through a few pages.

"There," she said. "That's the boardinghouse in its coal company days."

This time I could make out the coal miners, for they sat along the porch and the upper balcony with their sooty faces staring back at the camera. Some of them held knapsacks, some held lunch pails. There were also a few men who weren't miners—loggers, maybe, for the railroad—and a few women.

"Are you in this picture, Granny?" I asked.

"No, this would have been before her time. This

was taken about 1915 or so. When Clarissa Hart ran the boardinghouse for the company," Aunt Millicent said.

"Clarissa worked for the company?"

"Yes," she said. "Mom didn't start working it until the late twenties."

"I worked there up until about 1935," my grandmother added.

"Then what happened?" I asked.

"I got married," she said. "I think that's when the company went belly-up. At any rate, the company had sold the boardinghouse around 1918, I think."

"Well, the deed will tell me that much, as soon as I can get into Quentinton," I said.

Aunt Millicent pointed to another photograph on the next page. It was of Gert sitting on the front steps of the boardinghouse with one of her cousins. I recognized that it was a cousin, because I'd seen pictures of her before, but I couldn't remember which one. They were both about twelve or thirteen.

"What do you know about the boardinghouse?" I asked.

"It's bad luck," Millicent said.

I was a little surprised by her answer. "What?"

"Whoever owns it receives bad luck."

"Clarissa Hart lived to be one hundred and one years old and, having been at the reading of her will, I can attest to the fact that she had accumulated a good-sized estate," I said. "You call that bad luck?"

"You have no clue what her life was like," Aunt Millicent said.

"Enlighten me," I said.

"It would take more time than we have for me to tell you her life story. The coal company went belly-up," she said. "As much as I'd like to see you here in West Virginia, don't move into the boardinghouse."

"You're serious," I said, amazed. "I didn't know you were superstitious."

"I'm not," she said. "It's proven. That place is bad luck."

"Well, who else has owned it besides the coal company and Clarissa Hart?" I asked.

She looked at her mother for a second, as if she was waiting for Gert to say something. After a few moments, Aunt Millicent said, "Your great-grandmother, Bridie McClanahan. She was a widow at twenty-two and died at twenty-six. I'd say that's bad luck."

"What?" I asked. I whirled around to my grandmother, who was sitting quietly to my right. "Gert, why didn't you tell me she owned the boardinghouse?"

"I didn't think it was that important," she said. "She only owned it for a short time."

"So she owned it, and then after she died you went to live with her sister, and *then* you worked in the boardinghouse, after Clarissa bought it?" I asked.

"Yes," Gert said.

"Only Clarissa never bought it," Aunt Millicent countered.

"What do you mean?"

"Bridie left it to her in her will."

Okay, now I was truly shocked. But it made perfect sense. Clarissa was just returning what had once been Bridie's property to Bridie's family. It stung a little, though, to know that my grandmother had lived in poverty most of her life, sometimes having to work as many as three jobs at a time, and there sat Clarissa with the boardinghouse. She could have signed it over to my grandmother then. Why wait until now and sign it to me? Was there a reason she didn't want my grandmother to have it?

"All right, let me see if I have the chronology correct. The Panther Run Coal Company owned the boardinghouse up until 1918, when they sold it to Bridie McClanahan?"

"Actually, they sold it to her husband, Hank Seaborne," Aunt Millicent said.

"Okay . . . so they sold it around 1918 to Hank Seaborne, who in turn dies in a logging accident and leaves it to Bridie. Who in turn leaves it to Clarissa in 1926," I said. "But the whole time, miners for the coal company are still boarding there. Right?"

"Right."

"Then the coal company goes belly-up about 1938? Isn't that about right? And then the boardinghouse is just a place for tourists and the occasional logger."

"That's about right," Aunt Millicent said.

"Huh," I said. "Interesting."

"Sell it," she said.

"Oh, I have no intentions of moving out here, Aunt Milly, boardinghouse or no boardinghouse. I love New Kassel," I said. "I don't know what I'm going to do yet. Besides, the Harts may contest the will anyway."

"Oh, that would be just like them. Greedy ones, they are. Every last one of them," Aunt Millicent said. "And Maribelle likes to pretend that she's not, but she is. She didn't marry Prescott because of his enigmatic personality. She married him for his money. They are never satisfied."

I thought about Pastor Breedlove's sermon earlier today. Never satisfied. Were any of us?

85

"Do you know a man named Norville Gross?" I asked.

"Never heard of him."

"What do you know about two miners who disappeared from this area?"

She got the most peculiar look on her face. It was hard to determine exactly what she was feeling or thinking with the flickering candlelight playing across her face. "There were cave-ins all the time," she said. "I'm sure there are plenty of men who were swallowed up by the mountains. Plenty of them."

FOURTEEN

I AWOKE EARLY THE NEXT MORNING, TOOK A SHOWER, and threw on my very large and very comfortable teddy bear shirt, a powder-blue pair of shorts, and my thongs. My hair was the longest it had been in years, since those maternity vitamins make my hair thick and shiny and increase the speed with which it grows tenfold. It was actually long enough for me to pull it back in a twisty.

I grabbed a muffin from the kitchen and was very happy with myself for being stealth prego and making it out the door without my grandmother knowing I was leaving. I didn't want her to come with me on my errands today, because she would be bored, bored, bored, which would make me feel like I would have to hurry with my research. I'd just finished consuming the blueberry muffin as I came into the great room, with a spiral notebook under my arm and my purse over my shoulder, when out of nowhere I heard my grandmother's voice.

"Why didn't you wake me up?" she asked.

I was so startled I literally dropped my notebook and squealed. "You are determined to make me have this baby two months early, aren't you?" I asked.

Gert sat in the big brown wing chair, with her cane and purse clutched in her hands. Clearly, she was ready and raring to go for the day. She stood up and walked toward the door. "Come on," she said. "Let's go."

"Go where?" I asked her.

"To see Sheriff Justice," she said. "And then to the library at Quentinton and, if you have time, to the courthouse. Isn't that where you were going?"

Yes. That was exactly where I was going. To think my poor mother had been raised by this woman. "Gert—"

"We'll have to stop somewhere and get me some breakfast and coffee, since you didn't get me up early enough to eat something here," she said as she reached the door.

Guilt. Guilt. Guilt.

"Sure," I said. "Denny's?"

About an hour and half later, I pulled into the sheriff's department in Panther Run. Oddly enough, from the desk of Sheriff Justice, I could see both the Denny's, which had become our hangout, and the church we had attended yesterday. My grandmother sat quietly next to me. The sheriff looked tired.

"What can I do for you?" he asked me.

Out of my purse, I pulled the plastic bag that contained the burned pieces of Clarissa's will and laid it on his desk. "I didn't want to show you this at the boardinghouse with everybody there," I said.

"What is it?"

"The morning that I found Clarissa, I came downstairs to call 911. Mr. Gross accompanied me. I spied this in the fireplace. Dexter Galloway said that as soon as he found out Clarissa was dead, he went to her office to get her new will to put away for safekeeping, but it was gone," I said. I took a deep breath and continued. "Turns out her lawyer already had a copy of her new will. But I think these are the remains of Clarissa's copy."

"Really?" he asked, sitting up a little straighter. "How do you know?"

"I can make out a few of the words and they say things like 'of sound body and mind' and other familiar phrases," I said. "I'm a genealogist. I've read tons of wills."

"So then what you're driving at is somebody burned this copy of her will, thinking they were destroying the only copy of it and nobody would realize that the old one wasn't the new one," he said.

"Exactly."

"Thank you," he said. "Thank you very much."

"You're welcome," I said. "Any idea who Norville Gross was?"

"Well, I'm limited as to what I can tell you at this point, but I can tell you that he didn't have a record of any kind, based on his DMV record," he said. "As far as I can tell, he was an average guy, who just happened to be left a nice sum of money by Clarissa."

"Was he born here in West Virginia?"

"Yes, as far as I can tell. I believe it was something like 1942."

"I suppose we'll find out a lot more when the next of kin is notified," I said, hoping to glean just a little more information. Like, who was his next of kin?

"His father is coming in to identify the body. I kid you not, that is the only living relative," he said.

"Oh," I said. "That's a shame, because then most likely Norville was his father's only living relative, too, and his father's on his way to identify him. How far is he traveling?"

"Just from Morgantown," he said. "He can make the trip in less than four hours," he said. "Still, I know what you mean. He has to drive all the way down here not knowing if his son is alive or dead. Yeah, it's a sad situation."

Just then his phone rang. He picked it up and told whoever it was that he'd call them back in just a minute. Before he even put his phone back in the cradle, he went on talking to me. "We're waiting on autopsy results from both bodies. In my humble opinion, though, he did not die from a panther attack."

"What are you looking for in Clarissa's body?"

"We're going ahead and doing a toxicology and such," he said. "She was worth quite a bit of money."

"She left Torie the boardinghouse," my grandmother said like some parrot that had been trained to say three or four sentences. This seemed to be one of her sentences.

"Yes, I know," he said. "Look, I know you're pregnant and all, but I need for you to stick around a couple of days. At least until we get the autopsy results back."

"Not a problem," I said. "If you need me any more today, I'm going to be in Quentinton at the library, doing some research."

"On what?" he asked.

"On the boardinghouse. I'd like to find out a little bit about the place that I've inherited," I said. I stood up and put my hand out for him to shake. He shook it firmly and smiled.

"Why do you think Clarissa left you the boardinghouse?" he asked. It was a fair enough question, and I knew that there was no way that I could get out of being a suspect if Clarissa had indeed been murdered. Even so, it sort of unnerved me.

"I kept asking myself that question over and over," I said. "Then my aunt told me last night that my great-grandmother actually owned the boardinghouse and left it to Clarissa. Clarissa died before she could tell me why she'd left it to me, but she did say that it was a 'debt repaid.' I think, in her mind, she was just returning it to the appropriate family."

"Interesting," he said.

"I'm going to check it out today and make sure," I said.

He handed me a business card from a square glass dish sitting on his desk. "Let me know what you find out," he said.

"Sure," I said and smiled. Wow, a sheriff who didn't tell me to mind my own business. I kind of liked this guy.

FIFTEEN

"I'LL JUST SIT HERE AND BE QUIET," GERT SAID TO ME as we entered the library at Quentinton.

It was an old building made of red brick and a few white ones here and there to give it a speckled appearance. I'd say the building was probably about a hundred years old, tall with a white cupola. I got the impression that maybe it had been a courthouse or something else back at the turn of the century. The inside most likely had been redecorated sometime in the 1970s and hadn't been touched since. All the furniture was made of brown vinyl, which would stick to your skin when you sat on it in shorts or dresses. A distinct smell of mildew was ever-present and wouldn't go away no matter where in the library I went. I hate mildew nearly as much as I do mold.

Gert literally picked out a brown vinyl throne, sat upon it and never moved. I wasn't sure if that was so I could actually get something done or if that was to instill pity—derived from guilt, of course—for her having to sit there on such a gorgeous day. I have trouble deciphering her motives sometimes.

I walked up to the front desk of the library after searching the shelves for half an hour. I realize that the Dewey decimal system works no matter what state or city you live in, but sometimes different libraries would have different holding areas for local-interest things. And since I struck out in a half hour for finding what I wanted, I thought I'd go and ask.

The counter was empty until a woman about my age literally popped up from the floor below. She had impossibly curly hair and small, happy green eyes. "Oh, hi," she said. "I was tying my shoe."

"That's okay," I said and laughed. "I need to know if you have a special holding area for your local-interest stuff. And your local newspapers. Do you have them on microfilm? Oh, and for what years?"

"Yes, ma'am," she drawled out. "Local interest is here on the wall, our genealogy department is in the special holdings room behind it. Our newspapers are in the microfilm section on that little balcony area that you see up there."

My gaze followed to where she was pointing. There was a small balcony above the northeast corner of the library with about four microfilm machines.

"We do have one computer with Internet access, but you have to get on a waiting list," she said and smiled. Her accent seemed to drawl on forever, yet at the same time, her sheer energy level made it seem like she was babbling. "We have the Charleston newspapers up until about 1950, the *Quentinton Gazette* from about 1870 to the present. We have some of the smaller papers, like for Ellensdale and Panther Run, but they're not always complete. You know, we might have 240 out of 365 days one year, or we may have the whole year. Just depends."

"Thank you very much," I said.

"Is there something of particular interest to you? I'm guessing you're not from here," she said.

"Actually, yes. I was trying to find some information, historical information, on the Panther Run Boardinghouse," I said.

"Oh?" she asked.

"Yes," I said. "My great-grandmother used to own it."

"How cool," she said. "Was that . . . that's not the Hart family, correct?"

"No," I said. "Bridie Seaborne."

She got the most peculiar look on her face. Her small eyes tried their darnedest to open wide and look shocked. "Seaborne?" she asked.

"Yes," I said. "You know the family?"

"Elliott Seaborne works here in the library and I think he's related to that family," she said.

"Elliott Seaborne?" I asked, the excitement rising in my chest. "Elliott? Elliott works here?"

"You know him?"

"Yes, I know him. He's my cousin. I haven't seen him in quite a few years, in fact I haven't even talked to him in close to six months. The last I heard he worked for the archives in D.C.," I said.

"Ooh," she sang. "Let me go get him."

She was gone before I could say another word. I waved to Gert and motioned for her to come over to the counter. Her chair sat just a wee bit too low for her to get in and out of comfortably and it took her several tries before she finally managed to rise. "What's the matter?" she asked as she got closer to me.

"Nothing," I said. "Elliott works here."

"Elliott?"

"Elliott Seaborne, your brother's grandson," I said. Which made him my second cousin, since his father, who was dead, was my first cousin once removed and my mother's first cousin. I have this mental chart in my head on how to work all of this out. Some people make grocery lists, I make ancestor charts. There could be worse things.

Before I could explain further, Elliott Seaborne came around the corner out of the stacks, picking up his pace when he saw me. Elliott was about two years younger than me, so in his early thirties. He was fairly short for a man, stocky, with blondish hair and brown eyes hidden behind near Coke-bottle-thick glasses.

"What in heavens are you doing here, Torie O'Shea?" He grabbed me and hugged me, careful not to squeeze me too hard, lest he pop my belly. He then grabbed my grandmother and did the same thing, nearly toppling her over.

"I thought you were in D.C.," I said.

"Just moved back home about two months ago.

93

Mom's sick," he said. "Thought I should be closer. It was a sudden decision and I haven't had time to write to you to let you know. My God, you are pregnant, aren't you? You really should get e-mail, so I can e-mail you."

"Yeah," I said. "Heard that before. I hope your mother feels better."

"Thank you. So, why are you here and what can I help you find?"

I explained briefly what we were doing here and about Clarissa Hart leaving me the boardinghouse and the fact that she was dead.

"Our great-grandmother actually owned that boardinghouse?" he asked. "I didn't know that."

"Neither did I," I said. He seemed a little put off by this news and, I suppose, by the fact that Clarissa had chosen me to leave it to, when Elliott had the exact same relationship to Bridie McClanahan Seaborne as I had. Why had Clarissa not left it to him? I'm sure he had to be asking himself that question. If he was, he shrugged it off quickly and showed me to the local-interest section.

I pulled out several books on coal mining and local mining history. Elliott had agreed to check them out for me, so I wouldn't have to speed-read everything in the library and I could concentrate on the stuff I couldn't check out, which were the newspapers.

As usual, I was overwhelmed by the sheer volume of information available in newspapers. And as usual, I was thoroughly discouraged because it can take me six hours to go through three days' worth of newspapers. Three days out of a time span of about ten years. I needed to scan the papers from 1916 to 1926 when Bridie died. Gee, just three thousand six hundred and forty-seven days left to go through. I never trust that every mention of a specific subject is actually cataloged, which is why, if I have time, I like to go through the newspapers page by page. But I didn't have that kind of time, so I consulted the card catalog.

I couldn't even begin to figure out how many entries there were for the Panther Run Coal Company or the boardinghouse bearing the same name. I just started at the top and marked them off as I came to them.

What exactly was I looking for, anyway? What did I think I was going to find? I asked myself that question, not really thinking I could answer it, as I scrolled the machine down page after page.

I wasn't sure if this is what I was looking for, either. But it looked very interesting:

PANTHER COAL COMPANY SENDS IN THE BIG GUNS

November 21, 1916, Panther Run, West Virginia— In a decision some are calling cautious and others are calling confrontational, the Panther Run Coal Company has sent out its "secret weapon," Aldrich Gainsborough, to calm the riotous miners in this central West Virginia mining town.

"The situation is explosive," Gainsborough says. "Every effort to keep the miners happy and working is being made. The company wants nothing but a smooth, efficient mine and mining team."

When asked if it was true that he was actually being sent to Panther Run to thwart the interest in a union, Gainsborough told reporters that although this was not his business, it was still no secret that Panther Run Coal Company did not want a union. He would not comment further.

It is not known how long Gainsborough will be staying, but he will be at the Panther Run Boardinghouse for this visit.

I knew very little about the coal mine wars, other than the fact that the miners, who dealt with horrible working conditions, desperately needed and wanted a union, and obviously the coal companies wanted the opposite. I knew that the coal companies would hire African or Italian workers for cheaper rates if the local white workers raised a stink about their pay. I also knew that, on occasion, the situation turned violent. There had been literal shoot-outs between the opposing parties, like something out of the Wild West. That was about all I knew.

My stomach rumbled, reminding me that it was well past lunchtime. My baby took that same moment to move, settling low in the front. The blood would be cut off to my legs in a matter of minutes if I didn't get up and walk around.

After scanning a few more of the earmarked articles on the Panther Run Coal Company, I printed them out, rewound the microfilm, and put it in the return bucket. I picked up the stack of books Elliott had checked out for me and headed down to get Gert for lunch. On the way out, Elliott and I made plans for him to look up some more of the marked articles on the boardinghouse and the coal company. He was also going to come to the boardinghouse tonight and help me go through the stuff in the attic. Now that the body had been removed and the evidence gathered, I was hoping that I could actually get up there and see what Clarissa thought was so important. Important enough to give Dexter Galloway specific instructions that I see what was up there.

SIXTEEN

MY FEET WERE SWELLING, SO I DECIDED TO GO BACK to the boardinghouse and change into my tennis shoes, which I could leave open. My thongs were cutting into my feet and leaving marks on them. I also thought it would be cheaper if we just grabbed something to eat at the boardinghouse, rather than eat out.

Gert planted herself on the couch in front of the television, while I went upstairs to change my shoes. I opened the door to my room and found Craig Lewis, Maribelle's far too perfectly polite son, rummaging through my suitcase.

What to do in a case like this? If I hadn't been pregnant I probably would have marched up to him and demanded an explanation. The fact that I was pregnant made me hesitate, because it wasn't just my well-being that I had to consider. There was somebody else who depended on me breathing and staying alive. And besides, two other people had died recently under mysterious circumstances.

"Excuse me," I said.

Craig jumped, throwing a handful of my elephant-sized underwear into the air. He turned around and before I could say another word, one of my bras came down and landed on his head. If it weren't for the fact that I was fuming angry and a wee bit scared, I would have laughed. He tried desperately to speak.

"I—I—I can explain," he said, as he removed the maternity bra from his head and clutched it to his chest.

"Your suitcases are probably in your room," I said. "This is my suitcase. My room."

"Of course," he said. "It's just that . . . I . . ."

97

"I assure you that the ten-dollar nursing bra that you now have clutched ever so lovingly to your breast can be bought right here in West Virginia. It's from Wal-Mart. You have Wal-Mart, I'm sure," I said. "There's no need to steal mine."

He looked down at his hand and realized that he was indeed clutching my nursing bra for all it was worth. His pale face now turned a flushed red. "But I—"

"I won't tell a soul what your real preferences are, Mr. Lewis. As long as you get out of my room and stay out," I said. I'd made my way fully into the room now. He looked far too scared to actually inflict any harm on me, and what would he have done? Beat me with my own maternity bra? Wearing them was indeed torture, but I didn't think a person could be tortured with one.

Slowly, he began backing out of the room, taking my bra with him. "I was, I was looking for—"

"If you want my opinion, Mr. Lewis, you'd be better off to just let me think that you like women's underwear. Any other explanation you might come up with will most likely be far more damaging than you having a lingerie fetish," I said.

I really did want to know what he was doing in my room. But was he going to tell me the truth? Whatever excuse or explanation he came up with at this moment was almost certainly going to be a lie. So why bother? I just wanted him out of my room.

"The door was unlocked," he said.

Okay, I couldn't really preach at him too much over entering a room that had an unlocked door, because . . . well, I've done that myself a time or two. But this was *my* room, dammit. "An unlocked door is the greatest temptation. But, still. Try and refrain. Or I'll tell the

98

sheriff, and your mother, and then I'll tell that very young wife of yours."

"I thought that. . ." he said, creeping closer and closer to the door until he finally reached it.

"Mr. Lewis," I said. I held my hand out. "May I please have my bra?"

With that he literally leaped out of my room into the hall, where he disappeared nearly instantly. It was as if he just melted into the walls or something. Which was fine, except he melted into the walls with my bra.

This was definitely one of the more peculiar things that had happened to me since I'd arrived in West Virginia.

I didn't check to see if anything was missing. I think I'd interrupted him in the act, and the only thing I saw him leave with was my bra. God, that really irked me.

I turned the lock on the knob and shut the door, making my way back down the stairs to the kitchen. About ten minutes later, I sat down to the table with a turkey sandwich, sliced tomatoes, cottage cheese, and a Dr. Pepper. I know, I know. I'm not supposed to be doing the caffeine thing, but a man just stole the only extra maternity bra that I had with me. I was traumatized. I needed Dr. Pepper and his soothing ways. It was medicinal. I think I'd convinced myself enough to actually be able to drink it without feeling too much guilt.

My grandmother came in and sat next to me with a plate full of cottage cheese and tomatoes. She did not have a turkey sandwich, however.

"Did you lock the door this morning, Gert?" I asked.

"What door?"

"To our room. Upstairs."

"I don't remember," she said. "Why?"

"Because I just caught Craig Lewis with his hands in my . . . suitcase." I was thinking *underwear,* but realized how bizarre that would have sounded. "He was looking for something."

"Did he take anything?" she asked, her eyes all big and instantly worried.

"Relax," I said. "I think he's harmless. But he did make off with one of my bras." I said it as deadpan as I possibly could. Gert stared at me, a positively horrified look on her face.

"I know," I said. "It's not like his wife doesn't have underwear when the urge hits him. I'm not happy about it."

"He didn't touch any of *my* underwear, did he?" she asked. I could see her mind running through all of the perverted things that could have happened to her underwear. She was too old to be having thoughts like that.

Her fork, piled high with cottage cheese, just sort of hung in midair. She'd forgotten she was holding it.

"No, no. I think your virtue is safe," I said. I began to shake slightly as the realization set in that there had been somebody looking for something in my room. "Granny, what was he looking for?"

"Why are you asking me?"

"You're old. You're supposed to know everything," I said. I took a deep cleansing breath. "What is going on here?"

"What makes you think I would know?" she asked.

"We arrive Friday night. Clarissa is dead by sunrise, whether by accident or natural causes we don't know. By that evening, the quiet and dark stranger, Norville Gross, is dead. Again, we're not sure if it was an accident or not," I said, and finished off my sandwich. I

100

chewed for a few minutes and then took a drink of my soda and hoped my grandmother didn't notice that my soda was a soda. "Prescott is freaked out over my presence and angry because I inherited this tumbledown piece of garbage. Albeit a very meaningful, historic tumbledown piece of garbage. Somebody burned Clarissa's will, we can't leave town until the sheriff knows if it was murder or not, and now Craig is looking for something in my room. As if I have something that belongs to him. What the heck is going on?"

She gave me a blank look and blinked. "Is that a Dr. Pepper you're drinking?"

SEVENTEEN

"HERE'S SOME MORE ARTICLES ON THE BOARDING-house," cousin Elliott said to me. He stood in the great room next to the fireplace, looking at the far wall, which was the stairwell wall to the second floor. The one with all the framed photographs hanging on it. He gave a big sigh and shoved his hands in the pockets to his brown khakis. "All this time . . . I never knew it ever belonged in our family."

"You did know that Bridie worked here. And Gert and her sister. I don't think your grandfather ever worked here, though. You did know that, didn't you?" I couldn't imagine how he couldn't have known it. Stories about working for the company and the boardinghouse were the staple of my childhood.

"Grandpa mentioned it a few times that I can remember," he said. "He died before I really got into the family tree. By that time my father had forgotten most of the stories. There were a few, though."

101

"Come on, this way to the attic," I said and led him across the great room and up the picture stairwell. We reached the end of the hall where Clarissa's room was. I'd noticed earlier today that there was no crime-scene tape. "I'm assuming the authorities are leaning more toward natural causes than foul play, judging by the fact that there is no crime-scene tape," I said as I opened the door to her room. "Either that or they managed to gather all the evidence already."

The first door in the bedroom was her closet. I walked over to the second door on the far wall, by the windows that looked out upon the river. I opened the large, hand-carved oak door and was amazed that it didn't squeak. I was expecting it to squeak. "Dexter set the boxes in the middle of the room with my name on them. Technically, everything in the attic is mine, but apparently these things in particular she wanted me to see and take home."

The steps were steep and narrow. My foot barely fit on one of them and I wear a size six shoe. Something tapped me in the face and I swatted at it, thinking it a killer spiderweb or something. It was a chain for the light switch. Immediately I pulled it and tried to pretend in the new light that it hadn't just scared the bejesus out of me.

When we reached the top of the steps, I was more than a little startled to see Sherise Tyler standing over the boxes with a photo album in hand. What the heck was going on? First Craig went through my suitcase, and now Sherise was helping herself to my boxes.

She didn't act all nervous and startled like Craig had, though. She casually turned around and set the photo album, page open, on top of the open box. "You caught me," she said. "I am a reporter, though. I will not apologize for doing my job."

"Doing your job?" I asked. "I thought you already had your story. Isn't that what you said?"

Cautious eyes suddenly flicked toward Elliott. "Who's this?"

"My cousin Elliott Seaborne. Elliott, Ms. Sherise Tyler."

"Hello," he said quietly.

"You can't blame a girl for trying to make sure that she has every tiny bit of information possible," she said. I agreed with her on that, but her being here unnerved me, nonetheless. Why, I don't know. I was doing exactly what she was doing.

"What did you find?" I asked.

"Nothing. I've only been up here a few minutes," she said.

"What do you think is going on here?" I asked. "Why was Craig Lewis ransacking my belongings earlier today?"

A look of contempt crossed her pretty face. "What makes you think I can answer that?"

"No reason. Just thought you might have overheard something," I answered.

"No. I've heard nothing." She walked effortlessly past us to the stairway. She really held herself with great poise. If I had met her on the street, I would have sworn she was a ballet dancer.

She made a dramatic pause at the top of the stairs. "What do you think you're going to find up here, Mrs. O'Shea? A killer?"

"No," I said honestly. "I don't know that anybody has been killed. I'm just going through the things that Clarissa told Dexter to make sure I got. I'm anxious to see if there is anything up here that was my great-grandmother's. The woman died so young that there are very few mementos of her life."

She gave a smug smile and flipped her hair over one shoulder. "Right," she said and took one step down the stairs.

"I'm serious, Ms. Tyler. My interest in all of this is my great-grandmother. Not the Harts. Not Clarissa," I said.

"What about the vanished miners you keep asking about?"

How did she know that I'd inquired about them on more than one occasion? That sort of bothered me but I let it go. "I'll admit, I'm just curious."

"What is it you do for a living?" she asked me from the top stair.

"I'm a genealogist. Historian. I also work for the historical society of my hometown and give tours and such of the old buildings," I said. "Why?"

"Maybe you should consider being a reporter," she said and walked down the stairs. "You've got the nose for it."

When I heard the door downstairs open and shut, I turned to Elliott. "Sorry about that," I said. "She's been oddly confrontational."

"What do you mean?" he asked.

"Well . . . I can't explain it. It's like she's angry or suspicious of me, and I haven't done anything to her," I said.

"So, you gonna take her advice?" he asked. "Become a reporter?"

"No. My best friend Collette is a reporter. I hear all the juicy stuff from her. I don't do well in severe competitive situations like that," I said. "I believe things should stand on merit alone, not on how much I shove it down your throat."

"Yeah, me, too," he said and smiled. "So . . . what's in the boxes?"

Aside from the boxes in the middle of the room, there was a chiffonier, a chest, some sheet-covered furniture, and one of those dummies without a head that you hang old dresses on. I'm sure there's a word for that, but I'll be darned if I know what it is. The headless dummy wore a blue gown that, judging from the style of it, was most likely an 1890s evening gown. I know this because it was very similar in style to one of the gowns Sylvia'd had made for me to give tours in.

"Let's find out," I said. I handed him the photo album that Sherise had set on top. "You look through that and see if you recognize anybody."

In the very first box was an old wicker sewing basket with multicolored glass beads strung along a thick thread and connected to the lid. Two tassels that were dingy from the decades were attached in the middle where the beads came together. I opened the lid and inside were a wooden darner, paper patterns, a cloth measuring tape that looked like it was ready to disintegrate, and oodles of old buttons, thimbles, and thread.

"Oh," I said absently. "This is so cool. This must be Bridie's sewing basket. All of this stuff was actually touched and used by her." I felt goose bumps cascade down my arms as I thought about the fact that this was one of the few ways I could reach across time and touch an ancestor who had died nearly forty years before I was born.

"Look," Elliott said. "That's Bridie's dad. And that, if I'm not mistaken, is *his* father."

I looked over his shoulder to get a better look. And so it went for an hour or so, each of us oohing and aahing over our newfound treasures and photographs. Clarissa had attached little pieces of paper to most of the items

105

with a brief explanation of what they were, who they were used by, or what they were used for.

Indeed, I found a cracked cake plate, many many doilies, a shoe hook, a book of days, and a few things that had belonged to Gert and her siblings, like baby booties and bonnets. There was even Bridie's old box camera that she'd taken so many pictures with. And the main subjects of her photographs were the boardinghouse, the miners, and later her children. There were also plenty of pictures of Bridie and her friends, namely Clarissa Hart. But the boardinghouse and the miners seemed to be her main fascination. Some of the photographs were very artistic, nearly *National Geographic*-like in subject, lighting, and mood.

"Amazing," I said for about the tenth time. I finally came to the last box and opened it, nearly forgetting in my excitement that I was on the lookout for spiders with fifty legs. In this box was a quilt. The note attached to this read: "Sampler Quilt. 'Bridie's Secret.' Made 1920."

"Bridie's Secret?" I asked.

Elliott took the note off the quilt and read it. "I think that's the name of the quilt. A lot of quilters give names to their quilts, like people name estates, or paintings," he explained.

"Oh," I said. I unfolded it and it was huge. I'd say it would fit a queen-sized bed, easily. The main colors were indigo-blue and sun-yellow, although there were three or four other colors used throughout the quilt to accent it. "Look, each square is something different. A different pattern. And yet, the color scheme is all the same."

"Yeah," he said. "That's a sampler quilt. You get a

106

sample of a pattern but not a whole quilt. Sometimes they stay in the same color scheme, sometimes not."

"How do you know so much about quilts?" I asked as I scratched my neck. Digging around in old stuff always makes me itch. It's like the dust mites suddenly realize there's food or something.

"My mother is a blue-ribbon quilter," he said. "I spent more days in fabric shops and quilt shows than any red-blooded American boy should have to. Or ever have to admit to."

"You're so cute," I said. "Help me fold this back."

He helped me fold the monstrous quilt back into the neat rectangle that I had found it in. I put it back in the box and realized that my back was absolutely killing me. I can't get over the one long ache that I get after about the sixth month of being pregnant. Just one long backache. And once the child was here it would be an eighteen-year-long pain in the butt. I say that only because I'm pregnant. I actually adore my children.

"I want you to know that I'm going to have copies made of all of those pictures for you," I said. "She was your great-grandmother, too. And I want you to think about what you'd like to have out of these boxes. There's plenty here to go around."

"That's very thoughtful of you, Torie," Elliott said to me. He took his glasses off and rubbed at one of his eyes. His eyes were so weak that it actually looked painful for him to be without his glasses. He put them back on carefully. "Come on, let's get you downstairs for dinner."

"Are you going to stay for dinner?" I asked. "It would be nice to have an ally in the house."

"Not tonight," he said. "But I'm off tomorrow and I don't have any plans tomorrow night."

"Wonderful," I said. "Be here whenever you feel like it."

We had started toward the steps when he stopped and turned to me. "Why do you think Clarissa left you the boardinghouse?" he asked.

"Frankly, I believe it's because I was the only one of Bridie's descendants that she knew. I mean, I wrote to her a few times and she wrote back. I don't think she was really aware of anybody else," I said. "I also think it's because of what I do. Being a genealogist. She knew I would care about the place and the stuff in it."

"I'm a genealogist, too," he said.

"Yes, but she didn't know about you. I really think that's all there is to it," I said.

"Do you think she was murdered?" he asked. His expression was calm and inquisitive.

"I did find a pillow on her face," I said. "But I guess if she was wrestling around in her sleep it could have accidentally fallen on her face. It doesn't feel right that it was an accident, but at the same time, I really don't know."

"Are you afraid to stay here?" he asked.

"A little," I said. And it was the truth. "Initially, I felt fairly safe because now that the local authorities are actually here and involved, I can't believe that if there is a murderer, he or she would chance attacking anybody else. Especially a pregnant lady. But since finding Craig Lewis rummaging through my suitcase, I've been thinking about taking Gert and getting a hotel room tomorrow."

"It might not be a bad idea," he said. "You can sleep on my floor."

I smiled at him. "Well, thanks. I think Aunt Milly would probably let us stay with her, if it came to that," I said. "Besides, if I ever got down on your floor, I wouldn't be able to get back up."

EIGHTEEN

"RUDY?" I SAID. THE PHONE HAD RUNG ONLY ONCE AT my house, which is rare, and so I was a little startled when Rudy answered right away.

"Yeah. Toric?" he asked. "How are you?"

"I'm fine," I said. I stood in the great room of the boardinghouse, looking out across the river and the storm clouds that were slowly, but surely, moving our way. In fact, the front had nearly reached us and I could no longer see the sunset. "How are you?"

"Good," he said. "I thought you were your father calling."

"Why?"

"He and I are going fishing tonight. You know the fish bite better at night," he said.

"So do the snakes," I answered.

He ignored my remark. "Your mom said that you've run into some misfortune on your trip. That the old lady actually kicked the bucket while you were there," he said.

"That is incredibly insensitive," I said.

"Sorry," he said. "I just thought it was weird that she would call everybody together for the reading of her will and she wasn't even dead. Maybe she planned this. Maybe she knew that she was going to die, so that there could be an actual reading of the will. With a corpse. Like there is supposed to be. You know, your grandma Keith knew."

"I know," I said. He was referring to the fact that my father's mother all but predicted her own death. She called and told us all good-bye and everything. It is the most seriously creepy thing that has ever happened to me. "I don't think that was it, though. Maybe."

"Otherwise things are okay?" he asked.

"Yeah. What did Mom tell you exactly?"

"Just that Clarissa had died."

"Hmm. Well . . . do you miss me?" I asked. I don't know what it is about mileage, but put it between me and Rudy and I become this really insecure schoolgirl. Ridiculous, I know, but there nonetheless.

"Of course," he said.

"Don't forget to feed the chickens," I said. "And Fritz has a vet appointment tomorrow. That's why I was calling. To remind you."

And to hear your voice.

"Tomorrow? I'm playing golf—"

"Again?" I asked, a little perturbed. Rudy had taken the week off so that my mother would not have to bear the brunt of watching the kids while trying to plan a wedding.

"Again," he said. "I'm only gone a few hours. What's that supposed to mean?"

"Nothing," I said. *It's just that you're so busy having fun that I don't think you really miss me.* Admit it. We've all felt this way at some time or other.

"So," he said. "Gert's keeping you in line?"

"Yeah. Yeah, she's keeping me . . ." *Crazy* was the first word that popped out into my head. "On the straight and narrow." *Path to insanity.*

"Good," he said. "Well, honey, I don't mean to cut you off but your father is supposed to be calling me."

"Oh."

"I love you, sweetie," he said.

"I love you, too," I answered.

"Be good. Stay out of trouble."

NINETEEN

I TRIED TO IGNORE EVERYBODY AT THE DINNER TABLE while I read the newspaper articles that Elliott had copied for me. I intended to be rude, although I've never understood why reading something in the presence of others is considered rude. Reading is a staple of life, like bread or water. Or chocolate. Anyway, I really didn't want to be drawn into any conversation with Clarissa's family, and besides, Craig Lewis still had my bra.

"So, did you get what you wanted from my mother's attic?" Prescott Lewis asked me.

"She wasn't your mother," I said, without looking up.

"She was my mother-in-law for more years than you've been alive," he said. "She was just like my mother."

I thought about that. Having a mother-in-law for that long. I said nothing and went on reading. Gert had been extremely tired today and already had gone on up to shower and relax for the night. So I sat, without an ally, eating as fast as I could and trying to ignore everybody.

"So?" he asked. "Did you find everything?"

"They were my great-grandmother's things," I said. "As much as you feel that I am not entitled to Clarissa's things, so I feel that you are not entitled to Bridie's."

One more word from him and I was going to finish my dinner upstairs, in my room with my grandmother. Dinner was fried chicken and mashed potatoes, with beets, peas, and homemade biscuits. It would not carry well, but I'd take that chance rather than have to suffer through this dinner with him in the same room.

Maribelle decided to try and change the subject. Prescott was her husband. I don't know why she didn't just tell him to get lost or take a cold shower or something. It seemed as though he spoke all the time and she never heard him. Not one word. "Danette," Maribelle began. "Why don't you tell Torie what you found."

Quiet fell across the room and that was my cue to look up. Danette's Caribbean mop was piled high on top of her head with most of it deliberately falling down around her face and neck and in her eyes. Her eyes were lined with severe black kohl, and she was wearing one of the coolest oversized T-shirts I've ever seen, Albert Einstein's face peering out from a galaxy of stars. Does anybody actually make smalls anymore? When was the last time I saw somebody wearing a T-shirt that actually fit?

I looked around the room and nobody said anything. "What did you find, Danette?"

Danette would not look me in the eyes as she pulled a huge syringe out of her pocket and set it on the dining room table. I say it was huge, but then, all needles look twice as big as they really are. I was a little horrified at first. Germs, you know.

"What are you doing carrying that around in your pocket? Haven't you heard of AIDS?" I asked. "Or hepatitis?"

Danette just shrugged her shoulders. My gaze went from the needle to Maribelle and then to Prescott, to Lafayette, Craig, and finally Edwin. Everybody just stared at me. It seemed as though the table grew a hundred feet long and I sat at one end and they were all the way down at the other end. My jury. Them against little old me.

"That's interesting, Danette. Where did you find it?" I asked.

"Out in the yard," she said quietly.

"Anybody here a diabetic?" I asked innocently.

Nobody answered. Sherise Tyler came sauntering in and pulled out a chair next to me, unknowingly breaking a tense moment. She must have just gotten out of the shower because the smell of rose water was intense and the underneath side of her hair was still wet. She reached for the fried chicken and spied the syringe on the table, along with everybody's accusatory stares. At me.

She looked at me, and I think I saw real pity on her face. "What's up?"

"Danette found a syringe," I said.

"I see that. Danette, why don't you take that off the table," she said. "Needles are a hothouse for disease."

"Thank you," I said. "My thoughts exactly."

"What do you think a syringe was doing out in the yard?" Edwin asked as he leaned forward on his elbows.

"Don't put your elbows on the table, Edwin," I said. "Why would you think I would know that?"

"You know a lot of things, Mrs. O'Shea," Prescott said. "Don't you?"

"Actually, yes. I know quite a bit. About that syringe, I know nothing," I said. I began to tremble slightly, and put my chicken leg down on the plate lest people would think it was still alive.

"Awfully funny how you arrive and Mom just up and dies," Edwin said and snapped his fingers.

"Edwin. She was a hundred and one," I said. "She didn't just up and die. You guys have been waiting for it for twenty years."

"Who said that?" Maribelle asked, instantly defensive. "None of us have ever said that."

"Why would you think I had anything to do with this?" I asked. "And why didn't the sheriff and his deputies find that syringe when they were out scouring for evidence?"

Nobody said anything. I looked to Sherise, who seemed to know where I was going with this. "How long have you had it, Danette?"

Danette did not answer.

"When did you find the syringe?" Sherise pressed.

"Friday," she said, after a long moment filled with her eyes darting around the table and her chest rising and falling in nervous spasms.

"Friday," Sherise said. "Before Torie and Gert arrived?"

She nodded her head.

"You didn't tell us that part," Maribelle all but hissed across the table. Gasps and groans and general noises of discontent wound around the table until a single tear ran down Danette's face.

"You didn't ask," Danette said. Suddenly she turned to me, tears streaming. "I didn't know what they were going to do. Not until just now. You have to believe me."

"I believe you," I said. I stood up with my photocopies in hand. "Is that it? You all assumed when you saw the syringe that I poisoned Clarissa or something?"

"Nobody said nothing about any pizen," Lafayette said. I knew from my grandmother's momentary slips into her accent that he meant *poison*.

"Then what do you call this?" I asked. "Look, I got news for you people. It would be the stupidest thing in the world for me to have killed Clarissa. I knew nothing about the wills, either one of them. But guess what,

114

folks? Clarissa was just returning this godforsaken place to the right family."

They all looked at each other briefly. "What do you mean?" Maribelle asked.

"My great-grandmother Bridie owned this boardinghouse before Clarissa," I said. "She left it to your mother in *her* will. Clarissa was just giving it back. That's it. No conspiracy. Now, why don't you guys grow up? You don't even know how she died."

I turned to leave and then went back to the table and grabbed a chicken leg to go. It took a lot more than a confrontation to curb my appetite. "Or do you? You all seem to act as though you know it was foul play. And how would you guys know that if you weren't the ones who did it?"

With that I turned and marched toward the doorway of the dining room with my chicken leg in hand. I was feeling mighty brave and pious and so I turned for yet another one last word. "Craig, I want my bra back."

TWENTY

I SHUT THE DOOR SOFTLY BEHIND ME, AS GERT WAS fast asleep and snoring. I could never understand why her own snoring didn't wake her up. I can remember as a small child having to turn the television up because my grandmother's snoring in the other room drowned out *Starsky & Hutch*.

Rain began pelting against my window and I instantly recognized it as a gentle rain, without lightning or thunder to accompany it. There was no breeze to speak of and so this would be perfect sleeping weather.

If only I could sleep.

I locked the door behind me and then went and opened the window about two inches, so that I could not only hear the rhythmic patter of the rain better, but also smell its wonderful clean aroma. How is it that the smell of the wet earth, which equals mud, smells clean? Isn't that an oxymoron or something?

I turned the lamp on in my room and noted that the clock said seven-thirty. Gert was asleep early tonight. I laid the photocopies on the bed, took off my shoes, and climbed on top of the bedspread. Thus I prepared myself to read the rest of the newspaper articles and eat my chicken leg, whose grease had somehow managed to get smeared all over the photocopies. I swear I thought I'd been extra careful not to touch anything with chicken leg.

The baby rolled back and forth in my stomach as I read quietly to myself. When I'd finished eating the chicken leg, I tossed the bone into the trashcan between my bed and Gert's.

Somewhere around nine-thirty I found the article that I'd been looking for. It read:

TWO MINERS MISSING

September 8, 1917, Panther Run, WV—Doyle Phillips and Thomas MacLean were last seen on the August 31, a little over a week ago. Phillips, who worked the tipple, and MacLean, who worked in demolition, both for the Panther Run Coal Company, were not strangers to the townfolk here. Phillips came from Boggs and MacLean was from Blue Springs, and both were well-known and vocal about their stand on the UMWA. One reason the authorities are

116

concerned is because both men were wanted for questioning in the murder of Aldrich Gainsborough this past June. It is suspected that both men left the state to escape questioning, but none of their families or friends have heard from them, either, leaving authorities to wonder if some ill fate has befallen the two local mineworkers.

By the way Aunt Millicent had said that many a miner had been swallowed up by the mines, I had assumed the two missing miners had been lost in a cave-in, although that wasn't the impression I had received from everybody else. Providing, of course, that everybody I had asked about the missing miners was thinking of the same missing miners.

How likely was it that people of the twenty-first century would still be talking about two miners that had gone missing eighty-two years ago?

It would be fairly likely, I thought, if there was a conspiracy or secret that went along with the disappearance or some sort of theory that had gone unproven. There is nothing like a subject without closure to keep the gossip mill turning for centuries, eventually becoming legend. The supposed ghost of Victory LeBreau, back home in southeast Missouri, was a good example of that.

Wanna keep a secret, tell Bridie Mac.

I hadn't expected that to jump out at me from the recesses of my mind, but it did.

Why was it that the woman at Denny's, when we mentioned the boardinghouse, immediately brought up the two missing miners? She wondered if anybody would ever know what happened to the men. Was the boardinghouse connected to the disappearance of the miners? Or the owner of the boardinghouse? *Tell Bridie Mac.*

Who would tell Bridie MacClanahan?

Clarissa Hart.

Who would tell Bridie MacClanahan what?

What happened to the miners, maybe?

Nah, Couldn't be. I stifled a yawn and realized that I had to use the bathroom. I was not looking forward to this, because I'd have to leave the room and either take the key with me or leave the room unlocked. I was not leaving the room unlocked. Not after the bizarre things that had been happening here and the way people had been behaving toward me. If anything happened to Gert, I'd never forgive myself.

I went to the bathroom, brushed my teeth, and was quite relieved to return and find Gert safe and sound. I changed into my pajamas. I've never been able to figure out why all of the maternity pajamas have those little slits for breast-feeding in them. It's not like you breast-feed while you're pregnant. It can be a tad distressing to feel a breeze and realize that you're hanging half out of the slits in your pajama top. So to prevent such a horrible thing. I take a safety pin and pin them shut.

I sat back down on the bed and fingered the greasy photocopies once more. The miners had been wanted for questioning in the murder of Aldrich Gainsborough. I thumbed through the pile until I found the earlier article in which Gainsborough had just come to town and wasn't sure how long he would stay. How had I missed an article on his murder?

I found it about halfway through the stack. I assumed I just skipped over it because I wasn't looking for

118

anything on him, just on the miners, who now had names: Phillips and MacLean.

The article read:

SPOKESMAN FOR THE COAL COMPANY LYNCHED

June 29, 1917, Panther Run, West Virginia— Authorities are calling what happened in this sleepy little coal town nestled into the ancient mountains of central West Virginia an atrocity. A barbaric display of what man is capable of.

Late Tuesday night after leaving the Panther Run Boardinghouse where he was staying, Aldrich Gainsborough went to town to mingle and partake of the spirits with the locals. The details of the night are sketchy, but sometime around midnight he was seen leaving Rowse's. He was feeling good, but not drunk, witnesses say.

The next time he was seen was four o'clock Wednesday morning, hanging from a tree in the front yard of the Panther Run Boardinghouse. His neck was broken, the soles of his feet were burned, and there was quite a long list of other marks of torture.

Authorities believe that the boardinghouse and its occupants were never in danger, and are compiling a list of suspects.

At this point, given the tension between miners, who want to be unionized, and the Panther Run Coal Company, which is against unionizing, the list of suspects could include several hundred.

Impressive. The local townspeople had mentioned to me the fact that there were two miners missing when the

119

subject of Clarissa or the boardinghouse came up. But nobody, I mean *nobody,* had mentioned that there was a man *lynched in the damn front yard!*

What the heck was wrong with these people?

My eyes were droopy. I knew that even if I settled in to sleep, either my back or bladder would wake me up two hours later anyway, but I still had to sleep. I put the photocopies in between my mattress and box springs. Don't ask me why, just paranoid. I crawled back into bed but my mind would not wind down right away.

I thought about the boardinghouse. Aldrich Gainsborough. Bridie MacClanahan. Clarissa Hart. Two missing miners. The boardinghouse. I wondered if the only connection between Gainsborough and the boardinghouse was the fact that this was where he stayed on his visits or was there more to it? Were Phillips and MacLean residents here, as well, or did they live in town in the shacks owned by the company, with their own families? Was there any way for me to find out?

There were so many questions bouncing off the inside of my head I didn't think I would ever go to sleep. The next thing I remember was waking up at midnight to go to the bathroom.

TWENTY-ONE

IT WAS A GOOD NIGHT. I ONLY HAD TO GET UP ONCE AT midnight, so that meant that I got a six-hour chunk of sleep. Unheard of for me this far into a pregnancy. I awoke to chirping birds and the sound of the river rushing by outside, since my window was still up. For a second, I thought I was at home in my blue gingham bedroom in New Kassel. But I knew better. There were no children below making noise.

The breeze billowed the clouds just barely, and I was amazed to realize that it was a little on the cool side. I love cool mornings. They make me just want to snuggle back in the sheets and sleep all day. Or snuggle next to a warm body.

It was my first fully awake thought of the day, and so, of course, it had to be about Rudy.

I rolled over to see that Gert was not in her bed. This bothered me a little, so I did not allow myself the luxury of snuggling into the covers and thinking sappy thoughts about my husband several hundred miles away. I didn't even bother to put on my house slippers.

I did, however, put on my yellow and white checked robe and head out the door into the hallway to see if my grandmother was in the bathroom or eating breakfast already. She usually got up early, and I talked myself out of getting too worked up by rationalizing that she had gone to bed at seven the night before. Anybody would be up at six in the morning if they went to bed at seven.

She was not in the bathroom, however, and so I descended down the long picture stairway to the floor below to find her. The house smelled of biscuits and gravy, and I knew that Susan Henry was already up and cooking for the household.

I walked into the kitchen, and Susan scowled lightly at me. I'm sure she was afraid that I was going to start snatching at her food. She was dressed in a flower-print cotton dress and a paisley apron. It clashed something fierce, but this woman's arms were twice the size of mine and I was not going to comment on her fashion

121

faux pas. Besides, who was I, Miss Jeans and Tennis Shoes, to judge her wardrobe? Right?

"Good morning," I said. "Can I have a glass of juice?"

"Your house. You can have whatever you want," she said without looking up from the pile of dough she was kneading.

"I don't think, technically, this is my place just yet," I said. "I'll have that glass of juice, though, all the same."

I got myself a glass of orange juice and watched her silently working that dough. The ease with which she worked it made me think that this was something she had done her entire life. I couldn't exactly say how old she was, but I'd guess fiftyish. She was a bundle of contradictions. On one hand, her face was nearly wrinkle-free, but her hair held generous amounts of grey. Her body, however large, seemed to move with great ease, indicating somebody younger, but her style of dress was of somebody born in the late forties in the middle of nowhere and without access to fashion magazines or cable television. Either that or she just didn't care.

"What are you staring at?" she asked.

"Nothing," I said and wondered how she knew I was staring at her when her back was to me. "I was just curious if you'd seen my grandmother yet this morning?"

"Out in the dining room," she said. "Inhaled a bowl of oatmeal and a cup of coffee."

"Oh, thanks," I said. "So, how long have you worked for Mrs. Hart?"

"Thirty-four years," she said.

Well, I'd guessed her age about right. If she had been in her early twenties when she went to work for Clarissa

122

that would make her around fifty-five. "Good Lordy," I said. "That's a long time."

"All I've ever known is cooking for the missus," she said. "Nothing else."

"Have you always lived here or do you have family?"

"You're a mighty nosy one," she said and went about cutting out the biscuits with the biscuit cutter.

"Sorry," I said and finished my juice. I put my glass in the sink and turned to leave for the dining room.

"No," she said and slowly turned around. "I'm sorry. You've got a right to know everything. You're my new boss. My future is in your hands."

"Oh, don't say that," I said. "Look at me. You don't want your future in my hands. I can barely balance the checkbook. And I can't if my husband uses the ATM card. Throws me off completely."

"Oh, but I think you're quite capable in many other ways," she said.

"Capable of causing disasters wherever I go," I said.

"You didn't cause the flash flood," she said. "Happens all the time."

"I wasn't referring to the flash flood," I said and tied the tie on my robe just a little tighter, afraid that safety-pinned pajamas would become visible.

"You mean Mrs. Hart?" she asked. "She would have died no matter what: It was her time."

"What if somebody murdered her?" I asked.

"Then it was still her time, wasn't it?"

"Yeah," I said. "Sure."

"To answer your question," she said. "I have a daughter, she lived here growing up. She moved on with her life, though. Not that I blame her for leaving. The isolation is pretty tough. I see her about once a month. I never had no husband."

123

"Oh," I said. Why do I ask such personal questions if I'm not prepared to hear such personal answers? This was a serious character flaw of mine. "Did you like working for Mrs. Hart?"

There I went again.

"Yeah," she said and turned around to take the first round of biscuits out of the oven. "Nice woman. She always seemed sad somehow. I heard things. Glimpses of stuff every now and then. But I never asked."

Okay . . . *she* might not have asked, but I was going to. "Like what?"

"Wouldn't be right," she answered and shook her head. "Unless you *need* to know that as my employer."

No. I didn't need to know that as her employer. But I needed to know it as the nosy little busybody that I was. Now she was going to make me feel all guilty and everything if I pushed her to tell me. The scales go back and forth and . . . drats.

"No," I said. "I don't need to know that."

I walked into the dining room, thumping myself on the forehead with the palm of my left hand, amazed that her guilt trip worked on me. This should come as no surprise since my family uses it on me all the time. But jeez, if I can't manipulate a complete stranger, who can I manipulate?

My grandmother sat at the table, completely dressed, her cane and her purse sitting by her chair. She sipped her coffee, the spoon rattling in the blue and white china cup as she did so.

"Gert," I said as I sat down. "What . . . why are you up so early?"

"In case you tried to sneak out the door again this morning without me, I would be ready," she said simply.

My family wrote the book on guilt and manipulation. That had to be why they were all so perfect at it. I rose and headed back to my room to change my clothes, thumping my head as I went.

I was dressed, seated at the dining room table finishing my breakfast, thinking about the small hotel in town that I would go to and see if they had any vacancies today. I'd just swallowed the last bite of Susan's homemade biscuit with a generous portion of an excruciatingly delectable strawberry jam when there was a knock on the front door. I heard voices, and within a minute, Dexter Calloway stuck his pointy head into the dining room and informed me, with a rather pale shade to his face, that Sheriff Justice was here to see me.

"I'll be right there," I said.

"Don't bother to get up," Sheriff Justice said from behind Dexter. He slowly entered the room, removing his hat as he did so. A moment passed while my biscuit seemed to lodge in my throat, and only when I took a drink of my milk did it go down. I had a funny feeling about Sheriff Justice's visit at seven-thirty in the morning.

"Clarissa Hart was definitely murdered," he said.

It felt like my stomach dropped to the floor. "Oh, my gosh," I said. Until this point I think I'd half convinced myself that she'd just died in her sleep. Now, however, I felt very unsafe. "Shouldn't you be telling the family?" I asked.

"I'm goin' to," he said and rocked up on the balls of his toes. "Mrs. O'Shea, I don't know how to say this, but . . . well, you're a suspect."

"I . . . uh . . . I'm a s-s-suspect?" I asked. Why did this surprise me? I was the first one in the room. I knew

125

I would be a suspect if indeed she had been murdered. I guess hearing him say it just sort of creeped me out.

"I'm gonna have to ask you not to leave the boardinghouse. Don't leave town," he said.

"Should I call a lawyer?" I asked. That biscuit seemed to pop back up out of nowhere, and I swallowed extra hard trying to get it to go down.

"Up to you, really."

"What do you mean? Do you think I actually did it? Do I *need* a lawyer?" I asked, panic rising in my voice.

"You're not under arrest, although I will need you to come down and answer some more in-depth questions," he said. "You were the first one found in the room. And since the only other person in there with you is dead, that sort of makes it look bad."

"It doesn't help that I had the pillow in my hands, either," I said. I realized too late that since the only person who had seen me with the pillow in my hands couldn't testify against me, I needed to quit confessing to stupid things like that.

"Doesn't much matter about the pillow," he said. "She died of anaphylactic shock."

"Anna who?"

"An allergic reaction."

"Like some people are allergic to sulfur or shellfish?" I asked.

"Yes," he answered.

"Then how is that murder?"

"In her case, it was penicillin," he said. He threw a medical alert bracelet on the table, sealed in a plastic bag. "She wore that always. It was all over her charts. What's more . . . she hasn't been to the doctor or been seen by a doctor in over six months. She was not ill. Somebody put it in her food or something that she would ingest."

126

"But she ate dinner with all of us."

"There was probably penicillin in all of your food."

"How do you know it was penicillin?" I asked, just absolutely amazed at what he was telling me.

"There were heavy concentrations of it in her system," he said.

"Oh, how horrible," was all I could manage. After a moment of the sheriff standing at the edge of the table with his hat in his hand,

I motioned for him to take a chair. He did not take it. He did, however, pick up the bracelet and return it to his pocket. "Who else is a suspect?"

"Gross was," he said. "And if he was killed by a panther, I suppose he still could be."

"*If* he was killed by a panther?"

"Autopsy results are still not back yet on Mr. Gross," he explained. "If he was murdered, I'd say that he was innocent of Mrs. Hart's murder, but a victim because of it."

"You think that whoever killed Clarissa killed Mr. Gross, then. Is that what you're saying?" I asked.

"I would almost bet on it," he said.

"Then that would certainly look good for me," I said. "Since I doubt I could do that kind of damage to a man in my condition."

"That is most probable," he said, diverting his eyes to his shoes.

"Okay," I said. "Who else?"

"Basically, the will beneficiaries are who we are looking at right now," he said.

In other words, her children. I pondered this a moment. "So you are assuming that whoever killed her was after monetary gain only," I said. "Have you not considered personal reasons?"

He looked at me peculiarly. "Personal reasons?" he asked. "She was a very old woman. All her sins were ages old."

"An ages-old sin can come back and bite you in the butt just as easily as a recent one, Sheriff Justice," I said.

I could tell that he considered what I was saying by the look in his eyes. He put his hat back on his head. "Don't leave, Mrs. O'Shea," he said. And then he tipped his hat and disappeared out of the dining room's swinging doors.

Great. Just great.

TWENTY-TWO

"WHAT DID THE SHERIFF WANT?" GERT ASKED.

"Oh, nothing. He just wanted to drop by and tell me not to leave town and find a good lawyer," I said. "Actually, he said to not even leave the boardinghouse. He wants me right here."

"Hmm," she said. "When do they vote for the All-Star team?"

"It's midway, isn't it . . . Gert! I'm being serious. Can you stop thinking about sports and feel sorry for me or be appalled or *something*!"

"You're in a heap of cow turds," she said. "No matter how much you shower, you're still gonna smell like one."

"Oh, thanks. You're just so helpful," I spit, waving my arms all around.

"Don't get your panties in a wad, Torie. You may go into labor early. You know how worried you are about that," she said.

128

I stared at her, mouth agape. "What is your problem? Why are you deliberately being so blasé about my seriously compromised position here?"

"Your own damn fault," she said. "Keep your nose where it belonged and this wouldn't happen."

"Wait, wait a minute," I said. "You wanted to come on this trip. You were all for it. Now that I'm a murder suspect, suddenly this was all my idea."

"I didn't tell you to go murdering anybody," she said simply and tried to get up out of the chair. Of course, she did not make it on the first try.

"I didn't murder anybody," I said. "I said, 'Now that I'm a suspect.' Why am I telling you this? You *know* I didn't murder anybody."

"Yes, but if Clarissa hadn't gone and gotten murdered, you wouldn't be having this problem," she said.

You ever feel like other people live on a hamster wheel? I was beginning to feel that way. She strained and groaned and tried to get up out of the chair. It was her usual show, put in to make everybody aware that she was an old woman. She could get up without all that hoopla, because I've seen her do it when she thought nobody was looking.

"Are you gonna stand there all day with your mouth open or are you gonna help your old grandma up out of the chair?" she asked.

"Oh, get up yourself," I said and stormed out onto the front porch.

At times when I was with her I felt like I was fourteen. I didn't know if she just brought that out in me or if that was something you were just always supposed to feel with grandmothers. My father's mother had been dead since I was seventeen. I hadn't had the pleasure of finding out if she would have infuriated me this much, darn it.

It occurred to me, standing there on the weather-beaten front porch, that the tree I was looking at was the tree that Aldrich Gainsborough had been hung from.

It was a big oak with many thick branches that hung low enough for somebody to jump up and grab. There were also plenty of branches that were high enough for a tall man to swing from without his feet hitting the dirt.

I walked over to the tree and turned back toward the boardinghouse. The tree wasn't that far away from the house. It was almost at the road, so I'd say almost exactly halfway between the boardinghouse and the river. It was a straight shot from the great room of the boardinghouse and a diagonal line from where Clarissa's bedroom was in the present day. Who knew if that was the room she had occupied then?

How quiet they must have been. It made me wonder what they had done to Gainsborough to keep him silent when he would have obviously been in pain. Or maybe by the time they got him back here he was nearly dead, and there was no point in giving him anything to keep him from making noise. I assumed, of course, that they would have wanted him quiet long enough for the bad guys to get away.

Why here? Why bring him back *here?* Why didn't they dump him at the opening to the mine? Why not in town in front of the company store? Something that would have made more of a statement, for I was assuming that he was murdered over either union or coal reasons. Why bring him back to the boardinghouse a couple of miles out of town, a place where nobody but the rare passerby at three in the morning would see. It wasn't as if passing by a place was that easy back then. Most people did not have cars, and thus visiting another location would have entailed hitching the horses or walking.

There was a reason they brought him back here.

They wanted somebody here to see him. To find him. To find him hanging by a tree with no dignity whatsoever. Why would somebody do that? It was just as my cousin Elliott pulled up in the driveway that I realized the answer to these questions would come when I knew exactly who Aldrich Gainsborough was. And what his connection had been to the boardinghouse, or the people in it.

Elliott got out of his car with his khaki pants already wrinkled for the day. Either that, or he was like me and his clothes just wrinkled the minute he laid eyes on them. Surely, that must be a recessive gene of some sort. That's it. The wrinkle gene. As long as it remained confined to clothes and not my face, I supposed I could live with that.

"Hey, cuz," I said. "You're here early."

"There are a few people around that I thought you might like to talk to," he said. "Thought we'd get a head start."

"Oh, yeah?" I asked. "Like who?"

"Some old-timers, some sons of old-timers. They have lotsa stories," he said and smiled.

I looked back at the boardinghouse and thought about my grandmother inside. For all I knew she could still be trying to get out of the chair. "Gert's mad at me," I said.

"Why?"

" 'Cause I'm a murder suspect."

The expression on his face dropped at least an inch. "Clarissa was murdered? They've announced it?"

131

"Yeah, and I'm their A number one cookie," I said and rubbed my belly.

"Wonderful," he said. "My mom may not let me hang out with you anymore. You being such a bad seed and all."

"Shut up, you jerk," I said and laughed. Elliott snickered, quite pleased with himself at being a complete smart aleck.

"Did you know there was a man lynched here?" I asked after we'd had our good laugh. I studied his face closely, to see what he would give away. As usual, with Elliott, the expression I saw backed up his statement.

"Vaguely heard something about a hanging," he said.

"How is that?"

"What do you mean?"

"I mean, mountain people thrive on stories and tales, and the more colorful and dramatic the better. They love nothing better than a ghost story about double crosses, adultery, and murder. How is it there could have been a genuine, bona fide lynching right where we're standing and you *vaguely* heard about it?" I asked. "Doesn't make sense."

"How come I never knew that Bridie owned this place at all?" he countered.

"I'm the one asking the questions here. If you start asking them, then I'm going to get all confused," I said.

"Oh, sorry."

Dexter Calloway came out the front door, and briskly walked down the steps and around the corner of the house. Maribelle opened the window to her bedroom just in time for me to hear Preston's mouth running at fifty miles per hour.

"What's going on here, Elliott?" I asked as I watched the inhabitants going about their business.

132

"I'm not sure, cousin."

"No . . . no, I don't just mean right now, on the surface. I mean, what is really going on? Deep. Under the surface."

"I'm still not sure," Elliott said.

TWENTY-THREE

AN HOUR LATER I WAS SEATED ON THE GROUND underneath a very large tree that housed a very healthy bird and squirrel population. I'd dodged bird doodoo at least twice already, and I could no longer feel my feet. Sitting Indian-style on the ground at seven months pregnant was something one only did if she were *trying* to cut off the circulation to her feet.

But here I sat, with Elliott to my right and Chester H. Farnsworth the third sitting across from me. All I could think was what a good thing it was that Gert was mad at me, because she would never have made it up off the ground. And since Mr. Farnsworth the third had insisted we sit under the tree, on the ground, I would have had to go back to St. Louis in a few days with my grandmother permanently employed as Mr. Farnsworth's new scarecrow, or she would have had to ride on the hood Indian-style for twelve hours. See, some things happen for a reason. I'm just certain of it.

Mr. Farnsworth's house was set on a hill, nothing new there, and his yard overlooked the two-lane blacktop that snaked around the foot of the mountain. It was a lovely day, mid-seventies, sunny with an occasional wispy cloud. Oh, and don't forget the soggy ground from the rain the night before that would now

133

have a permanent dent in the shape of my butt. All I could say was this had better be good.

Chester himself was about ninety thousand years old, and at his age I couldn't imagine being able to even find my legs, much less contort them into the position in which he now sat. I bet he had never taken yoga. I bet he never jogged, ran a race, took karate, ate low-fat, low-sugar, low-caffeine, low-calorie, or low-carbohydrate foods a day in his life. And yet the man was the perfect embodiment of everything healthy and everything I absolutely despised.

I wouldn't mind being more health conscious as long as I didn't have to think about it.

"This is Torie O'Shea," Elliott began. "Torie, this is Chester. His father was a miner for the Panther Run Coal Company and lived at the boardinghouse."

"Nice to meet you," I said.

"Who are you, exactly?" the old man asked.

"Clarissa Hart left Torie the boardinghouse in her will," Elliott said.

Chester's heavy grey eyebrows rose about an inch, and then he took aim and spit about six inches from where I was sitting. Wonderful. Made me wonder what else I was sitting in, besides dirt.

" 'S 'pose I should say congratulations," he muttered.

"Torie was wondering if you could give her some information on the building. On the boardinghouse itself," Elliott said.

"Like what?" Chester asked.

"I don't mean to be rude," I said. "But what year were you born?" What year he was born would determine my line of questioning. There was no point in asking him things that he wouldn't begin to know because he wasn't alive yet.

"I was born on the twenty-seventh of February, 1910," he said with his head held high.

Well, that made him pretty darn ancient, but not quite old enough for some of the things that I was curious about. For instance, he would not have a conscious memory of Bridie or her husband, other than through the eyes of an eight- or ten-year-old. "What do you know about two men named Doyle Phillips and Thomas MacLean?" I asked.

"Been years since somebody asked questions 'bout them. People still talk about 'em, but I ain't been asked no questions in a long while," he said. "Why do you want to know about 'em? Seen their ghosts?"

"No, no, I haven't seen any ghosts." His question did not make me think he was off his rocker or anything like that. Ghost stories were a staple of mountain life, especially ghosts involving unsolved disappearances, murders, and star-crossed lovers. "Did your father ever talk about the men?"

"Sure," he said. "Lily-livered sons a, uh-hem, excuse me. Forget myself sometimes. My dad always said them boys deserved whatever it was they got, 'less a course they were on a beach in Hawaii or something."

"Why?" I asked. "What did they do?"

Chester scratched his paper-thin white hair and spit again. Had he forgotten how to swallow? After a moment he stated, "Don't know. Dad never told me. Don't know if Dad even knew."

"Okay," I said. "Exactly what do you know about them?"

"I know that there was a dance a-goin' on that night. Down at the fairgrounds. Everybody was there. Doyle and Thomas showed up in their best clothes, all spit shined and scrubby," he said. " 'Bout an hour into it,

135

they started tellin' people that they had to go. They had dates. Kept tellin' everybody that they was in for a good time and that they'd tell 'em all about it the next day."

"Good," I said. "That's good. What happened?"

"They left and nobody saw 'em again. Ever."

"That's not so good," I said. "Is there nothing else that you've been told?"

"There was rumors aplenty. Some said that Bridie knew where the miners had gone. Others said that Bridie kilt them."

"What?" I all but screeched.

"Nobody believed that. She had no business with them. What reason would she have to do something like that?" he asked. "Nope. Most nobody believed that. But most everybody believed that she knew where they'd gone off to."

"Why? Why did people think that Bridie knew the fates of the miners?" Elliott asked before I had a chance to.

"Best as I can tell, when she was questioned about 'em, she all but said that she knew their whereabouts. When they went and pushed her about it, she said that it wasn't up to her to make people awares," Chester said with a smile on his face, as if he was proud of her. "Since there was never no crime committed, she didn't do nothing wrong."

I unfolded my legs, but stayed seated on the ground. I stretched them out in front of me, trying to get the blood to return to my feet. I wiggled my feet and rolled my ankles. "What do you know about the lynching?" I asked finally.

"I saw that body," he said. "He'd pissed himself but good."

"That's nice," I said and nearly hurled my breakfast

right then and there. Then I thought about what he'd said. He couldn't have been more than seven or eight. How would he have seen the body? I'd lock my kids in the closet before letting them see something like that. "H-ow did you . . . Weren't you terribly young?"

"Sure," he said. "My dad had to quit mining because of the seventeen."

"Seventeen? What exactly does that mean?"

"The cave-in of seventeen. Broke his back. Couldn't mine anymore," Chester explained. "So, to try and make extra money, before school I'd walk up to the boardinghouse and get the mending, ironing, things like that, and take them back to my mom. She got paid for doin' that sort of thing. It was 'long about five-thirty when I got there and there's a big crowd. Just a minute."

Chester jumped up and took the steps up to his house two at a time. I gave Elliott an amused look and he smiled back at me. Not even a minute later, Chester was back and handed me a picture. "That's me," he said and pointed to a hollow-faced boy who peered back at the camera with sharp eyes in a dull body. He stood in a crowd of people, who stood around a body hanging from the tree that stood in the front yard of the boardinghouse.

We desperately needed the voice of Danette here so that she could say her usual *oh, gross.* I said it for her. "Oh, gross."

"Let me see," Elliott said and took the picture from me.

"What do you know about him? Why would somebody do that?"

"Why?" Chester asked. "Why not? Big-shot company man. He could have your job in a second. Always tryin' to squeeze the local man out and bring in some

137

foreigner that would do the job cheaper. There's a hundred people that coulda done that."

I thought that Chester was still a little touchy over this particular subject and that I needed to be very careful about what I said and how I said it. Elliott handed the picture back to me and I studied it. I tried to look at the body without really looking at the body, as if the evil presented there could somehow jump out of the picture and invade my safe world. As if just by looking at it, I was bringing his misfortune to myself.

"All right," I said. "I understand that. But seriously, who could have done it?"

"Oh, they caught the guys that did it," he said. He snapped his fingers and tapped his temple as if that would help him remember exactly who they were. "Arlo Davis and William Gross."

I heard the words that Chester said, but I didn't really hear the words that Chester said. That was because I was engrossed in looking at the lynched man in the photograph. I thought about how unusual it was that in the only photographs of this man that I had ever seen, he was dead. This was Aldrich Gainsborough.

And this was the man in the casket in the photograph that hung above the fireplace at the Panther Run Boardinghouse.

TWENTY-FOUR

"WHAT DOES IT MEAN?" ELLIOTT ASKED ME. HIS brown eyes were serious and yet somehow there was a certain look of wide-eyed disbelief to them. He downshifted the gears in his Eagle Scout as we came to a four-way stop at the foot of the hill. How brave he was, I thought, to drive a stick shift in a mountain state.

"I don't know," I said and gazed out the window at the supreme foliage all around. "Why would Clarissa have a picture of a dead guy hanging above her fireplace? Since 1918, I might add. Why would Clarissa hang a picture of the *superintendent* of the Panther Run Coal Company above her fireplace?"

"In his casket, no less."

"Yes, we've established that. Creepy in and of itself," I said. "Then add the fact that he was lynched in the front yard . . ."

Elliott turned his vehicle to the left, and we headed up over a mountain. "Okay, so the superintendent of the company gets lynched in the front yard of the boardinghouse, and Clarissa forever hangs a picture of him in his casket above her fireplace."

"Do you think it was a reminder?" I asked.

"A reminder of what?"

"Of the fact he was lynched? I don't know. I read in one of the books you checked out for me that the superintendent was pretty much loathed within the community. I didn't really get a chance to read *why* he was loathed, but suffice it to say that he was. So why would she hang a photograph of him in his coffin in her house?"

"Maybe Gainsborough did something really horrible to her and she wanted to see his dead face every day as a reminder that he was dead," Elliott said and shifted gears yet again.

I sort of stared at him from the corner of my eyes. "You have an active imagination," I said. "I'm almost afraid to ask where that came from."

"Well, think about it. Let's say . . . he killed her father or something horrible like that. She absolutely despised

139

him and wanted her own revenge. Now, we know that tiny Clarissa Hart couldn't lynch a man all by herself, so that's out of the question. But somebody else *does* lynch him and makes her day. So, she takes his picture and hangs it in the boardinghouse as a reminder every day that the guy got what he had coming to him," Elliott said, all worked up at his own devices.

I thought about it a moment while Elliott waited for me to reply. "Well, your theory holds merit. In fact, it's the best theory we've got so far . . . but Lord, it sounds like a plot to a Monday night movie or something."

"You know they get ideas for movies from real life," he stated.

"Okay," I said. "Say you are correct. Where's the connection between him and the miners, Phillips and MacLean?"

"Who said there has to be one?" Elliott asked. "Maybe they were suspects in the Gainsborough lynching. Nobody ever said they actually did it, and besides, Chester said they caught the guys that really did it. You know, if the papers print that you are suspected in the murder of Clarissa Hart, we all know that you didn't do it, but somebody eighty years from now may question it, like you're questioning Phillips and MacLean right now."

I gave him a sideways glance and pondered what he'd just said. "Well, that's comforting," I said. "So you don't think that there is a connection between the Gainsborough lynching and the missing miners?"

"I didn't say that, either," he said.

"Oh, for Pete's sake, Elliott. You're giving me a headache," I said.

"What does any of it matter?" he asked. "I mean,

seriously. Does any of this really help determine who killed Clarissa Hart? Can it possibly help?"

"I think it could," I said. "You'd be surprised how many thorns from the past pop up in the present day."

"I suppose you're right. We could just as easily be wrong," he said. Elliott pointed up to the top of the mountain where an absolute mansion sat gleaming in the summer sun. "That's where we're headed."

"Wow," I said. "Don't hit any really big bumps."

Before we could even get out of the Scout, two very large and well-fed German shepherds came to greet us. Large and absolutely beautiful, the two barked at us as if they'd never bark again but did not bare their teeth. They were interested, and maybe slightly alarmed, but not ready to attack.

"Nice doggy," I said as I stepped out of the truck. I made no sudden moves and kept my hands palm down and to my sides. They sniffed and sniffed and I really wished that their owner would come and call them off. "Nice big doggy."

The house was an amazing piece of modern architecture with more points and angles to it than I thought possible in a building. I swear there had to be rooms that had five or more walls instead of your standard four. It was a white sandstone with what I assumed were large solar panels along the roof. The yard was immaculate, and every pane of glass seemed to be a veritable commercial for Windex.

"Can I help you?" I heard a deep voice ask from behind. I jumped as if I had been shot and was comforted by the fact that Elliott actually shrieked.

I turned to find a *large* black man in overalls and a navy blue thermal underwear shirt. His boots were clean

141

and his face freshly shaven. I looked to Elliott, hoping he would speak up, because I had no clue as to who we were there to visit.

"I . . . I . . . jeez, you scared the vinegar out of me," Elliott said, still trying to catch his breath. The dogs had calmed down and were seated on their haunches. "I'm looking for Robert Miller."

"What's your business with him?" the man asked in that voice that seemed to grow from his chest.

"Uh . . . we're wanting some help with some local history," he said.

The man looked at Elliott's vehicle and spied his West Virginia license plates. "You're local."

"Yes," I interrupted. "But I'm not and I've just inherited the Panther Run Boardinghouse."

The man eyed me, I swear, all the way from the top of my head down to my toes, which were sticking out of my sandals. "I'm Bobby Miller. What do you want to know?"

"You're Robert Miller?" Elliott asked.

"What's the matter? You weren't expecting a black man in this big mansion on the hill?" he asked.

"Well, actually," Elliott began. "I . . . I don't know what I was expecting. I was told Robert Miller had been a miner, and I've never seen many miners end up in houses like that one."

Bobby Miller was at least six feet three, with forearms the size of my thighs. Okay, my normal thighs, not my pregnant ones. He was maybe fifty years old, which was only alluded to by the grey at his temples. Otherwise, there were no wrinkles, except around his eyes, and he was as fit and firm as any thirty-year-old.

"Come on in," he said and walked up to his house with the dogs quickly on his heels. "Been trying to keep

142

the panther off my property at night. I'm not having any luck."

"How are you attempting that?" Elliott asked.

"I put up an electronic fence two acres out. She doesn't seem to care," Mr. Miller said. "She's a mean one."

He led us into his house and showed us to the family room where he told us to sit while his wife brought us iced tea. I didn't ask if it had caffeine or not. I drank it, hoping that it would have caffeine and I would be innocent of any wrongdoing.

"What is it exactly that you're wanting to know?" he asked as he sat down in a large tan recliner. The living room had floor-to-ceiling windows, which was really cool in the daytime because you could see forever and see all the wildlife. The flip side meant that at night anything and everything could see right into your living room. Surely there must have been some sort of miniblind system that I just couldn't see.

Bookcases were built into the walls, with a fireplace made out of a cream-colored marble taking up the only space not covered in books or windows. The floor was an expensive tongue-and-groove. Being the practical person that I am, or else the pessimistic negative wonder that I sometimes can be, I could only think of what a pain in the butt it must be to keep clean. There were pluses to being lower middle class, in a small house with yucky brown carpet. Only having to vacuum twice a week was one of them.

"Mr. Miller, my name is Torie O'Shea, by the way," I said. "Is this house really run on solar power?" I don't know where that came from. I was all prepared to ask him about the boardinghouse and the mines, and instead that question just sort of tumbled out of my mouth.

143

"Call me Bobby," he said, and smiled. "And, yes. It is."

"Oh, that is just too cool," I said and looked up at the ceiling.

"You didn't come here to ask me about my house," he said.

"No, you're absolutely correct," I said. "Forgive me."

"It's all right. My house has been in quite a few magazines. It is one of a kind."

"You were a miner?" I asked.

"When I was a child," he said. "I was eight years old the first time I stepped foot in the mines. My father took me in."

"How long ago was that?" Elliott asked.

"Nineteen forty-eight," he answered.

He was older than I thought, but still not quite old enough to actually remember the era that I was most interested in.

"Thought I'd die of claustrophobia," he said. I looked at his house with all of its bright open spaces and twenty-foot ceilings. Windows that went all the way to the sky. His confession was no surprise to me. "I swore I was not going to end up like my father or his father or his father."

"What happened?" I asked. "How did you break the cycle?"

"Clarissa Hart," he said. "She married a man who was educated and was on his way to being somebody. They had money. One day she was down at the mines—"

"Why?" I asked. "Why would she be down at the mines by that point in her life?"

"She would come down and visit every now and then. Just so happens I'd come down with the flu or something that day and my father sent me out ahead of

144

him, early. Said for me to go on home. Clarissa saw me coming out of the mine and she stopped me. She asked me a few questions, like if I could read and write, which I could. My mother had made sure of that. Clarissa said that no boy who could read and write should be wasted in the mines . . ."

"I don't understand," I said.

"Most of the children who worked in the mines couldn't read or write," he explained. "She said that there were plenty of things that I could be doing. She made me promise her that if she got me out of that mine that I wouldn't waste my life on things like whiskey and gambling. That I would go to school and go to college and be somebody. I said I would."

"So, what happened?"

"She paid my father whatever I would be bringing in mining, plus an extra ten dollars a week. In exchange I was to go to school, but as soon as school was out, I had to come to the boardinghouse and do whatever odd jobs there were, plus read to her every day. That was all she wanted me to do. I did that for nine years," he said with a smile on his face. "I told her once when I was leaving for college that she'd saved me. She shook her head and told me that my mother had saved me by seeing to it I knew how to read and that I'd saved myself by being willing to work and learn. She refused to take any credit for it at all."

"So do you come from a long line of miners, then?" I asked.

"My father was a miner for fifty-two of his sixty-three years. He came down with black lung. They started making his coffin before he was even dead," he said.

"W-why would they do that?" I asked.

"There was no hope. As soon as they diagnosed him . . . everybody knew," he said. "His father worked the mines and his father before him, and my great-grandfather was a slave over in Shenandoah. The miners weren't much better off than the slaves, but at least the miners could vote, were free to go where they wanted, and didn't have to worry about their children being sold out from under them. I'm not exaggerating when I say the life of a miner back then was close to slavery. We've been told it was a free country, but at the time . . . to people who worked for the company . . . it wasn't. Nothing free about it."

What do you say to something like that? "Did your father ever talk about the old days? Or your grandfather? I'm looking for the scoop on the Panther Run Boardinghouse and the coal company. I know that the superintendent was lynched there."

"Why?" he asked, and I noticed a slightly distrustful tone.

"I've inherited the boardinghouse and I'm curious as to its history. Once I started getting a little bit of information I just couldn't get enough," I said. And it was true.

"That place was at the center of bloodshed for many years. My grandfather told me about the lynching once," he said. One of his dogs had laid his head in his lap, and Mr. Miller absently stroked the fur on its head. "Gainsborough wasn't always the superintendent."

"No?" I asked.

"No. He was sent in to take over because the first superintendent was missing for two weeks and then found floating in the river. They brought Gainsborough in, and at first he was just an official guest of the company. He'd been a superintendent at several other mines, and from what I understand had whipped them

146

into shape in nothing flat. He had a reputation coming in. After a while, he decided to take the position of superintendent," Mr. Miller said. "It was his fatal decision."

Mr. Miller looked as though he was growing tired of the conversation, and I felt a little peculiar sitting in this man's house asking him all sorts of personal questions. But not peculiar enough to refrain from asking one more.

"Do you remember what was hanging in the great room of the boardinghouse when you were a child? Right above the fireplace?" I asked.

He smiled at me and stopped petting his dog for a minute. "Yes," he said. "The photograph of Gainsborough's funeral."

"You ever ask her why it was hanging there?" Elliott asked.

"Yes. Yes, as a matter of fact I did," Mr. Miller said.

There was a pregnant pause, and not just because I was in the room. "Well? What was her answer?"

"She said 'Forgiveness comes when you forget.' "

"What the heck does that mean?" I asked. I hadn't meant to say that out loud.

"I don't know exactly," Mr. Miller said. "But I never asked again."

"Well, we've taken up enough of your time. I can't tell you how much I appreciate your taking a moment to answer the questions of a complete stranger," I said and stood up. I smiled at him and he smiled back.

"I figured if Clarissa left you the boardinghouse, you must be okay," he said. "She had a keen sense."

"Oh, thank you," I said.

"Can I ask you a question?" he said as he got up to show us to the door.

147

"Sure."

"Why'd she leave it you?"

"She said it was a debt repaid," I answered as Elliott and I reached the foyer. Mr. Miller opened the door and the brilliant yellow sunlight spilled in across my face. "My great-grandmother Bridie MacClanahan had owned it originally and left it to Clarissa."

"Bridie Mac," he said. "You don't look much like her."

"How would you know what she looked like?" I asked, aware of the fact that she'd been dead fourteen or so years before he was even born.

"Oh, I've seen pictures. At Panther Run. We've all seen pictures," he said.

You would think that at a moment like that I would be able to think of something to say. Instead I thanked him again and stepped out into the brilliant light with Elliott, just as confused as I, by my side.

"I want to go home," I said.

TWENTY-FIVE

"RUDY?"

"Yeah, Torie?" he asked. I knew that he was several states away, but if I closed my eyes and pressed the phone up to my ear as close as I could get it, I could almost imagine we were in the same room.

"What's going on?" I asked as casually as I could. "How was fishing with my dad?"

"Miserable."

"Why?" I asked.

"Because he caught about twenty fish, and the only thing I caught was a case of malaria from all of the blasted mosquitoes," he said.

148

"Take more vitamin B-twelve," I said. "You know, Elmer can tell you every vitamin you need to take for every ailment. He claims vitamin E will do the same thing that Viagra does."

"I don't need any help in that department," Rudy said. "Or do I?"

"Considering my present state, I think not."

"You miss me?" he asked.

"Of course," I said. "How's Mom?"

"Fine. She's finally come to the decision that you will look just as good in peach chiffon as you would in seafoam-green . . . satin or whatever it was that you were supposed to wear," he said. "I think Colin's getting a little nervous."

"Good," I said. "It will put hair on his chest."

Rudy laughed and then seemed to teeter on the verge of saying something. "What is it?" I asked.

"Your grandmother called earlier," he said.

"Oh, did she tell you that she's all mad at me?"

"No. She did say that you guys wouldn't be able to come home because the old lady was definitely murdered and that you were the biggest suspect," he said. "Do you need me to come out there? Do you need me to call our lawyer?"

"We don't have a lawyer. Do we? Honey, what do we have a lawyer for?" I asked.

"My father has one. I can get him," he answered.

"That's very sweet of you," I said. "And it makes me feel good. But things are . . . under control." I knew as soon as I said it that it was a bad choice of words.

"Under control? Torie, what is going on?"

"Nothing. There's nothing . . . Look, I didn't do anything and it will be cleared up before you know it. I should be home as planned late this weekend," I said.

149

"There's nothing to worry about."

"Which means I need to worry very, very much."

"Thanks a whole heck of a lot," I said.

"Don't get touchy, Miss Torie," he said. "You're like a magnet for trouble."

"You've been talking to my mother. I'm so underappreciated. I remember a time when you used to be on my side," I said.

"Oh, hush. How are you feeling? Baby okay?"

"Yeah," I said. "We're fine. How are the kids?"

"Fine."

"Okay, well, I've got to go. Elliott is taking me square dancing," I said.

"Elliott."

"Seaborne."

"Oh, yeah, your cousin," he said with just a tad of relief in his voice. "Square dancing?"

"Yeah. Figured I should get some fun in, while I'm here. It's in town and everybody's going. I think I'm even going to get Gert to go along," I said.

"Just don't let her dance," he said. "She won't be able to move for a week."

TWENTY-SIX

A FEW HOURS LATER I FOUND MYSELF PONDERING things like, just what is a do-si-do, anyway?

It was actually more of a party than an actual square dance. There was plenty of do-si-doing to go around, but they also had some nice waltzes and slow dances and foot-stomping, almost rock-and-roll type music. I just thanked God there was no crying-in-your-beer music, because what's the point of crying-in-your-beer

150

music if you couldn't have any beer to cry into? Besides, I can only take so much crying-in-your-beer music and then I want to shout from the top of my lungs, "Get over it, already!" I grew up on it, though. If they mapped out my chromosomes, somewhere in there they'd find Tammy Wynette and George Jones.

It was nice to see Danette out and having fun. Somehow she'd managed to find some other lonely tattooed and pierced teenager, whose parents were not claiming him as far as I could tell, to hang with. I'd seen nothing in the way of adult supervision around him. I don't think that this was their particular venue, but they were making the most of it.

"Do you want to dance?"

I turned to find Dexter Galloway standing next to me with his hand outstretched. He was dressed in a pair of jeans that looked like they'd just come off the rack and a black Western-style shirt. I hated to turn him down, since he was being so polite.

"As long as you don't mind dancing with your arms way out in front of you," I said. "My stomach tends to get in the way of dancing."

"Don't mind," he said and led me out to the dance floor. He tried his hardest to lead me into one of those dances where your feet slid across the floor and made a box. I always misread signals and end up trying to take the lead away, and then I step on somebody's foot.

"Oops," I said as I stepped on his foot. I had known he would not be immune to my maiming feet. "Sorry. I'm not very good at this."

He just smiled and kept up the pace. It was so simple. Why did I have to think about it so much?

"Dexter, can I ask you a question?" I had to raise my voice somewhat to be heard over the band, which had not just one but two fiddle players. He nodded. "Why do the Hart children care so much about the boardinghouse? It in no way equals her other property and investments. What is the big deal with it? Are they just upset because Clarissa left one tiny morsel to a mouse instead of the big cats?"

"Funny how the only other person who inherited anything is dead," he said. "That means whatever he inherited is theirs now, too."

"Is it your intention to make me uneasy, Dexter? Because if it is, I just want you to know that you've succeeded and you can stop any time now."

He gave a half-smile and shook his head. "I just want you to be on guard. Edwin is not above breaking the law to get what he wants. And Prescott is without a conscience," he said.

"Oh, wonderful," I said.

"There's more to the boardinghouse and the property it sets on than meets the eye. And they all know it," he said.

"Like what?"

He looked around the room, suddenly uncomfortable. Pastor Breedlove was on the dance floor with, I assumed, his wife. Although I didn't know for sure.

"You're asking the wrong person," he said.

"Who should I be asking?"

He said nothing.

"Dexter?"

"Ouch! Could you pay a little more attention to your feet?" he said.

Heat rose in my cheeks as mortification set in slowly. "Sorry," I said. "Maybe we could do one of those dances where you just go around in a circle."

"Like the teenagers do at the eighth-grade dances?"

"Yeah. Like that."

152

He smiled at me, and for at least a minute, I didn't think that he was going to let me have my way. Finally, he stopped making me go in a square, and we settled into dancing in a circle. I could do this and talk at the same time. I was confident.

"Dexter . . . who should I be asking about the property?" I repeated. "You do know that I am a suspect in Clarissa's death. If you don't help me . . ."

"There's not a thing I can say to you that is concrete," he said. "All I can do is give you the paranoid suspicions of a middle-aged groundskeeper." It was amazing listening to him slowly enunciate every word. He spoke very slowly, regardless of what he had to say. I, on the other hand, get faster and faster depending on how excited or upset I am about something. If I'm talking slowly and carefully, it's usually because I think you're stupid.

"Look, you simply can't be any more paranoid than I am, so fess up," I said, and smiled a big smile with my eyes as wide as I could make them. Man, my charms were just not working on these people.

"I've paid attention when I shouldn't. I've been like a little mouse hiding in a corner," he said. "And I still know nothing."

"I don't believe you," I said. And I didn't. "I think you want me to believe it because you don't want to be the one to spill the beans to me. I mean, look at the way you let me know about the fact that there was an exit from Clarissa's room. You want me to know. You just don't want to tell me."

His eyes flicked from person to person as we danced slowly around the dance floor. It seemed as if he was making sure that nobody was in hearing distance.

"What are we talking about?" he asked. "Exactly."

"The fact that you know something you're not telling me."

"I know a lot of things that I'll never tell you, Mrs. O'Shea. I don't know who killed Clarissa," he said. "Nothing you say can make me suddenly know that."

"Then why are you so sure that I didn't do it?"

"I just know," he said.

"How?"

"I just do."

"You know something about the boardinghouse . . . or what happened years ago. How about the lynching? Is that what you're hiding?" I asked.

His eyes took on a bemused expression as he looked down at me. The music ended, and he held my hand for a moment and gave it a squeeze. "You've been doing your homework," he said.

I rolled my eyes in frustration. He leaned in and said softly, "The Hart children are the most spoiled, self-righteous, loathsome, pampered bunch of people I've ever seen," he said. "I hope you find what you're looking for. And when you do, I only hope that it will be something so awful that it will make each and every one of them disappear from sheer humiliation."

With that he walked away and left me standing in the middle of the dance floor without a partner. Without a partner and with a gaping mouth. I hadn't expected such venom.

Never fail, Pastor Breedlove saw me standing alone and came my way. I looked down at his huge belly and then looked at mine.

"There is no way that you and I are going to be able to slow dance," I said to him just as he reached me.

"That was not my intention," he said, and smiled. "You're a smart cookie."

"Thank you."

"I was hoping I could buy you a 7Up and talk to you a moment."

Somebody who wanted to talk to me? Like I would turn this down? "Sure," I said. "Love to."

Pastor Breedlove led me to a dark corner where we sat with our 7Ups at a square table about three feet by three feet. I'm assuming his drink was straight. I would give him the benefit of the doubt. God, I wanted caffeine. I'd already given Rudy instructions that he was to bring a cooler of Dr. Pepper to my hospital room right after the Apgar score was given to our new baby.

"I wanted to talk to you about your present predicament," he said. He was straightforward; I'll give him that. A little refreshing, actually.

"I'm listening."

"The Harts are good people," he said.

I couldn't help it. I snarfed my 7Up all over the place. "Oh, excuse me, Father. I mean Pastor, or Brother. What exactly is it I'm supposed to call you?" I asked as I wiped at the plastic tablecloth to make sure my snarfed soda had not invaded his side of the table. How humiliating. First I stepped on Dexter's toes, now I'd snarfed soda on a man of the cloth. What was happening to me?

"You can call me whatever you like," he said.

"Okay," I said. "Sorry, Mr. Breedlove."

"Why did you react that way?" he asked.

"Well, it's that I've been told just the opposite. And if I went by the Harts' actions, I'd have to say that my welcome hasn't been the warmest," I explained.

"All right. Edwin isn't worth much and Maribelle means well," he said. "She's just easily influenced."

"I believe she was born with a spine, the same as all of us," I said.

"Don't judge, Mrs. O'Shea—one of the first lessons of Sunday school," he said. "My concern is Laffy."

"Laffy?"

"Laffy Hart. Lafayette, I mean. Sorry, it's an endearment since childhood," he said.

"Why are you so concerned with . . . Laffy Hart?" I asked and tried not to giggle.

"He wouldn't have killed his momma, Mrs. O'Shea. You have to know that," he said and stroked his white fluffy beard.

"Nobody is saying that he did," I said. "The last time I checked, I was the number one suspect."

"Yes, I know," he said, his eyes lighting up. "If you could just—"

"Just what? Confess? Rig evidence so that I'm convicted? Is that it?" I asked, incredulous. The band started up again. They were playing that swinging song by John Anderson. The one that talks about him sitting on the front porch and eating some kind of pie and he was just a-swingin'. Silly song, but I liked it.

"Nothing like that," he said. "I want you to find out who did it."

"You what?" I asked. I thought about it a moment, and then something popped into my head. "Oh, I get it. You want me to find out who murdered Mrs. Hart and make sure that it isn't Laffy. I mean, Lafayette. Is that it?"

He had the decency to look slightly embarrassed. I glanced around the room to find my grandmother sitting at a table with ol' Laffy Hart. She'd been very short with me all evening.

"It wasn't Lafayette. But I'm afraid that boneheaded

156

sheriff might get it in his thick skull that Lafayette did do it and then there would be no stopping him. See . . . if you find out who did it, it won't be Lafayette because he didn't do it."

I shook my head, thoroughly confused. "Wait a minute. If Lafayette didn't kill his mother, then the sheriff will know this."

"Not necessarily," he said. He hunched his shoulders inward and leaned toward me. "Things have a way of ending the way the sheriff wants them to end."

I know I must have looked totally appalled, because, believe me, I wasn't buying this for one second. He was actually trying to convince me that Sheriff Justice was crooked? Or at the very least incompetent? I've seen my share of sheriffs and this one knew what he was doing. "Are you suggesting—"

"I'm not suggesting anything, Mrs. O'Shea," he said.

"If I continue this conversation with you I'm gonna need a real soda," I said, pushing my glass away and resting my head in my hands. "What do you know about Mrs. Hart?"

"I know that she was a very generous lady," he said and smiled at me. "Obviously."

"Yes, obviously." Ooh, I hate it when people get nasty. "Are you angry because she didn't leave you anything for your church? Is that it?"

His skin turned as white as his beard. "No, of course not."

"Then hurry up, Mr. Breedlove. I need to get back to my grandmother. Can you help me or not? I need to know what happened to Clarissa when she was a young woman. Other than witnessing a lynching in her front yard," I said.

The pastor shook his head. "I wasn't even born yet,"

157

he said. "But I heard how that changed her. She wasn't ever the same. Never."

"No, I imagine not."

"No, I mean it was so bad that she had to leave."

"What do you mean, leave?" I asked, suddenly interested.

"Couple months after the lynching, she left. Left the state, as far as I know. Least that's what my daddy told me. Said she was gone about a year. One day she came walking back on up the road, stopped at the boardinghouse and asked your great-grandmother for a job. Nobody knows why she left," he said and then raised his eyebrows. "Rumor was your great-grandmother knew. People said that Bridie knew where she was the whole time."

"Just like they say she knew where the miners had gone, as well," I said.

"No amount of coercing would make Bridie talk. Not even the cross burning."

"The cross burning?" I asked. I could feel my eyes bulge out of my head. "What cross burning?"

"The sheriff back then was a KKK member. He was convinced if Bridie was scared enough, she'd tell. So he rounded up about eight members and put switches on her doorstep. When that didn't get her to go a-running and confess what she knew, they burned a cross in her front yard," he explained.

"Man, that front yard has seen a lot of action," I said.

"I imagine we will never know the half of it. Regardless, Bridie knew where Clarissa had gone off to, but she never would tell. My daddy said that Clarissa came back a haunted woman, wasn't never the same."

"When did she leave?"

158

"Couple months after Gainsborough was lynched. Uh . . . I think it was about a few weeks after those miners went missing. The whole county was thinking that Clarissa was another missing person. But she came back," he said.

"From where?" I asked more for myself than for him. "Where did she go?"

TWENTY-SEVEN

THERE WAS AN ALFRED HITCHCOCK MARATHON ON television at the boardinghouse when we returned from our night out of do-si-doing. Or my night out of stepping on people's feet and dancing in a circle. There's nothing square about my dancing.

I love Alfred Hitchcock. I also am the biggest Cary Grant fan in the world, so I was doubly upset when I found out I'd missed *North by Northwest*. It wasn't as if I hadn't seen it a dozen times already, but I wanted to see it again. My spirits rose when I realized I would get to see *Suspicion*, because even though it was not one of my favorites, I'd get to see Cary.

So, there I sat with my swollen feet propped up on a pillow on the sofa, trying to get them higher than my head. I had a stack of oatmeal-raisin cookies and a glass of milk, and watched Cary Grant play a not-so-nice character, wishing I was at home in New Kassel listening to my chickens cluck and watching my dog Fritz snore.

As far as I could tell, everybody was retired for the evening. I was at the part in the movie when Joan Fontaine argued with the portrait of her father. In her mind, the portrait was telling her to be suspicious of her

159

husband, and she defended him. I looked over my shoulder at the portrait of Aldrich Gainsborough in his casket and wished it would talk to me.

Then I looked up at the gallery of pictures on the stairway wall. I took a bite of cookie and then a drink of milk. I never dunk my cookies because I can't stand anything that is soggy. Soggy is bad. I finished off my glass of milk and set it on the table as I stood up. Leaving the television on, I walked over to the stairwell wall and flipped on the switch.

I probably knew everybody on this wall, but I could not recognize them because many of the pictures were baby portraits. I can't explain my fascination with and love of old pictures. A moment in time captured. A snippet from the evolutionary time scale. A door to another time.

I found the same picture my aunt Millicent had of the boardinghouse with my grandmother standing in the front yard. There was a picture of Clarissa and a man that I assumed was her husband. She wore an elegant dress from the forties with a string of pearls around her neck. And then I noticed a photograph of Bridie. She stood in front of a quilt that hung draped over the porch railing. A few photographs down the wall, I found another one of her. Only this one was a studio portrait in which she wore a small dark hat and the looser clothing that had become popular in the early twenties. Draped across her lap was a quilt.

I stepped back down one step and looked at the earlier picture and then back at the studio one. It was the same quilt. It was the same quilt I had upstairs in the attic in a box that Clarissa had wanted me to see.

Okay, sometimes I'm really dense and I don't get things. Other times I'm extremely paranoid and imagine

160

theories that could never be true. So I had to be very careful with what my next thought was. Yes, every now and then I do have control of my mind.

Was Bridie photographed with this quilt several times for a specific reason? Was it the only quilt she ever made? I doubted that seriously. Why had Clarissa chosen those pictures of Bridie to display in frames on her picture wall? Did it mean something? Or was it just a coincidence? More than likely it meant nothing at all. Still . . .

I went up the stairs and to my room, where I got my keys out of my purse and headed on down the hall to Clarissa's room. As I reached to unlock the door, I noticed that it was already unlocked. I supposed that Dexter was no longer keeping it locked. The door to the attic was unlocked, as well.

I waved my hands out in front of me in the suffocating darkness, trying to find the string that was the light switch. I finally found it, turned it on, bathing the stairs in a dim golden hue, and went on upstairs. What I found, although disturbing, wasn't really a shock to me. Somebody had gone through all of the things in my boxes that Clarissa had set aside for me. This was the second time things of mine had been searched. What was somebody looking for?

I couldn't tell if anything was really missing because it was all just sort of piled into the boxes without being in any order. I spied the quilt and took it, along with the photo album, and then grabbed the sewing basket, as well. As I turned around, I saw somebody out of the corner of my eye and I screamed. It wasn't a little stifled shriek, it was a full-fledged, full-lung-power scream. I also dropped the sewing basket, sending buttons and thread and stuff all across the attic floor.

161

It was Vanessa Killian, the cleaning lady. "What in the hell are you trying to do?" I asked. "Couldn't you have cleared your throat or something?"

"I'm sorry," she said. "I didn't mean to scare you."

"I don't believe you," I said and began picking up all the stuff that had spilled from the brown antique basket. "I think you enjoyed that very much. I think all of the people in this house have a morbid sense of humor and you're all trying to drive me crazy. That's what I think."

"Now, tell me what you really think," she said and smiled. She was about thirty, stocky, and reminded me of one of those nasty women in a Three Stooges movie with a bad Eastern European accent. Except she had no accent.

"What do you want? It's at least midnight," I said.

"That's exactly correct, Mrs. O'Shea. I might ask what you are doing up here at midnight?"

"No, you may not ask," I said from the floor as I was about finished picking up all of the renegade notions. "If you must know, I came up here to get the quilt because I wanted to have a closer look at it. I barely glanced at it the other day when I was up here."

"At midnight."

"Yes, Ms. Killian. I couldn't sleep." She looked at me blankly. "Have you ever been pregnant? You're so sleepy you could drop, yet you can't get comfortable enough to sleep, so you wander around the house doing really odd and stupid things that you normally wouldn't do when you weren't pregnant."

"I see," she said. Boy, she had no sense of humor at all. Made me want to ask her if she had a stash of penicillin somewhere. I would refrain, however. I do remember a few things that my mother taught me. You

162

know, it matters not what I teach my children, because when they grow up they'll flip through their mental file of "Lessons by Mom" and use what they want and throw out what they don't want. Just like I do all the time.

"Can I help you with something?" I asked, and stood up.

"I just heard the noise, I wanted to see if . . . if there was a prowler."

"Oh," I said. Maybe I'd misjudged her. "Have you heard anybody up here earlier? My things have all been gone through."

She looked away quickly and then gave a curt, "No."

"Did you go through my things?"

"No, ma'am," she snapped.

"What is going on? What is it they're looking for?"

"You should go home as quickly as possible," she said and turned to leave.

"Why?" I asked. "Don't you know when you tell somebody to leave quickly, it's only going to make them stay? Because curiosity killed the cat."

"Let's hope it doesn't kill the pregnant lady," she said.

"Are you threatening me?" I asked and moved over closer to her. I didn't look all that intimidating, considering I was pregnant, barefoot, had my hair all messed up, wore cookie crumbs on my lips, and was holding a handful of junk.

"No. I'm trying to help you."

"Well, for your information, I can't leave," I said.

"Why not?"

"The sheriff told me I had to stay put at least for a couple of days. He thinks I killed Clarissa, you know," I said and raised my eyebrows in exaggeration.

163

"We're aware of what is going on. The Harts are the ones going through your stuff," she said and descended the stairs.

"Why?"

About halfway down she turned back to address me. "They're looking for it."

"For what?" I descended the steps with her.

"A few years before their father died, he told them that somewhere on this property was something that would make them wealthy. They've been looking for it ever since."

"What is it?"

"Nobody knows."

"When?"

"When what?" she asked, confused.

"When did their father die?"

"I dunno. Sometime in the sixties," she said. "Go to your room, Mrs. O'Shea. Do us all a favor and stay there."

Man, oh man. I hadn't been told to go to my room in at least a couple of months. I supposed that would change now that my mother would be moving out in August. It was one good thing about her upcoming nuptials.

I was on my way to my bedroom, honest I was. When I smelled this incredible aroma coming from downstairs. It was spicy and cheesy and . . . oh, my gosh. Somebody had ordered pizza! If it was any of the Harts they'd be far too snotty to share their pizza with me, but it might be somebody else, and what did I have to lose? Other than a nice gooey piece of pizza?

I entered the dining room, and there sat Sherise Tyler with a bottle of Rolling Rock and a pizza with the lid opened. The box took up a good two feet on

164

the table, and I could see the round red layers of pepperoni on top.

"Hi, Sherise. I'm going to be rude and ask if I can have a piece of pizza. I'll gladly pay you for it," I said, eyeing the box.

"Don't be silly. I won't eat the whole thing. Sit down and help me," she said and slid the box a few inches toward the empty chair at the head of the table.

"Did you find somebody who delivered all the way out here?" I asked. I disappeared into the kitchen to get a small plate and a glass of water.

"No," she said as I came back in the room. "I picked this up on the way home."

"It smells great. What is it about eating pizza at midnight that is so much better than eating it any other time of the day?" I asked. I sat down and put two pieces on my plate. They had mushrooms, sun-dried tomatoes, and onions on it, in addition to the pepperoni I'd already spotted.

"I don't know," she said. "But, to me, everything's better at night. I'm a night person. I know what you mean, though. What is it about a warm, breezy, starry night that makes people want to be close to the one they love, more so than straight-up noon? Or why is that your husband is so much sexier when you're in his parents' basement? Ever notice that? I suppose the context is everything," she said.

"Yeah," I said and sunk my teeth into the pizza. Wonderful. "Mine is candles. Light the place with nothing but candles and everything looks better. The whole world seems to fall in place and all is right. From a stupid candle."

We were quiet a moment while we ate our pizza. "Baby keeping you up?" she finally asked.

"Yes," I said. "I think he's laying a weird way. Everytime I lay down he sits up or something like that. So, I'm just not laying down."

"That's fine for a while," she said. "You gotta get tired eventually."

"I have an incredible amount of energy, Ms. Tyler. I think my mind just shuts off the valve that says it's tired. Either that or I've convinced myself I'm a failure if I don't get thirty hours out of every day. It's a sickness, I'll grant you."

"I was like that in college," she said.

"Oh, yeah? Where'd you go?"

"SIUE."

"SIU . . . Edwardsville? You went to Edwardsville? In Illinois?" I asked.

"Yup."

"That's just across the river from—"

"St. Louis. Yes, I know."

"That's interesting," I said. "But you're originally from here?"

"Yes."

"So, then . . . tell me what it was like."

"What what was like?" she asked.

"In the coal town. Tell me what it was like to live under the Secret Service known as 'the company.' I've not read a whole lot, and believe it or not, my grandparents have told me very little," I said.

"What makes you think I can tell you?"

"I think that the 'story' you've got involves the coal company. Or something along those lines. I think you know more than anybody else that's here and willing to talk to me."

She smiled and flipped her hair over her shoulder with the hand that wasn't holding the pizza. "You sure

166

you're not a reporter? You're awfully good at this."

"At what?" I asked.

"At asking the perfect questions," she said.

"I don't think so," I said. "I think I'm just incredibly nosy and just ask all the questions I can think of. Eventually one of them will be right."

"Give yourself more credit than that," she said.

"I suppose it's from tracing my family tree. You come to a dead end so many times on the same ancestor that eventually you start asking yourself some of the more improbable questions to try and solve the puzzle," I said.

"Like what? Give me an example," she said.

"Okay . . . like, I had this ancestor whom I could track to the census in 1860. His last child was born in 1863. After that he disappeared. I assumed he died, but because of the years, I couldn't get death records, and I could not find him in any cemetery around. Now, because it was the area that is now West Virginia, and because of his age, it never occurred to me that maybe he died in the Civil War. We all know that plenty of West Virginians fought in the Civil War, but because of its stance *against* the war, it actually became the state that it is today. My mother always told me West Virginia didn't fight. I found out later that isn't exactly the truth. But what happened was this. I found out my ancestor *had* gone off to war, and he died in a prison camp in Illinois. Thus, he was not buried anywhere in West Virginia. But because I eventually asked the improbable question, I found out that several other ancestors or ancestors' siblings fought in the war," I said and took a drink of water.

"On my dad's side, there was this ancestor who just dropped off the planet after 1861. Not one person ever mentioned that he'd fought in the war. Not one. And my great grandparents knew him personally. So I checked it out, and sure enough. He not only fought but died in it. It changed my whole way of thinking. Anytime I come across an ancestor who just dropped out of sight with no death record or will, I check to see if that was the year of a war. Any war. I can't tell you how many times this has helped me."

She'd stopped chewing and was staring at me.

"What?" I asked, suddenly self-conscious.

"You should see yourself when you talk about your family tree. You get this glazed look in your eye, like you're visualizing the charts and stuff. You actually see your ancestors, don't you?" she asked.

"Don't be silly," I said and blushed. It was true.

"Don't deny yourself that. That is passion. That is what makes the world go around. Not love. Not money. Passion. It is passion that drives everything," she said. "It proves you are one of the living."

"My point being," I said, "that I suppose I carry some of that over into my real life. If I come up against a wall, I just back up and go at it from a different angle. Or I parachute down on it. Do you understand what I'm saying?"

"Oh, completely," she said.

"What made you want to be a journalist?" I asked.

"Same thing. Absolute burning desire to know everything. And if you tell me I can't know it, it pisses me off so badly that if I have to steal to know what I'm not supposed to know, I will," she said.

"Wow," I said, impressed with her confession. "So, then. You'll understand when I ask again. Tell me what it was like to live in a coal town."

She smiled and prepared to tell me what I wanted to know.

TWENTY-EIGHT

BEFORE THE BEAUTIFUL SHERISE TYLER WOULD TELL me anything, she went and got herself another Rolling Rock and lit up a cigarette, apologizing again for smoking in my presence. I assured her that as long as she opened the window, I would breathe shallowly.

"I always feel bad when I read those statistics. You know, the ones that say some ten thousand children are admitted to the hospital every year because of second-hand smoke," she said. "I feel bad until it's time to light up another cigarette, and then I feel bad for me. I'm terribly selfish."

"Maybe you just can't commit to quitting," I said.

"And admit I'm weak? I'd much rather be selfish," she said.

"Okay, selfish it is," I said. "Feel better?"

"Yes, thank you."

For some strange reason I knew that she was wanting me to agree with her on this. It was some sort of penance. She admitted her guilt. I agreed. And then she could move on.

"Seriously, though. If it were bothering me too terribly much, I'd go get a gas mask or something," I said, joking.

She laughed finally, ready to move on to telling me all about life in the coal town of Panther Run. She tied her long silky hair in a knot, something I've only been able to do once in my life when I was very young and my hair was long and straight. She pulled her feet up under her and took a drink of her beer. I had a big sparkling glass of ice cubes and water.

"Okay," she said. "First of all, your life was the

company's. Throw out whatever patriotic notions you've got about freedom of speech and the freedom to go anywhere. Throw out the insane ideas that men are created equal, they get equal pay for an honest day's work, they have the right to improve their position. It didn't exist."

"Go on," I said.

"First off, the miner was paid by the carload. Not by the hour or even by the day. Which meant that the operators had any number of ways to cheat the miner. Which is why so many of the miners began bringing their sons in to work alongside them. To try and produce more coal," she explained. "Which enabled all the money to go into the one home."

"How did the operators cheat the miners?" I asked. I should have been taking notes, but I wasn't about to run upstairs to get my notebook and pencil. I had a feeling she was only going to talk for so long and that was it. I didn't want to give her time to think about it and change her mind while I was upstairs.

"Well, one of the ways was that the company got all of the coal that was knocked off or fell off the cars. See, the miner would load a car and put his number on it, and then it would go and get weighed, and that was how he got paid. The company kept anything that fell or got knocked off. That was coal that no miner got paid for, the company got it free and clear. In some cases, the operator would change the shape of the car to hold more coal. So instead of the miner taking a day to fill it up, he might take a day and half or two days, but still get paid the same amount of money."

"Well, that's crappy," I said. "How fair is that?"

"Fair? Throw it out. That word is not in the miner's dictionary," she said.

"Oh, sorry."

"Forget it. Second, the operators would enlarge the holes in the screens so that larger and larger pieces of coal would fall through, and these pieces were the company's, free and clear. And the operators weren't beyond rigging the scales," she went on. "See, that's why the owner/operators didn't want a union. Because the union would threaten the operators' ability to make a profit except through the efficient production of coal. But that's neither here nor there at the moment."

"What else?" I asked and took a drink of water.

"The biggest way the company really stuck it to the miner was by using what was called 'scrip.' "

"Scrip? What was that? Some kind of bad coal or something?"

"No," she said and put her cigarette out in the empty pizza box. Okay, that was gross. "Scrip was bogus money."

"Bogus money. Forgive me if I'm sounding really stupid. It is one-thirty in the morning," I said. "What do you mean, bogus money?"

"Miners were issued scrip instead of money. And scrip could only be used at the stores, doctors, barbers, and so on in town. And guess who owned the stores and barbershops and doctors?"

"The company?"

"Bingo. The company owned everything in the town. They owned the houses that the miners lived in, so who did they pay rent to? The company. In scrip. The company owned the doctor and his office. So who benefited from the miners' use of those establishments? The company," she said. "The store carried everything from fresh produce to furniture, all with excrutiatingly high price tags. The miner was forced to patronize the

171

very places owned by the company because his scrip was no good outside of the coal town."

"Wait, wait, wait," I said and held my hand up. "Isn't that a felony or something? Isn't that against the law?"

"Yes." That was all she said. She did not elaborate.

My head hurt thinking about the horrible cycle that those people had been in, the desperation they must have felt.

"What's more, the company made the miners sign contracts stating that they could be evicted after ten days' notice. There are stories of how peddlers would come through the town selling produce or something, and the superintendent or his henchmen would throw their wares into the river. They didn't want the mining families to patronize anything or anybody other than the company."

"How would they be able to anyway if they were paid only in scrip?" I asked.

"Because sometimes their wives would make money from other things, like sewing or housecleaning in the next town. Or sometimes it was strictly a barter or trade. You know. I'll give you this brand-new pair of socks if you give me a pound of tomatoes," she said.

"Oh," I said. "I understand."

"Do you?" she asked. "The superintendent was the one in charge of all of it. He decided who would be evicted or who wouldn't. He decided everything. You know, it's hard to get ahead when every dollar you earn is in turn given back to the very company you're breaking your back for."

"How horrible," I said. "How did they ever break the cycle?"

"They either didn't or the union came town by town, company by company. The union opposed forced

172

buying in the company stores and cheating on weighing and that sort of thing. Plus, there were an awful lot of miners' daughters who never married."

"What do you mean?" I asked.

"Meaning, they saw what their parents went through. They lived in a coal town; who were they gonna marry? Coal miners. They saw with their own eyes what kind of life that was, and so they stayed unmarried or else in the middle of the night they'd just run off and never come back. Thus breaking the cycle."

I thought about Clarissa Hart taking off after the lynching of the company's superintendent. "Where would they go?"

"Most likely Charleston. Follow the river, and you end up in Charleston. From there you could catch a train or barge to anywhere. If you had the money. Some just walked until they dropped, and that's where they stayed," she said. "It's quite suffocating to be the child trapped in your parents' nightmare. Almost as suffocating as it was to be a miner."

"Wow," I said. "I can't thank you enough for all of this background. I had no idea."

"That's just the tip of the iceberg. Things are a whole lot better for the miner today. But think about the living conditions back then," she said. "The entire town was covered with a thin layer of coal dust. There were explosions and there was the risk of cave-ins. Most of the time mothers sent their boys, starting at eight years of age, off to that blackness known as the mine. They'd be carrying their lunch pails of food that the rats would most likely eat before they could get a chance to."

"Okay," I said. "I think I've heard enough. I probably won't sleep tonight, and it won't be due to my back for once."

She smiled and downed half of her bottle of beer. "And then there were the deaths."

"D-deaths?"

"Every family in a mining town could boast at least one son or husband who was dead or maimed. If your husband was a miner, you knew that when he went off to work, he might not come home."

"Sort of like a cop's wife" I said.

"Very much," she said. "Except it's much more honorable to be killed in the line of duty while saving damsels from ne'er-do-wells than to be blown to bits in a coal mine. Or buried alive."

"I got the picture," I said. Her energy was building with each sentence she spewed.

"I'm just getting started. If you didn't die in the mine, well, then you had to look forward to that pesky little thing known as black lung. Or pneumoconiosis. For a long time it didn't have a name. The government didn't want to acknowledge that there was such a thing."

"Reminiscent of HIV. How many people had it infected or killed before they actually gave it a name?"

"Exactly. *The X-Files* isn't too far off when they quote 'Deny everything.' "

There was a sound outside and I jumped. It was the panther. She was back. I wondered if it was just one panther that I'd heard several times or if there were several. And why did I always refer to it as a she?

"Panther," she said.

"Yes. Startled me," I said. "Anyway, back to the black lung."

"Well, the miner in general was a completely deteriorated individual after forty or fifty years of mining. I mean, he would have had multiple fractures or

174

broken bones in his lifetime. Often miners were stoop-shouldered or burned. Their blood was weak—"

"Why?"

"Because the air that they breathed in the mines was full of gases. As a result, they did not have oxygen-healthy blood," she said.

"Oh," I said, feeling totally stupid.

"And it was full of coal dust. Thus the black lung. The pores in their lungs would become clogged with it. They would cough and spit up black stuff," she said.

I think she was feeling her beer because every word she said now was overenunciated and filled with venom. Gee, I was really sorry that I had brought up some obvious sore spot. But I was very happy to have the information that she'd supplied.

"Do you know how many little girls never even got to see their fathers?" she asked with a haunted look.

It takes me a while, but eventually I catch on.

I think I understood where her rather unexplained venom was coming from. She obviously had lost somebody in a cave-in or explosion or something. That last remark was just a tad peculiar.

I cleared my throat, and she came out of her reverie, swiping at a lone tear as she arrived in the present. "Have you got a good picture of it now?"

"Yes," I said. "Thank you. You mentioned some of the girls just leaving. Heading to Charleston. What if they didn't have the money for trainfare once they arrived? Was there a particular place they could go?"

"Actually, there was. There was a women's hospital there. Mostly for prostitutes or unwed mothers. Good deal of syphilis cases there, as well. I know, I've checked this out. Otherwise, there was a halfway house, where women could go and maybe get a job, or

175

whatever. I mean, they didn't have counseling like you have today."

"Really," I said, thinking back to what Pastor Breedlove had told me earlier about Clarissa just taking off one day, only to return a year later.

"But they did help people," she said.

"Would you happen to remember the name of this place?" I asked. I think if her judgment had not been impaired, she would not have answered this question. But because of the state she was in, all of her own doing, mind you, she was willing to talk. Did I feel guilty about this? Surprisingly, no.

"VanBibber something or other."

"You're joking," I said.

"No, why?"

"It's just that . . . well, some of my ancestors were VanBibbers."

"Hmph," she said and rolled her eyes. "Well, this particular branch of that family were Methodist and really into helping people."

"Wow," I said. "How cool."

"I would have just left," she said.

"What do you mean?"

"If I had gotten out of this godforsaken hellhole, I wouldn't have stopped in Charleston. No, siree. I would have kept going. Sometimes women had people waiting for them on the other side," she said.

"Other side of what?"

"You know . . . just wherever. The other side. Meaning other than here. Like the Underground Railroad, only not as much cloak-and-dagger," she said.

Lord. The beer was really getting to her. "What do you mean?"

"It's a fantasy of mine. I like to imagine some young

girl leaving in the middle of the night, with nothing but the clothes on her back—"

"Bridie did that. Only she absconded. Got married to somebody the family didn't exactly like. He was a divorced man," I said in a whisper.

"Anyway," she said, irritated with my interruption. "I fantasize that this girl has an aunt or a cousin in a faraway state who helps her to freedom."

I know my expression was indescribable, because I, for one, wasn't sure how to take her confession of such a romantic fantasy. I knew that the "slavery" known as coal mining was nowhere equal to that of actual slavery. Sherise, however, had gotten it into her head that it was a form of slavery, and there was no convincing her otherwise. I wondered if she was this melodramatic about everything in her life or just this particular subject.

"Haven't you ever read about the Underground Railroad? You know, how they used quilts to communicate. Like a map or something. Certain patterns meant certain things. Well, kinda like that. That's my fantasy. She makes it to Charleston and in the train station is a big map printed on the station floor, only nobody sees it because of how big it is. You have to be up high. The girl eventually finds it and knows what train to take. And she lives happily ever after," she said with a rather sad smile. "That's what I like to imagine."

"A map," I said. "Did you say a map?"

TWENTY-NINE

"NORVILLE GROSS WAS KILLED BY A PANTHER."

The news sort of shocked me, really. I'd convinced myself that he had been murdered. I'm not sure which

177

was worse, actually. Being attacked by a panther and afraid the whole time that you were going to die, or being attacked by a person and afraid the whole time that you were going to die.

Sheriff Justice's uniform was crisp and his hat kept the sunlight from his face. I stood out in the front yard, beneath the lynching tree, wondering why he was telling me this at all. It kind of looked bad for me, though. If Norville had been murdered, then the sheriff would have had to seriously consider somebody else for the murder of Clarissa Hart. My alibi, if Norville had been murdered, was my third-trimester stomach. Everybody and their uncle knew that I could not have committed a brutal crime like the attack on Norville Gross in my present state. His being killed by a panther sort of made Clarissa's death look more like my fault.

I didn't do it. I swear. Where would I get penicillin, anyway?

"Have you dusted for prints?" I asked.

He smiled at me, although I could not read his eyes. "Why would I do that? Any and everybody has touched any and everything."

"I mean in the attic."

"What do you mean?" he asked.

"The entrance to the attic is in Clarissa's bedroom. Somebody could have snuck up there and out through the window while I was discovering the body," I said. "If you dusted for prints around that window, you might be surprised to find that they're not mine."

He was quiet a moment. I was happy. After I had gone to bed last night, I could not sleep. How could I with everything Sherise Tyler had just told me? After I'd finished mulling over all of her information I had begun to work on a way to prove I *hadn't* killed

Clarissa, rather than who had. I remembered Dexter telling me that he saw the window in the attic open. Around three in the morning, I thought of the fact that they'd probably left fingerprints. Now if I could just convince the sheriff.

"Well?" I said. "Are you going to check?"

"I'll get right on that," he said.

"Thank you. You know, Susan Henry is the one who had access to all of the food, Sheriff. Not me. And . . . and Clarissa's son Edwin came in and gave her a chocolate bar," I said, snapping my fingers. I'd forgotten all about that. He could have easily poisoned the chocolate bar. "Did you find a candy wrapper or anything like that in the room?"

"I'm not at liberty to discuss that with you," he said. "I said I'll dust for prints and I will. And please don't tell me who is a suspect and who isn't."

Well, he didn't have to go and get his panties in a wad over it. He seemed a tad more professional and irritated with me than he had the day I visited his office. "Did Mr. Gross's father ever make it into town?"

"Yes," he said. "He came in and identified the body and then took it home. Took a matter of hours."

"How sad," I said.

"Mrs. O'Shea," he said. "Do you have a lawyer?"

"Yes," I blurted out before I even thought about it. My heart pounded in my chest, and my face was instantly flushed. "Why do you ask?"

Like I really needed to ask that.

"I think you know why," he said. "Do you have any priors?"

"No, of course not," I said. "Well . . . actually, I was arrested once. But it was a total misunderstanding and that sheriff is deeply regretful."

179

He raised an eyebrow.

"Seriously. Fingerprints, Sheriff Justice. Don't forget to check for those fingerprints."

"What have have you found out about the place?" he asked and pointed to the building in front of us that seemed to have been the center of so much activity in the first couple of decades of the twentieth century.

I could play snotty and tell him I didn't have to share my information with him. And I really wanted to, but no use in making him more angry. "Actually, I have learned so much. But I don't think any of it is getting me any closer to solving who killed Clarissa," I said.

He cut his eyes around quickly, and I could feel the coldness coming from them. "That is, if I were trying to solve her murder. Which I'm not. Of course not. Because if I were, that would probably be interfering or something like that, and I would never do that," I said.

And yes, my fingers were crossed.

"What have you found?" he asked again.

"Bunch of stuff on the Aldrich Gainsborough lynching. Some stuff on Clarissa leaving shortly after that and not coming back for a year. That sort of thing."

"Why do you want to know about that?" he asked brusquely.

"I didn't say I wanted to know about it. That's just what's come up. You know, when you're researching something, you don't know until after it's all over which path would have been the most direct. When you're in the process of it, you get a lot of stuff thrown at you that you can just dismiss. Hindsight is twenty-twenty, you know," I said. "I really must get going. The day is getting away from me."

With that I walked into the boardinghouse, passing

Dexter, Maribelle, and Prescott on the way. I headed up the steps just as Danette came around the corner. "Good morning, Mrs. O'Shea," she said.

"Good morning, Danette." I took a few more steps and was stopped by Danette's voice yet again.

"Why do you always take the stairs?" She asked. "You're pregnant, you know."

"Can't forget it," I said.

"Well, Granny's elevator works just fine. Nobody will care if you use it," she said.

"Oh, no thank you," I said. "I have severe claustrophobia and an old rickety thing like that is . . . well, it is a disaster waiting to happen. With me in it, no less. Thanks for the offer, though."

"You're welcome," she said and went outside onto the porch.

I ignored everybody else in the great room and finished my trek upstairs to find Gert. She was seated on the edge of her bed rubbing her feet. I was amazed by this because I didn't know she could get her feet in her lap.

"Gert, what are you doing? You'll fall over," I said.

"Oh, shut up," she said. "My feet hurt from dancing."

"Did you dance?" I asked.

"Me and Lafayette danced one dance. Around in a circle, because neither one of us could remember how to make a square," she said.

"Oh, Gert," I said, laughing. "You are so mean."

"I've had plenty of practice," she said.

"You still mad at me?" I asked.

"I'm not mad at you. I thought you were upset with me," she said.

"Well, I'm always upset with you in some form or another," I said. "I thought—"

181

"Forget it," she said.

Her feet had bunions the size of quarters. Her big toes grew crooked and I often wondered how her feet held up at all after she had waited tables for thirty-something years. She still had an exceptional arch, though.

"How come you never told me that Lafayette's nickname was Laffy?" I asked.

"How silly is that? That's horrible. Poor guy. Why would I want to deliberately spread something that silly around?" she asked.

"Oh," I said. "I see your point."

"Have you talked to your mother lately?" she asked.

"I talked to Rudy yesterday," I said. "I'll talk to her today probably."

"They still think you're a murderer?" she asked and put her shoe on.

"Yes," I said. "Oh, and Sheriff Justice came by and he said that Norville Gross was definitely killed by a panther. So that's comforting on one hand. There isn't some crazed psycho killing off the boarders of the boardinghouse. On the other hand, that means Clarissa's murder looks more like I did it. But on the other hand, we have a crazed panther on the loose. Wait a minute, that was three hands."

Gert shook her head and clicked her tongue. "How do you do this to yourself? How do you get yourself in such messes?"

"I . . . uh, well, if it makes you feel any better, I don't try it," I said, duly scolded. "How was I supposed to know that picking up a pillow could lead to all of this? Would you have known that? I think not."

A long, frustrated sigh exhaled from her body. "That wasn't a panther attack, I don't care what anybody says. What are your plans for today?"

182

"My plans for today are as follows: I need to get to the courthouse to look at some vital statistics. And I need to find out where Clarissa went for a year."

"What do you mean? What are you talking about?"

"It seems that after Gainsborough was lynched, she left town for, like, a year and then came back. At which time Bridie gave her a job," I said. "Sherise said that she may have stayed at a halfway house or its equivalent in Charleston. Would you know why?"

She thought about it a moment and then finally answered with a bewildered look on her face. "No. Mom never told me any of that," she said. "Well, I guess you don't want me tagging along today, then."

"Gert," I said with my hand on my hip. "Don't do that. It's not that I don't want you to come along. I'm always worried that you're getting bored. I tell you what, though. I do have a really important project for you."

"I quit doing laundry ten years ago."

"No, that's not it." God, I could just shake her when she got like this. I walked over to the closet and pulled the quilt down off the top shelf. I spread it out on the bed that she wasn't sitting on. "I think this is what everybody has been looking for."

"What do you mean?"

"I mean, Vanessa Killian told me that Mr. Hart told his children that there was something on this property that would make them all very wealthy. And then last night Sherise mentioned something about quilts being like maps to the slaves for how to make it north. I got to thinking, what if this quilt is a map?"

My grandmother looked at me over her glasses like I was crazy.

"Don't give me that look. Think about it. Clarissa made sure I got this. It's never been used. And there are two photographs of Bridie on the stairway wall in the great room, and in both of them she is pictured with this quilt. Maybe there is something on this property and Bridie made a map for it," I said. "It's plausible."

"Why didn't she just tell somebody?"

"Maybe this was a safety precaution in case something happened to her. Or, or, maybe she was too afraid or something, but she wanted to give somebody in the future a chance to find it. Maybe it was time-sensitive," I said.

"What do you mean?"

"Maybe she couldn't do anything about it until a certain time, so she made the quilt as a map so that she either wouldn't forget or it would be there in case she was dead by that time. And she died. Early," I said.

"I suppose you could be right," Gert said finally. "But what am I looking for?"

"I want you to get a piece of paper and pencil and write down the names of the squares left to right, top row, then second and on down," I said.

"I don't know the names for all of these," she said.

"That's why I'm having Elliott bring some quilt pattern books. There's one book that has ten thousand patterns with all of their different names. 'Cause you know some patterns can have several different names, depending on what part of the country you're in and such," I said.

"Okay," she said. "I'll do it. As long as you are back here by noon to take me to Denny's for lunch."

She could be such a pain in the butt. It was the only pain in my butt that I loved very, very deeply. "You got a deal. I'll even buy."

"I've heard that before."

Very, very deeply.

184

THIRTY

A MICROFILM READER CAN BE YOUR BEST FRIEND. LIKE all best friends, it can suddenly become possessed and behave in a completely un-best-friend-like manner. It can become temperamental, jerky, confusing, and downright annoying. What to do in this case? Do what we would all love to do to that best friend, but won't: Give it a good swift punch. Which I did and I bruised my hand in the process. Love hurts.

Elliott had gone down to Charleston and was searching vital statistics for some dates and facts on Clarissa and her husband. I'd spent the better part of the morning checking out the Soundex for the 1920 census to see if our boys Doyle Phillips and Thomas MacLean had shown up anywhere else in the state of West Virginia, which they had not. The library had a few of the 1920 Soundexes for the surrounding states, as well, and so I checked them, too. Unless Phillips and MacLean had changed their names, they were not in any of the surrounding states, either. Now, that's not to say that they hadn't taken off to Hawaii, but most of the time, people went wherever there were family and friends in times of trouble.

After the fight with the microfilm machine, which I embarrassedly admit it won, I headed off for the courthouse.

I love courthouses. I love everything about them. Except for the woman working behind the counter, who'd been working there forty of her sixty years and was genuinely pissed off about it. This courthouse was no different. The pins in Ethel Mae Crutchfield's hair succeeded in pulling her hair so tight that her eyes were slanted and the skin around her scalp was white. Her cat glasses hung around her neck by a chain that had long ago turned from silver to dingy grey. Ethel Mae would pick up her glasses and hold them to her face every time she needed to read something. Why didn't she just put them on, for crying out loud?

"Excuse me," I said. "I was wondering if you could point me in the direction of will and probate records?"

She pressed her lips together and chewed on the inside of her lip. "Down the hall to the left. Photocopies are a dollar, no exceptions. Please don't mark in the books, tear out pages, or trace the documents. No drinks, smoking, food, or chewing gum allowed. Please sign in," she said with a nasty tone and shoved a book and a pen in my face. She said all of that without even looking up at me from the letters that she was stamping.

You know, there were times when I wished I could be mean and rude right back at people. I didn't care if she hadn't gotten any sleep last night. I didn't care if she was bored with her job. I didn't care if her dog had made a puddle beside her bed, she had forgotten her bologna and cheese sandwich on the counter, or if she had gotten a speeding ticket on the way to work. None of that had anything to do with me. And furthermore, I didn't care if I appeared stupid or dumb to her. She was the expert. She was the one who got the paycheck for working here. Of course I wasn't going to know anything when I asked her for help. So therefore, she should be polite to me.

Just a little soapbox of mine, and I felt much better now. I signed the guest book as Margaret Thatcher and went down the hall to the designated room.

It had never occurred to me to check for a last will and testament for my great-grandmother, Bridie

186

MacClanahan. She was a woman who died in the twenties, and most women back then did not have a will, unless they were well off. And besides, she'd remarried, and so I also assumed that she had no property at the time of her death to do anything with. Boy, have women come a long way.

A few minutes into the books I found the will for my great-grandmother Bridie. And yes, she'd left the boardinghouse to "my dearest of all friends, Clarissa Hart. May you take over from here on out." Just what the heck that meant, I hadn't a clue. But then, that wasn't really anything new, now was it?

She'd had savings of sixty-three dollars, and for back then that was a pretty good sum. Part of it would go to pay her funeral expenses, and the rest was to be divided between her children. Her new husband was not mentioned. She specified that each of the children was to go live with a different aunt. I assumed that the reason she'd made a will at all, considering she was in her twenties, was because she knew she was ill, and she did own a piece of property. If she hadn't specified, her new husband would have gotten it. Smart woman.

I decided, just for kicks and grins, to look and see what I could find on Phillips and MacLean. I hauled out the marriage book and scanned the years 1910 to 1920, since I wasn't sure how old either Phillips or MacLean was. MacLean was not married, at least not in this county during those years. Doyle Phillips, however, was. He married in 1915 one Amanda Sherise Reynolds. Sherise. *Sherise.*

Goose bumps shot down my arms as that name echoed through my groggy head. What were the chances that this was a coincidence? Amanda Reynolds had to be the grandmother or great-grandmother of

187

Sherise Tyler. She had to be. Sherise was obviously connected to the boardinghouse. She kept referring to her "story" and wanting to prove it.

What were the chances that one of the men missing in connection with the lynching of Gainsborough would have married a woman with the middle name Sherise without there being a connection to Sherise Tyler? It's not like the name was Ann or Elizabeth. Sherise wasn't that popular a name even now.

Of course, the next leap my mind made was to Clarissa Hart.

Could Sherise have murdered Clarissa as some sort of revenge for her grandfather or whatever his relation would have been? But why? And why wait until Clarissa was ready to keel over anyway? Why didn't she do it years ago? What would she have gained from it?

The door opened at that moment and in walked one of Sheriff Justice's G-men. One of the ones with lots of muscles. He smiled at me and I smiled back, suddenly crashing from my adrenaline high. I wrote down the information as fast as I could.

"Whatcha looking for?" I asked the deputy. Not that it was any of my business, but how else should I have started a conversation with him? Gee, your uniform sure is tight? I guess I could have tried the old "Hey, I just had a contraction" line on him.

"Nothing," he said.

"Sheriff Justice didn't send you in here to spy on me, did he?" I asked.

"No, no. I'm not spying. I don't care what you do. But I'm supposed to make sure you don't leave town and you'd been in here too long," he said and took his sunglasses off.

"Why would you blow your cover like that?" I asked, dumbfounded.

"I'm not trying to hide from you. In fact, if people know we're watching them, they tend not to run. Honesty is the best policy," he said. "What are *you* looking for?"

"Oh, you know. I'm trying to save my ever-stretching skin, Deputy. It appears that I look fairly guilty where Clarissa Hart's murder is concerned and I'm trying to make sure I can go home on Saturday," I said. "All honestly, of course. I'm not breaking any laws."

"You're not?"

"Nope. This is all public domain. Freedom of Information Act and all that stuff. In fact, my mother's fiancé would be very proud of the fact that I've minded my *p*'s and *q*'s quite nicely while I've been here," I said. I put the marriage book away while I talked to the deputy. "To be perfectly honest, I was hoping that Norville Gross had been murdered."

He raised an eyebrow. It was his only reaction.

"If he had been, it would look more like a double murder and there would be no way I could be guilty of it," I said. "My grandmother's just convinced that those marks on him were not made by a panther. But what does an old lady know, right? Certainly not more than your forensics department."

"What could you find in here that could help you?"

"Lots," I said. "What's your name again?"

"Russell. Deputy Benjamin Russell."

"Kinda got that James Bond thing going, huh? Well, Russell, Benjamin Russell, I'm finished. I'm going to take my grandmother to Denny's for lunch. Has Sheriff Justice got that window upstairs dusted for prints yet?" I asked as I picked up my spiral notebook and headed for the door.

He opened the door for me after a moment's hesitation. "I'm not at liberty to discuss that sort of thing," he said.

"Why not? I won't tell anybody."

THIRTY-ONE

I ARRIVED AT THE PANTHER RUN BOARDINGHOUSE just in time to stop a catastrophe. Screaming assaulted my ears before I even reached the steps. I ran inside the building, letting the rusted screen door bounce behind me. About the time I was halfway into the room, I realized that it was Gert who was screaming.

"Gert?" I yelled. My pulse quickened and seemed to stop in my throat. "Gert?"

The rising hysteria in my voice alarmed me. I hadn't realized that I was so afraid until I heard it come out of my own mouth. The screaming was weak, but seemed to come from upstairs. I back-tracked and took the stairs as fast as my short legs would allow, considering they had a huge belly to contend with, as well.

"I'm coming, Gert!"

Why was nobody else helping her?

That would be because, so far, I hadn't seen another living human being.

When I reached the top of the stairs, I immediately turned to the right and was ready to check our room first. A noise that came from my left, however, stopped me cold.

It was the elevator.

I turned to find my grandmother tied up on the floor of the elevator. Through the metal bars I could see the bungee cord around her wrists. Sweat broke out along my spine, and I shook from head to toe. But it was not fear that made me shake. It was fury.

"Gert, my God," I said. I reached the elevator and yanked on the door, and it was locked.

Keys. Keys. I dumped the contents of my purse on the floor in front of the elevator and rummaged through all of the junk until I found the rabbit's foot key chain. I picked it up and began trying the different keys.

"What the hell," I said. "Who did this to you? Are you okay? Tell me you're okay. Please, God, tell me you're okay."

"Just get . . . me . . . up," she said.

"Where is everybody?" I asked. Key number four, number five, number six. Bingo! The right key. The lever released, and I yanked the door open, only to find another door. Mercifully, that one did not need a key.

I leaned on the elevator floor next to her and untied the bungee cord. And then I yanked on her arm to try and get her up off the floor. She didn't budge. She was too weak.

"Gert, you're going to have to help me. I can't lift you. I'm pregnant, you know. I—"

"I know. You don't . . . want your . . . water to break," she said, breathless.

"Or rupture something. You have to help me," I said. "One, two, three, heave."

She was almost up. One more try and she'd make it. "One, two, three, heave," I said and she came up off the floor.

She staggered and swayed a little, and a shaky hand went out to the railing to hold herself steady. I, however, thought I was going to need a wheelchair, I shook so badly. Unexpectedly, tears streamed down my face.

"Who . . . who did this?" I asked as I swiped away tears.

"I don't know. I've got to lie down."

I walked her back to our room and helped her into the bed. This was no time to have an antique bed that was nearly four feet off the darned floor! "Wait," I said and went to get a suitcase. "Here, step on this."

She used it to step up on, and got into the bed, where I fluffed her pillows and went about examining her for bumps or bruises. Other than the marks from the bungee cord, and a seminasty knot on the back of her head, she seemed fine. No blood.

"What happened?" I asked, somewhat calmer.

"I was in here working on the quilt. You know, trying to figure out what all the blocks were," she said.

"Yeah?"

"And . . . oh, my gosh, my derriere hurts. And all of a sudden this, ouch! You know, right on my head. And I think you're right. I think it is a map. Oh, my gosh, I don't think I'm gonna make it," she said.

"Make it where?" I asked. "Have you been shot or something?"

"No, no. I just feel funny."

"People don't die from feeling funny, Gert. Are you seriously hurt?"

"I'm not sure. They took the quilt."

"What?" I asked, a chill settling into my bones. "They took the quilt?"

"Yes."

"Then that means . . ."

"You were right. Oh, Lordy . . . everything's all fuzzy."

"So, somebody coldcocked you and locked you in the elevator to get the quilt," I said. "Did you figure it out?

Did you decipher it?"

"You know, I could be dying, here! All you care about is that stupid quilt!" she shouted.

"Are you dying, Granny? Are you?"

"I could be."

"Are you?"

"No," she said begrudgingly.

"Exactly. Did you decipher it?"

She hesitated a long time, obviously irritated with me. "I'm pretty sure. I think it's only because I lived here, though. I don't think an outsider coulda figured it out."

"What is it? What is it a map to?"

"Torie?"

I looked up to see cousin Elliott standing in the doorway looking excited and frazzled. He took a big gulp of air and then a wonderful sparkly smile spread across his face. "You are not gonna believe what I found," he said. He took a moment to study his surroundings and then he asked, "Where is everybody?"

"I don't have the foggiest idea," I said. I filled him in briefly on what had just happened. He was duly attentive to my grandmother, checking her head for the bumps I'd already checked for. My grandmother glowed in his attention. Why hadn't she glowed when I checked her head for bumps? I'm convinced grandmothers like boys better than girls.

"What did you find?" I asked.

"Okay. . ." he said. He took a deep breath, straightened out his shirt, and cleared his throat. "Aldrich Gainsborough never did anything awful to Clarissa like I suggested."

"Huh?"

"The reason his picture is hanging on the mantel is

because Clarissa was in love with him!" he said, all proud of himself.

"How do you know?"

"Because, you wanna know what Clarissa Hart was doing for the year that she left Panther Run? She was in Charleston having a baby. She had a baby boy," he said.

"How do you know?" I asked, amazed at what this could mean.

"In vital statistics there is a child born to Clarissa in the year that she was gone. She named him Owen Gainsborough."

"She gave him his father's last name," I said aloud. "What happened to the boy?"

"I don't know," he said. "I'm assuming he died."

"Why do you say that?"

"Because if she'd given him up for adoption, wouldn't the birth records be sealed or something like that?" he asked.

"I'm assuming," I said, just as unsure as he was about it. "I know that they are sealed today. Back then, though, most kids weren't actually adopted. They were raised in orphanages and such. Nowadays they go to foster parents, if they're not adopted."

We both looked at each other, wide-eyed. "We need to check out the orphanages," I said.

"The orphanages!" he echoed.

"What does any of this have to do with who killed Clarissa?" Gert asked, slightly annoyed. That quickly, my grandmother looked at Elliott pleadingly. "I need an icepack, Elliott. Do you think you can get me one? My head is throbbing."

"Gert, what did you find out about the quilt?" I asked.

"There were several blocks that were called things like, Picket Fences, Pumpkin Vine, Snail's Trail," she said.

"Which mean what?"

"Meaning that, back in the twenties, if you followed the picket fence that used to run along the property, you'd eventually run into the pumpkin vines by the pumpkin patch and then finally to what we called the snail's trail," she said, rubbing her head. "Oh, my toe is hurting. I think I might have jammed it."

"Why did you call it the snail's trail?" I asked, ignoring her toe remark.

"Because it was this very narrow path and you could only go single file and very slowly," she said.

"To where?" I asked. "Where did the trail lead?"

"The old abandoned mine shaft," she said.

"What mine shaft?" I asked. "Are you telling me there is a coal mine on this property?"

"Yes," she said. "When I was a kid, the mine shaft was boarded up. As far as I know, it's never been any other way. Clarissa owned it and she refused to let it be mined."

"You're joking?" I asked. "My gosh, she could have made a fortune. Either starting her own company or getting a commission from another coal company to mine it."

"Wait," Elliott interrupted. "Are you saying that the coal mine that is on the property then belonged to the Panther Run Coal Company?"

"Yes, and when they sold the ten acres and the boardinghouse to Bridie and our great-grandfather, the mine must have come with it," I said.

"Then why didn't our great-grandparents ever mine it?" he asked.

We all three were silent and stared at each other. "That's a good question," I said. "You're sure that this is what the quilt said."

"Yes," she said. "For one thing, I held the quilt up to

195

the light and the actual quilt motif that my mother quilted over each block was in the shape of a coal car."

"I don't believe it," I said.

"Who do you think did this to Aunt Gertrude?" Elliott said.

"I don't know."

"Is it our killer?"

"I don't know that, either. It kind of smells that way, though. But then, why didn't he kill her?" I asked. I worked my lower lip between my finger and thumb, thinking about what to do. "Can you get us to the mine, Gert? Do you remember how to get there?"

"Yes," she said. "But my head hurts too much."

"Okay," I said to Elliott. "Here's the plan. Let's take Gert to the hospital and have her checked out. We need to call the sheriff, as well, and file a report. Then you and I need to check out the orphanage records. If they exist and if we can go through them."

"One other thing," Elliott said. "I found an old woman whose mother worked at the VanBibber House. You know, the halfway house."

"Yeah?"

"She would have been about ten when Clarissa was there," he said.

"Wait, how do you know Clarissa stayed there?"

"The birth record asked for an address. I looked the address up and it was the VanBibber House," he said.

"Wow, Elliott. I feel so close to you at this moment. Kindred souls, you know? I thought I was the only one," I said in a melodramatic voice. He blushed and shrugged his shoulders.

"Maybe it just runs in our blood," he said. "Anyway, I called and she said that we could come by. She lives in Lockwood now."

"Great, right after we call the sheriff and we get Gert looked at by a doctor," I said.

THIRTY-TWO

"Seriously, Mom, Gert is fine. Just a bump on the head," I said.

My mother's voice was taut and suspicious. So much so that it came through loud and clear even over the long-distance lines. "This sounds serious."

"It's not, really. I'm taking her to stay with Aunt Millie," I said. "Her days of staying at the boardinghouse are over. I should have done it yesterday."

"Then why didn't you?" she asked.

Yes, why didn't I? Disbelief that anything would really happen? Disbelief that anybody would actually try and hurt her? I'd been expecting something threatening to me. Not her. "Well, the sheriff told me not to leave town. He actually said not to leave the boardinghouse. I took him at his word."

The phone rustled a minute and then the next voice I heard was not my mother's. Unless she was having serious testosterone problems.

"What exactly happened?" Sheriff Colin Brooke asked. Great. My mother's fiancé was acting like . . . egads! A member of the family!

"What do you care?" I asked.

"What happened? What exactly is going on?"

"Well, as I said earlier, Clarissa was poisoned with penicillin—she was allergic. I'm the number one suspect because I was found in her room, even though no one knows where I would get—or know how to

197

administer—penicillin. Norville Gross was killed by a panther, not murdered. Although my grandmother refuses to believe it," I said, taking a deep breath. "There's a woman reporter who I think is the granddaughter of one of the miners who has been missing since 1917 or so. And the cleaning lady said that there was something hidden on this property that would make the family rich. So, they've been looking for it and I think Gert found it and that's why she's been hit on the head."

There was silence on the other end of the line.

"Do you need to know anything else?"

"J-just take Gertrude to your aunt's house. And you should stay there, too," he said in a way too bossy tone.

"I can't," I said. "The sheriff here, who is very professional by the way, said that I couldn't leave the boardinghouse."

"Why?"

"Because he said so."

"When have you ever listened to what a person of authority has said?" he asked.

Oh, so he wanted to get nasty, did he?

"I guess when I find one that's worthy of his uniform, I'll listen!" I said. I was instantly sorry. "I didn't mean that. I'm sorry, Colin." I really didn't mean it. I was just really stressed and ticked off and, well, he sort of got too close to the truth. When did I ever listen to anybody who wasn't my mother? When? Never.

"I . . . I just took him at his word because I am an outsider here and I've never been suspected of murder before. I wanted to make sure that I did everything he wanted."

"Well," Colin said, "that makes sense."

It did? "It does?"

"Of course," he said. "The sheriff cannot order you to stay in a specific hotel or anything. He *can* order you not to leave town."

"Then why would he tell me that I couldn't leave the boardinghouse?"

"I would guess because it's just easier if you stay there. He knows where you're at. And he doesn't think you're in any real danger, because he thinks you're the murderer. You're of no threat to yourself. Of course, that just goes to show how little he knows about you."

I let that remark go.

"Not to mention, if it's a small town—"

"It is," I said.

"Then he's probably got people inside the boardinghouse that he trusts to watch you. If you left the boardinghouse, he would be flying blind," he said. "Of course, this means that you are a serious, serious, serious suspect."

"Yes, but there is absolutely no evidence, Colin. They've found no vial of penicillin anywhere in my possessions and nothing with my fingerprints on it. If it ever went to trial there would be no way they could convict me. I don't know how I can even be arrested."

"You were found in her room and she was dead."

"Yes, but she wasn't suffocated, for crying out loud."

"People seeing her alive and then seeing her dead with you in the room is a strong persuasion," Colin said. "Watch your back, Torie. It sounds to me like somebody is out to get you."

THIRTY-THREE

BEFORE ELLIOTT CAME TO TAKE ME TO VISIT WITH THE old lady who had worked at the VanBibber House, I rapped lightly on the door of Oliver Jett's room. After a moment he answered the door. "Mrs. O'Shea," he said.

"Mr. Jett, may I speak with you?"

"Surely. I was just packing up to leave. I should have left yesterday."

"Why didn't you?" I asked.

"I have a brother who lives in Panther Run. I wanted to spend a day or two with him. May as well, since I was here and all," he said and went to the closet to pull out the only two suits that were hanging in there. "What brings you to my room?"

"Did you hear about all the commotion earlier?" I asked.

"Yes. I can't believe nobody was here," he said.

"Well, somebody was obviously here, they're just not going to admit it," I corrected.

"Well, whoever it was knew that it was shopping day for Susan Henry, and Dexter Calloway always visits his father in the nursing home."

"Where was Vanessa Killian?"

"From what I understand, she had a doctor's appointment. Unusual for nobody to be here, but with Mrs. Hart dead, Vanessa didn't see the harm in leaving the boardinghouse unattended," he explained.

"And where were you?" I asked.

"Visiting my brother."

"So, basically my grandmother was left alone in the boardinghouse with nothing but the Hart children and grandchildren," I said.

"Yes, well. You left her," he said.

"Right."

"Is that what you wanted? You could have found that out from Dexter," he said. "I think there is another reason for your being here."

The round, pudgy, nervous man that I had met the day Clarissa was murdered was a tad more sure of himself today. I'd only seen him briefly this past week and hadn't really had a chance to speak with him.

"There is," I said. "I was wondering if you would let me see Clarissa's will. The first one. The original one."

"That would be unethical," he declared.

"Would it be more unethical than letting a killer go?" I asked.

He stopped in front of the dresser and let out a long, exasperated sigh. I seemed to have that effect on people. "Mrs. O'Shea, last I heard, that killer would be you."

"But it's not."

"Am I supposed to believe you just because you're pregnant and you say it's so?"

Well, yes, I thought.

"I have no motive for killing Mrs. Hart. Somebody obviously burned her will in the fireplace either after they murdered her or after they found out she was dead. I think you know that I was left nothing in the first will. What would I have to gain from killing her? She'd already changed her will so that I received the boardinghouse. And burning the new will certainly wouldn't have helped me any," I said. "I would just like to see how much she changed it."

Ollie wiped the sweat off his brow and turned to look at me from the dresser. "Just for the record, I do not believe that you could harm anybody. And it's not just

201

because you're pregnant. Your eyes are far too honest to be a killer's."

"Oh, thank you," I said.

"I will not show you the will. But I'll tell you how she changed it. That way, I won't feel so damned guilty about it," he said.

Whatever. What did I care why he told me just as long as he spilled the beans? I smiled at him and sat down on the edge of the bed. He gave a sheepish grin as he looked down at my bare feet.

"There's a reason that 'barefoot and pregnant' became a quote. You can't wear shoes if your feet swell. Mine are swollen something fierce today," I said.

"The original will was basically the same as the revised one. With the exception of the boarding house and the fifty thousand dollars. Oh, and a few small personal items that she decided she wanted somebody else to have. She gave a list of items that were in a box out in the garage. She left about ten old books to a black man who used to be a miner. Never could figure that one out."

"Robert Miller," I said. I was touched by that, and it was evident in my tone of voice.

"You know him?"

"And his story. Quite touching, actually," I looked at him with pleading eyes, hoping that he wouldn't stop there.

"Originally, the boardinghouse went to Dexter Calloway and the fifty thousand dollars went to Sherise Tyler," he said.

"Did they know this?" I asked, the breath stuck in my throat.

"I don't know if Clarissa ever expressed the contents of her will to them or not. I'm assuming Dexter at least knew," he said. "Just because he's had access to so many of Clarissa's personal things for so many years."

"Why?" I asked, dumbfounded.

"Why what?"

"Why did she change it? What made her change it? Did something happen?" I asked.

"I'm not sure," he said. I did not believe him. Maybe he didn't know every single detail, but I believed that Clarissa had told him something.

"Why Sherise Tyler? What was her connection to Sherise Tyler?"

"I'm not clear on that, either. All I know is that Sherise was here a lot. Off and on. Especially when she was younger," he said.

"Is Tyler her maiden name?"

"For some reason I want to say no. I think she's divorced," he said.

"Thank you, Mr. Jett. You've been a big help. Have a safe trip back to Charleston," I said.

"Thank you," he said. "You be careful, too."

Just as I reached for the intricate cut-glass doorknob, Mr. Jett stopped me. I don't know if it was for drama's sake or if it was because he'd just remembered something. Or maybe he'd been unsure if he was going to say it. Whatever it was, I was all ears. I turned around and waited for his words.

"Take the boardinghouse," he said. "You won't be sorry."

"I might argue with you on that. This place seems to be full of bad luck," I said.

"Yes," he said and then lowered his voice to a whisper. "But it is also full of coal."

THIRTY-FOUR

"LOOK, ELLIOTT, I'M TELLING YOU THERE IS SOME sort of connection with Sherise Tyler," I said. "You don't leave somebody fifty thousand dollars just because she hangs around your boardinghouse. Gosh, if that were the case, Chuck Velasco would leave my husband his pizza parlor, his ex-wife, and his dog."

"I agree, but I'm not sure how. And short of asking her why or how, I can't figure out how to find out," he said. His brown eyes were watching the road, but it was almost as if he wasn't seeing it. After a moment's hesitation he added, "Why would Clarissa take it away, though? Why leave her fifty grand then take it away?"

"I don't know. But think about it. What if Sherise was counting on that money to help get her 'story' published, and then she found out she wasn't going to get it. Enough to kill for?" I asked.

"For some people, yes."

For some people. I guess that's what it really all came down to. Who was capable of doing what for how much? What was worth killing somebody for in Elliott's eyes could be totally different in my eyes. I could kill somebody in self-defense. Of course, that theory had already been proven. You never know until you're tested. It's a stupid question to ask somebody, because you really don't know what you would do.

"Maybe Clarissa found out that Sherise was planning on publishing a story about the whole Aldrich Gainsborough thing," I said. "That would be reason to cut her out."

"That's just so horrible," Elliott said and made a left-hand turn. "Think about it. Of all the people to fall in love with. The one person who would be despised by everybody that you knew. The entire coal town, all of the miners and their families despised their superintendent. Gainsborough. And Clarissa loved him."

"Yeah," I said, thinking. "I've thought of that myself. And then think about it. She finds the man she loves, the father of her child, hanging from a noose in her own damn front yard. Not just hanging there dead. Badly beaten and bloody and hanging there dead. I'm surprised she didn't go crazy."

Elliott steered the car off the road, down a driveway that was so steep, I lost my stomach going over the edge of it. I gripped the seat with one hand and door handle with the other one. "Good Lord," I said.

"You gotta put your houses and your driveways wherever you can in this state," he said. "Otherwise you'd have a population of about twelve."

"Well, you think they could have at least put some sort of warning up there," I said. "If I had been driving, I would have probably wrecked the car."

"Well, I think this is the house. Her name is Louanne Hill," he said.

Louanne Hill answered her own door wearing a powder-blue dress, with a bright yellow shawl draped around her shoulders. She wore wire glasses that rested peculiarly on the bridge of her long slender nose. Elliott introduced us and she invited us in.

"All I have to drink is milk and bottled water," she said. I noticed a slight tremor in her hands as they gripped the afghan tighter.

"Oh, we're fine," Elliott said. I nodded my head in agreement. She led us through a narrow hallway to the living room and told us to sit. I sat down on a fluffy

205

brown couch that had to be at least thirty years old. Gold shag carpet was covered with those rope rugs that you find at the flea market for five bucks. Daisy doilies were draped over the back of her couch and chairs. She had a walker tucked away in the corner of the room and the television was on.

Louanne Hill slurred her words when she spoke and moved as slow as molasses. It took her three minutes just for her butt to make contact with the chair. She seemed forever hovering above it. This ninety-year-old woman made me think of Sylvia back home in New Kassel. Not that she resembled Sylvia in any way. Rather the opposite. Sylvia was so completely different than this woman. Tall, proud, and crisp as she could be. My gosh, did I actually miss her? I would never admit to it.

"Mrs. Hill," Elliott began. He was such a good ambassador. He smiled and spoke softly and immediately put everybody at ease. "I talked to you briefly. We are interested in the VanBibber House. A woman named Clarissa Estep, later Hart, went to stay there around 1917 and gave birth to a baby boy."

"Yes," she said. "I remember that like yesterday."

I had trouble believing her, but didn't say anything.

"Why is that? Was there something special about her?" Elliott asked. "Or do you remember all of the women who went there?"

"Part of the reason I remember it is because it was my first summer there. My mother worked there. When school was out that summer, I came to work with her. I had nobody to stay with because my daddy had gone to Massachusetts to visit a business colleague and my oldest brother had just gone off to war," she said. She stopped and looked at me. "World War One. The first

206

one. 'Course, we didn't call it that back then, because how were we supposed to know there was gonna be another one?"

Made sense.

"Mom didn't trust me with my next-eldest brother who was fourteen. He was a wild one," she said. "So I went with her to the house and helped work."

"And the other reason?" Elliott asked.

So far I had not said a word. I didn't have to. Elliott was doing a fine job.

"Well, Clarissa had that baby and she was intent upon keeping it. Three, four months went by, and she decided that she just couldn't provide for it and she couldn't stay at the VanBibber House any longer. In fact," Louanne said, "she'd already stayed past her alotted time. Six weeks after a baby was born was usually when they'd move on."

"Oh," I said, thinking how absolutely lame it sounded.

"Other than becoming a streetwalker, there wasn't much she could do. She looked for housekeeping jobs, since she'd run the boardinghouse, but there was nothing open. She had no formal schooling, so she couldn't teach or anything like that. Finally, she decided to surrender him. Lord, how she cried."

"I can imagine," I said. Again, how lame. What words could I choose to express that I could feel Clarissa's anguish adequately? None. There weren't any. In fact, Clarissa's decision was such a heart-ripping one, I don't think I could even seriously imagine having to make it without breaking down and crying about it. I believe she did what was right. I think Clarissa knew it was what was best, which made it all the more painful to do.

"In fact," Louanne went on, "she cried so hard that all the blood vessels in her eyes popped and she had red eyes. Poor girl. Well, Mom couldn't stand that. Just plain ol' couldn't stand it."

"So, what did she do?" I asked. I know something was coming.

"She adopted that baby. It made Clarissa so happy that her baby wasn't going off to strangers that she cried all over again. 'Course, Mom made her sign papers saying she wouldn't try and get him back, which Clarissa did."

"Wait," I said, looking to Elliott. "I . . . I think I may be a little slow here. Are you saying that Clarissa's baby that she had by Aldrich Gainsborough is your adopted brother? Is that what you're saying?"

"Yes, ma'am," Louanne said, smiling. "See why I remember it so well?"

Sort of an understatement, really. "Can I ask you a question?"

"Sure," she said.

"Is your brother still alive?"

"No," she said. "He died back in seventy-two."

"Did he have any children?" Elliott asked, obviously on the same path that I was. We were acting like a couple of dogs who hadn't been fed in a week, begging for scraps. Hot on the trail of the trash pile. How pathetic we were. How excited.

"Yes. He had a set of twins. A girl and a boy. The boy's still alive. Up in Morgantown," she said. "The girl died in a car accident back in the late eighties. Imagine making it all the way to sixty and then dying in a car crash. Doesn't seem right. Seems like there should be some point in your life when you're safe from that sort of thing."

208

"Louanne," I said slowly. I took a deep breath and then asked the next question. "What was your maiden name?"

"Gross was my maiden name," she answered. "Germans from Pennsylvania. Why do you ask?"

THIRTY-FIVE

I WAS STUNNED INTO SILENCE AS WE LEFT LOUANNE'S house. And believe me, I can count on both hands how many times that has happened to me. In fact, I was so stunned that I didn't even blink as Elliott backed up his car to get a "run" at the hill known as Louanne's driveway. Normally, that would have sent me into a panic. I didn't even blink.

We were finally on our way back to the boarding-house when Elliott spoke. "Are you all right?"

"No."

"Do you want something to drink?"

"Yes."

"What would you like?"

"Dr. Pepper. Real one. Stop at the next gas station."

"How about Burger King up here about half a mile?"

"Fine." Caffeine and bubbles. I would be very happy.

"What do you think?" he asked, smiling at me.

"Pretty trees," I said and pointed out the window.

He laughed this time. "No, silly. About what Louanne said. What do you think?"

"I . . . I . . . Can we just drive in silence until I get the caffeine? I want to think about this," I said.

"Sure," he said. "I can deal with that."

And so we did. We drove in silence for the next three or four minutes until we reached the Burger King and

Elliott handed me my supersize Dr. Pepper. Although the straws are never long enough for those supersize drinks. It's like, okay. Supersize bladder requires supersize straw.

"Tell me this is okay," I said before I took a big drink.

"It's okay," Elliott said, still smiling at me.

I took a very long and much-needed drink and then let out a breath nice and slowly. "I think, obviously, that Norville Gross was Clarissa's great-grandson, that's what I think. I think that somehow or other Norville found out that Clarissa was his great-grandmother and contacted her. Whether or not he was thinking in dollar signs at the time he contacted her, we'll never know. In fact, since he was from up in Morgantown, he really had no way of knowing if Clarissa had money."

"So, why doesn't the rest of the family know who he is?"

"I don't know. Maybe Clarissa was going to announce to everybody at the reading of the will just who he was, and she was interrupted, of course," I said. I threw the paper from my straw into Elliott's immaculate ashtray.

"I agree. But why wouldn't Clarissa leave the money to Norville's father? Why skip him and give it to Norville?"

"Why did she leave me the boardinghouse and not you or your sister, or our other cousins? Maybe it was as simple as Norville's father not being interested in meeting her and Norville was. Believe it or not, some people could care less where they come from," I said.

"I can buy that," he said. "That sounds plausible. But what about Sherise?"

"I still haven't proven it, but I think she is the

descendant of Doyle Phillips," I said. "The really strange part is, why would Clarissa feel compelled to leave Sherise something because of that? I mean, why not leave money to everybody who was descended from anybody in the mines? There has to be another connection."

Elliott was quiet a moment. "What about Dexter Calloway?"

"What about him?"

"Why do you think Clarissa changed her mind about leaving him the boardinghouse?"

"I don't know. Unless she'd found me by then and just felt compelled to return it to the correct family. If it truly is cursed, maybe she liked old Dexter too much to leave it to him," I said.

"Seriously, Torie. Think about it. Who better than Dexter to know all the nooks and crannies of the boardinghouse? What if he knew he was supposed to get that boardinghouse and had his heart set on it? What if he were the type of man to kill for something like that?"

"Or get me arrested hoping the will would revert back to the original will? Is that what you're suggesting?" I asked, the hair slowly rising on my arms.

"Or else, get revenge on you by seeing you in jail for half a century."

"Eek, Elliott. You have an absolutely twisted mind," I said. "I like it."

"I'm just curious about one other thing," he said.

"What's that?"

"Do you think anybody else has this much fun with genealogy?"

THIRTY-SIX

ELLIOTT AND I WERE GOING TO TAKE MY GRANDMOTHER out for dinner. Not to Denny's this time, but someplace a little fancier. Like the Village Inn. Am I imagining things or does every town with a population under five thousand have a Village Inn or its equivalent? But dinner would have to wait until after we found the mine entrance.

I wouldn't have taken Gert hiking into the woods to locate the entrance to the old mine even if she hadn't experienced the bump on her head earlier today. But she drew us a map and told us about how far to go. Of course, that was in her language of measurements. "You go here a jag, and then up the hill a ways, and down over a stone's throw." How did we ever make it to the millennium?

I basically went along just in case something happened to Elliott. In fact, if the trail got too steep I was going to sit down right where I was and wait for Elliott, because I didn't think mountain climbing in my present state was a very smart thing to do.

Lucky for me, however, the "snail's trail" wound around the base of the mountain and only raised itself enough to go over a slight hill and down the next valley. Which is where, hidden behind overgrown vines and weeds, we found the entrance to the mine with rotted boards nailed to the front of it. A big KEEP OUT sign was set askew on one of the boards, and I looked around the valley feeling all creepy and everything.

"I just had a really awful thought," I said.

"I thought that was my job," Elliott said as he yanked on a handful of vines.

212

"No, I'm serious," I said.

"What is it?"

"What if Norville Gross was looking for the same thing?"

"What about it?"

"He came back dead."

"That was a panther," Elliott said.

"Oh, yeah," I said. "Oh, yeah! What if the panther gets us? I don't think they are very particular about their victims."

"Relax, it's broad daylight."

"So what? Does the panther know that people will see it in broad daylight?" I asked.

"No, it's just with civilization moving in closer to the panthers' habitat, they usually make themselves pretty scarce during the day," he said.

"Well, Norville Gross was killed during the day."

Elliott stopped and looked at me. "We're fine, Torie. Don't obsess."

"I'm not obsessing," I said. "Who's obsessing? What are you doing anyway? Do we have to see inside to know that the mine is here? Isn't this what we were after? Just to know that it was here."

"Yeah," Elliott said. "I just want to look to see if any old equipment or anything is visible from the entrance."

"You're not planning on going in there, are you?" I asked, hysteria rising in my voice.

"No, no. I'm not stupid. That thing could cave in on me just like that," he said and snapped his fingers. "I just can't help myself. I want to look inside."

"Oh." I supposed I could understand that. Just because creepy enclosed places were not the least bit interesting to me didn't mean that they wouldn't be to Elliott. In fact, there are some things that I would probably do that Elliott wouldn't. So, I should just breathe and calm down over this. He just wanted to look inside. Curiosity. I knew all about that.

Elliott stopped, frozen. One hand held a piece of vine and the other hand rested on a rotted piece of wood. His face turned ashen and all of the color drained from his lips. I'd never seen grey lips before. Except on a dead person.

"Elliott, what is it?" I asked.

"I think I found Phillips and MacLean," he said.

"What? No way, let me see," I said and shoved him aside. Sure enough, there were two skeletons leaning up against the south wall of the mine. Their clothes were tattered and dusty, and the clothes looked two sizes too large for the skeletons, since there was no meat or muscle to fill the clothes out. I squealed as a rat ran out of the shirt on one of the skeletons and disappeared into the eye socket.

"Oh, gross," I said. I quickly put my head between my knees. Well, as close as I could get to my knees, anyway. "I'm gonna puke."

"Oh, don't do that," Elliott said all in a panic.

"I can't help it. I am. I'm gonna puke."

"Oh, Torie," Elliott said, shaking his hands. "What . . . what do you want me to do?"

"Hold my hair."

And then I puked.

Ten minutes later as we walked along the snail's trail, my hands were still shaking involuntarily. "Thanks for holding my hair back," I said.

"You owe me, big time," Elliott said.

"Sorry," I said. "Just be happy I didn't have anything particularly chunky for lunch."

214

He had to laugh.

Just as we came back over the hill and could see the boardinghouse, I stopped. Elliott bumped into me, catching his balance and me as he did. "What is it?"

I pointed down to the boardinghouse. "The sheriff is there," I said.

"Why does that bother you so much?"

"Every time he's been here lately it's to tell me something more incriminating. I'm afraid of what he's got to say."

"You're obsessing again," he said. "Do you do this all the time? Rudy must have a heck of a time with you."

"Why is it everybody assumes that Rudy has a tough time with *me?* Doesn't anybody ever stop to think that maybe I have a tough time with *him?*" I asked.

"Sorry," Elliott said and shrugged his shoulders. "I've only met Rudy twice. I've not only seen you more, but I've had a heck of a lot more phone conversations with you. You're obsessing."

"So what?" I asked as we came off the footpath. "Does that hurt something? Has a little bit of obsessing ever hurt anybody?"

Elliott just looked at me. It was a look that I received often, so I knew I must have been feeling more like my old self.

As we reached the boardinghouse, the door opened and out came Deputy Benjamin Russell. I hadn't really thought about him since this morning. He hadn't followed me back to the boardinghouse after running into me at the courthouse. I had assumed he had other things to do and would catch up with me later. Sure enough, there he was. I have to admit, I felt a slight bit of relief when I saw him and realized that he was not Sheriff Justice.

"Are you here to see me, Deputy Russell?" I asked as we reached the porch.

"Heard about your excitement here today," he said.

"I can tell you that I think everybody has an alibi except the immediate family. All of the staff were other places," I said.

"I'll pass that along. I came out to fingerprint that attic window," he said. "It must have slipped the sheriff's mind because he didn't tell me or any of the other deputies to do it, so I just came on out here and got it done."

"Well, thank you, Deputy Russell." It was nice to see that somebody was thinking of me and my guilty-looking hide.

Deputy Russell walked down the porch steps and around his patrol car to the driver's side. He opened the door, and just as he was about to get in, he said, "What were you guys doing up in the woods?"

Elliott and I both looked at each other with momentary panic. We hadn't discussed what we were going to tell people. We'd only just found the bodies and we hadn't really decided what to do. Obviously, we would tell the authorities eventually. I cast my eyes downward, hoping that Elliott would read my mind.

"Looking over the property that Mrs. O'Shea just inherited," he said. "She'd never seen the whole thing."

It must have sounded plausible to the deputy because he nodded and disappeared into the patrol car. Within a minute he had backed out of the drive and onto the road.

"What do you think?" Elliott asked.

"About what?"

"About the bodies. If they truly are Phillips and MacLean?"

"You want my honest opinion?"

216

"Yes," he said and nodded.

"I think that they lynched Gainsborough and I think Clarissa invited them back to the boardinghouse that night to kill them. I don't know how, poison probably. And I think somehow our great-grandmother Bridie either found out about it, or walked in on it. They hid the bodies in the mine shaft and Clarissa went off to have Gainsborough's baby in Charleston. And Bridie never breathed a word of it. That's what I believe."

"What about the two men who were arrested for Gainsborough's murder?" he asked.

"I think they were wrongly accused. There was a lot of pressure put on the authorities by the coal company to find his murderer," I said. "I think the fact that the two bodies are in the mine shaft is a pretty good indication that the other two men were patsies."

"That was pretty much what I was thinking, too. It makes sense. All that talk about Bridie being able to keep a secret. And how she'd done Clarissa a favor and all. I think you're probably right on the money. Although we will probably never know exactly. Why do you think Bridie made the quilt?"

"I think her conscience was bothering her. I think she had to leave it for somebody to find out. She knew as long as Clarissa lived nobody would set foot in that mine shaft," I said.

"Do you think Clarissa was going to confess all of this to you?" he asked.

"Yes. Yes, I do," I said.

"So what does any of this have to do with who killed her?"

"I hate to admit it, but I'm thinking about Sherise Tyler," I said.

"Why?"

217

"If she is the granddaughter or great-granddaughter of Doyle Phillips, maybe she somehow suspected that Clarissa murdered him. Think about it. If Phillips's child was raised fatherless . . . maybe they suffered terrible hardships," I said.

"Why not kill her sooner?" he asked.

"Maybe it was only when Clarissa changed her will that Sherise felt she needed to get rid of the old lady. So she killed her and then tried to destroy the current will, thinking that Mr. Jett had not yet received the new one," I explained.

"How are you going to find out?" he asked.

"I don't know."

THIRTY-SEVEN

THE NEXT DAY I WENT BACK TO THE LIBRARY. ELLIOTT had to work that day, having taken two vacation days already this week. I'd checked the 1920 census for Doyle Phillips, but I hadn't checked it for his widow, Amanda Sherise Reynolds Phillips. She was in Huntingdon with one child, Rosemary Sherise Phillips.

Several hours later, I learned from the obituaries that Rosemary Sherise Phillips had married a man named Jack Henry. In the obituary for Amanda Phillips, who never remarried, they listed one of her survivors as her daughter, Mrs. Jack Henry. For some reason, the women lose all identity. They didn't list her daughter by name. They didn't list her as Rosemary Henry. No, it was Mrs. Jack Henry. Also surviving Amanda Phillips were her grandsons, Phillip and Michael, and her granddaughter, Susan. Susan Henry.

Susan Henry, the cook.

"Elliott!" I whispered loudly. He was working behind the counter and looked up to see me at the microfilm machine. He excused himself and made his way toward me.

"What is it?"

"Susan Henry is the great-granddaughter of Doyle Phillips," I said. "Susan, the cook at the boardinghouse."

"You're joking," he said. "Doyle Phillips. Does this mean she is Sherise's mother?"

"I think so. I've run out of ideas on how to get more information. Nobody is going to turn Sherise's birth certificate over to us, since neither one of us is her. All I can do is come out and ask Susan," I said. "Or Sherise."

"What do you think it means?"

"I think that it clears things up. It explains why Sherise spent so much time at the boardinghouse. Her mother had worked there her whole life. It also explains why Sherise was so dramatic when telling me the history of the coal mining towns. She'd lived it. Her mother had lived it," I said, swiping my hair behind my ears. "It would also explain why Clarissa had left Sherise something in her will. She felt guilty for Sherise's and Susan's lives being the way they were. Because she'd started it all by taking Doyle Phillips's life."

"Yes, but chances are if Phillips and MacLean had seen a jury, they'd have been sentenced to life in prison or worse. You do remember what the Gainsborough body looked like, don't you?" Elliott said. "Phillips is responsible for all of this. Not Clarissa."

"Yes, but you know Clarissa's sense of guilt and loyalty. She would have felt guilty."

"Yes, but why change the will, then? Why did she renege and give the money to Norville Gross?" he asked.

"I'm assuming, in her mind, her sin against Norville was bigger than her sin against Sherise."

"But then why not give Sherise the boardinghouse? Why cut her out completely? It makes no sense," he said.

"You're right," I said. "Something must have happened to change Clarissa's mind."

"Do you have any idea what it was?" he asked.

"No. Not a clue."

"You know," he said. "Susan Henry could be the murderess. Maybe she found out that Sherise was being cut out of the will, and in her anger, she killed Clarissa. She did have access to the food that Clarissa would eat."

I thought about it a minute. "You know what, though? Who's to say one of Clarissa's own kids didn't get ticked off because of the will and kill her? Maybe one of them learned who Norville Gross was and feared him suing for more than fifty thousand? Edwin is always in debt—"

"And Susan has an alibi for what happened yesterday to your grandmother," he said.

"*If* that was done by one and the same person," I said. "It's all too confusing."

"I fear we may never know who killed Clarissa," he said.

"I could live with that as long as I knew *I* wasn't going to be blamed for it," I said. "I'm not prepared to breast-feed behind bars."

"Go talk to Susan," Elliott said. "I'm going to try and find something on Sherise."

"Like what?"

"Like anything."

"She went to school in Illinois. Just across the river from St. Louis. Maybe there is something there," I said.

I looked around the room, noticing that people were looking at us funny. We were, after all, having a fairly intense and animated discussion. At least it would seem that way to anybody seated halfway across the room. I smiled sheepishly and lowered my voice. "I don't see how you'll have time. It could take you weeks to come up with something."

"I'm on it," he whispered.

THIRTY-EIGHT

YOU EVER NOTICE HOW, WHEN THERE'S SOMETHING that you really don't want to do, your stomach gets those little jittery things that feel like they are going to fly up your esophagus and out of your mouth? It sort of reminded me of how I felt when I had to explain to Rachel what a condom was for. I tell you, I nearly buckled and told her it was a swimming cap for her Barbies. I didn't, though. I was the good mother and bit the bullet.

Well, I sort of felt that way right now.

Susan Henry stood in front of me with flour up to her elbows and a hair net on. "I understand you're not going to be here for dinner any longer," she said.

"Yes, that's correct. I took my grandmother to my aunt's house. Considering what happened to her, I thought it would be best."

"What do you want, then?" she asked

"First of all, I'd like your opinion on who you think did that to my grandmother. You have an airtight alibi," I said.

"Nice to know, after years of service, I'm still trusted," she said.

221

"Don't take it personally, Ms. Henry. I don't know you from Adam," I said.

She smiled slightly and tilted her head. "Of course," she said.

"You are right. I've talked to Lafayette and he said the whole family went into town for the funeral arrangements. Visitation starts tonight and the funeral will either be tomorrow or the next day."

"I didn't ask that. I asked who you thought did it?"

"I think it was Edwin," she said bluntly. I was a little surprised that it didn't take more coaxing.

"Why?"

"They've been looking for it for a long time."

"Looking for what?"

"Their father told them that there was an antique, an heirloom that would reveal the location of something that would make them all very wealthy," she said.

"The entrance to the mine isn't that hidden," I said. "I've been to it."

Her smile only faltered slightly. "The mine? A coal mine?" She laughed and shook her head. "It was evident for you because that is what you were looking for. They haven't a clue what it's supposed to be. They were all just waiting for Clarissa to die so that they could begin searching all the antiques in the house for the map. Then Clarissa threw them a curve ball and left everything in the house to you. The only way they could search the stuff was to take it from you, or search while you were gone."

"Well, they are damned lucky all my grandmother had was a bump on her head."

"You don't understand. I don't believe they meant her any harm. I think they are just interested in money" she said.

222

"Yes, but the ironic part is that 'thing' that would make them all rich is located on *my* property. It can't be removed. So they won't be rich, after all. Well, no richer than they'll be with all of the other things that she left them in her will."

"I'd like to see their faces," she said. "When they find out it's a mine and Clarissa has left it to you."

"What about your daughter?" I said. "What's her alibi?"

Her head snapped up, and I could see by the look in her eyes that I had guessed correctly. Sherise Tyler was her daughter. A slow smile played across her face, and she turned toward the stove and began dropping dumplings into the chicken broth. "Clarissa was right about you."

"What about me?" I asked.

"She said that you were the best choice to give the place to. You would set things straight. You cared about the past," she said. "What she didn't say was that you care about everybody's past. Not just your own."

"It is a fault of mine. I admit."

"Oh, don't," she said and turned back to me. "Don't apologize for something that you're good at. Don't apologize for who you are."

"So, Sherise is your daughter. You're the great-granddaughter of Doyle Phillips. One of the missing miners from 1917," I said.

"I'm amazed," she said and held her hands up in exasperation.

"Public domain. Freedom of Information Act. It is a wonderful thing," I said.

"Yes, Sherise is my daughter. I was never married. Her father died in a mine explosion before we had a chance to get married," she said. "Clarissa felt personally responsible. She gave me this job. She paid me more than I earned. She was always trying to pay her debts."

A debt paid.

"I could tell you why she felt that way," I said.

"You don't have to. We all know. We all suspected for years. Just nobody ever came out and confirmed it," she said. "Clarissa killed my great-grandfather and Thomas MacLean for what they did to Gainsborough. I've imagined it many times, her inviting them over for dinner and slipping poison in their food. Then she called upon your great-grandmother, Bridie, to help her dispose of the bodies. And then she tried to pay for her sins for the rest of her life."

"Did you know that she was pregnant?"

"What?" she asked, genuinely surprised.

"Just like you. She was pregnant with Gainsborough's baby, but he was killed before they had a chance to get married. She surrendered that baby boy when he was four months old and moved back here to the boardinghouse," I said.

A tear welled up in Susan's eye. "I never knew," she whispered.

"Norville Gross was that child's descendant."

"Oh, that explains a lot," she said.

"So, Ms. Henry, I'm going to ask you this and I don't want you to get angry. I just need to ask it. Did Sherise have an alibi for yesterday when my grandmother was attacked?"

"I don't know," she said. "I imagine she did. My daughter did not kill Clarissa. Believe it or not, she admired Clarissa greatly. She tried to pretend that she didn't. You see, Clarissa had two big mansions. One in Charleston and one up in Wheeling. She only lived in them for a few years back in the forties and fifties.

Every other moment was spent here. In this boardinghouse. With her picture of Gainsborough in his casket."

God, it was so sad. I couldn't imagine her life. I couldn't imagine being a hundred and one years old and having eighty-something years to look back on the tragedy. I wonder if it ever got easier. Did it ever become less painful? "What about you?" I asked. "Did you kill Clarissa?"

"No," she stated vehemently.

"Did you know about the will? That Sherise had originally been left the money that Norville Gross ended up getting?"

"No," she said. "I'm flattered that Sherise was even considered. But, honestly. Norville should have had that money if he was really her great-grandson."

"Are you upset that you weren't left anything?" I asked.

She smiled a warm and caring smile. She wiped her hands on a towel and then took the hair net off her hair. "Mrs. O'Shea, I didn't need to be left anything. For one thing, she provided for me my whole life. She paid for Sherise's college. But the main reason I didn't need to be left anything in her will was because she'd already given us our inheritance. Me. Dexter. Vanessa. Ten years ago, we all got a savings account for Christmas with seventy-five thousand dollars in it, and an IRA to boot."

"What?" I asked. I felt warm and fuzzy all over thinking of Clarissa's generosity. Was it me or did they just not make people like that anymore?

"Clarissa was a very introverted, aloof woman. You could not get close to her. She was not warm and cuddly. Other than discussing menus, I bet she and I

225

never had more than twenty conversations in all the time that I worked here. But she was the kindest person I've ever met. With the largest sense of honor I've ever seen in a human being. I would not—I *could* not—kill Clarissa Hart. I don't think Dexter or Vanessa would be capable of it, either. Those who are capable of it are her children."

With that she dismissed me by turning around and putting the spices back in the spice rack. She was finished talking. That was that. If she spoke the truth, then she had cleared up a lot. I couldn't help but wonder, though, if her daughter Sherise Tyler honestly felt the same way toward Clarissa that Susan did. There was something about Sherise that just didn't fit. One thing was that Clarissa had taken the fifty thousand away. Clarissa had enough money. Why hadn't she just given Sherise and Norville fifty thousand each? No, it was as if she was punishing Sherise.

But for what?

THIRTY-NINE

I WAS SEATED AT AUNT MILLIE'S ROUND OAK DINING table, consuming the roasted chicken and vegetables she had made for us. I have to admit that Gert did look a little shaken today. There was something in her eyes. But have no fear, Aunt Millie was being quite the doting daughter, bringing her whatever she needed, interpreting her grunts and groans, and serving her favorite minced-meat pie for dessert. Aunt Bethany always said that Aunt Millie was allowed to dote because she didn't have to put up with her all the other days of the year. Whatever; my grandmother needed this attention today.

"Have you decided what you're going to do with the boardinghouse?" Aunt Millie asked.

"God, no," I said and rested my head in my hands. "The Harts may still try and contest the will, especially now that we know the property is worth beaucoup bucks because of the coal mine on it. I just wish I didn't have to think about it."

Aunt Millie smiled at me, sending sparkles into her eyes.

"Think about it," I said. "This is so unfair. My whole life I've always played with that old joke 'I can't wait until my rich uncle gets out of the poorhouse and leaves me something.' You know, you wait for this kind of opportunity your whole life. I mean, not for somebody to die. Nobody wants that. But for somebody to just hand something over to you. To win the lottery or something. Whatever. You think, oh, if only I had this much money or that much property that I didn't have to pay back. What all I could do with it. Kids' college fund, trip to Scotland, whatever. Now it's actually happened to me and I don't want it. I don't even want to think about it."

"That is pretty bad," Aunt Millie said. "I didn't mean to scare you the other day when I told you that the boardinghouse was cursed."

"Oh, but it is. I truly believe that it is," I said. "On the one hand, I'd love to keep it. It's got such a rich history. Bridie actually owned it, for crying out loud. On the other hand, if I never see it again with its lynching tree and its rotted screens, I'll be perfectly happy."

"You are in a dilemma," Aunt Millie said.

"Take what you want from it and sell it," Gert said.

227

"You and Rudy are busting at the seams. You could use a new house."

"Oh, but I'd feel so guilty," I said. "Just selling it like that. Especially after Clarissa left it to me because I cared so much for antiques."

"Clarissa's dead," Gert said. "She won't care."

I rolled my eyes. It didn't make me feel any better. Nothing would make me feel better other than to wake up last week and not make the trip to West Virginia at all. I didn't think that was very likely. It wasn't like I was trapped in one of those really bad TV dramas. Although it felt like it sometimes.

The phone rang and Aunt Millie answered it on the second ring. "Sure, just a minute," she said and handed me the phone. "It's Elliott."

"Oh," I said and took the phone. "Elliott? What's up?"

"I found something on Sherise. I stayed as long as I could without the janitor kicking me out. I e-mailed a couple of people who owe me favors and told them that I absolutely had to have this information by this evening. You really should get on-line, Torie."

"What? What is it?" I asked, ignoring his comment about the information superhighway.

"I have no idea if it matters in the least . . . but Sherise has been married twice. Divorced twice. This last time was to some hotshot investigative reporter up in Boston."

"Okay," I said, wondering where this was going.

"He disappeared without a trace."

"What do you mean?"

"I mean, Sherise divorced him, only she didn't get the settlement that she thought she was going to get. Two weeks later he turns in a story to his editor about unsolved crimes of Appalachia—wonder where that idea came from—and then is never heard from again."

"How did you find this out?" I asked, absolutely amazed.

"Well, once I figured out who she was married to, I just followed the newspaper trail. It was all over the Boston newspapers," he said.

"Was she suspected?"

"Suspected of what? There's no body. No crime. Plus, he had a new girlfriend who gave a statement saying that he'd gone fishing, by himself, off the coast of Key West," he said.

"Huh."

"Did that help?"

"I'm not sure."

"Oh, but get a load of this."

"What?"

"Her first husband was none other than Sheriff Thomas Justice," he said.

"You're joking!"

"No."

"How bizarre. They acted as if they didn't know each other," I said.

"Well, from what I understand it was a nasty, nasty, nasty divorce. She tried to prove he was a deviant and he tried to prove she was a lesbian. Neither of which, I think, are true," he said. "You know how desperate people get sometimes during divorces. Some people will make up anything to win."

"How did you find this out?" I asked.

"Well, again, once I found out who she married, I followed the trail. They were married in Edwardsville, Illinois, by the way. I paid a visit to an aunt of mine on my mother's side who knows all the trash on everybody within a hundred miles. She told me all the scuttle. Even though Sheriff Justice and Sherise were living in Illinois at the time, Sheriff Justice's mother still lived here. And his mother went to church with my grandmother, who in turn told my aunt everything."

"God, I love small towns."

"I know."

"Well, I haven't a clue if this means anything. I wouldn't think it does. Surely if the divorce was that bad, the sheriff wouldn't be up to helping Sherise kill somebody. What would be his motive?" I asked.

"That's pretty much what I thought, too."

"Thank you so much, Elliott. I'm going back over to the boardinghouse tonight. I want to talk to Danette about yesterday. See if I can get anything from her. She's been pretty cooperative with me. So, if anything else comes up, call me over there."

"Sure thing," he said. "Do you want me to come with you?"

"No," I said. "I think everybody will mind their *p*s and *q*s since it's known that my grandmother was attacked. I think they won't want to slip up."

"Okay. Call me if you need me."

"I will."

Huh. All very interesting information, but there was no way of knowing if any of it meant anything.

FORTY

I PULLED INTO THE DRIVE OF THE PANTHER RUN Boardinghouse at about six thirty that night. I had totally forgotten that Clarissa would be laid out tonight and that more than likely Danette would not be here. I think the family waited so long to make funeral arrangements because not all of her grandchildren could be here until today. Nevertheless, somebody was at the boardinghouse, because there were a few lights on and the door was open.

"Hello?" I called.

Vanessa Killian came from around the corner with her purse in her hand. You could just tell by looking at her that she was ready to go somewhere. Her hair was freshly combed, and I think I smelled some sort of lavender perfume. "Mrs. O'Shea, I was just leaving for Clarissa's visitation."

"Yes," I said. "I'd forgotten. My grandmother and I will attend tomorrow. Is there anybody else here?"

"Danette is in her room, hiding," she said. "She said she couldn't face it."

It wasn't as if Danette hadn't already seen her great-grandmother dead, because she had. I suppose funerals just creep some kids out. Especially if they've never been to one before and the first one they go to is for somebody they loved very much. I could relate to that.

"Actually, that's exactly who I came to see," I said.

A muffled version of some extremely heavy metal music could faintly be heard coming from down the hall of the first floor. Nobody else was home. She was going to take advantage of it and jam. I did the same thing when I was her age.

"She's in her room," Vanessa said, declaring what I already knew. "Dexter said he would be back early, around eight. So I expect him anytime. And one of Maribelle's other children has just come in, he is driving up from the airport as we speak. Otherwise, nobody is here."

"Okay," I said. "Thank you."

She gave me a curt nod and went out the front door. Just as I was about to head for Danette's room, there was a knock at the door. I assumed it wasn't Vanessa or she would have just let herself in. I answered the door and, to my surprise, it was Deputy Russell.

"Well, hello," I said. "Are you here to see me?"

"Actually, yes. I didn't want to interrupt your dinner at your Aunt Millie's," he said. "So I followed you here."

"Good Lord," I said. "You know everything. You're not James Bond. You're Big Brother."

"I wish I did know everything."

He had a rather pensive look to him. His mind was here with me, but it wasn't. There were other things on his mind that were overlapping. I could see it in the way he looked at me. "What is it?"

"I don't know how to say this," he said.

"Well, then, let's say it over food. That's always good. Come on, I know that Ms. Henry keeps a stash of cookies on top of the refrigerator."

"Okay," he said and smiled.

I led him back to the dining area, where he sat down, and then I went into the kitchen and got the tin down off the refrigerator. I'd only been proclaimed owner of the boardinghouse for a few days, and already I knew where all the good stuff was hidden. It's those nights with no sleep. I'm terribly nosy.

I know it's not a very enviable trait, but there could be so many worse things.

"Here ya go," I said and set the tin on the table. "Oatmeal raisin."

"Thank you," he said and took a bite of cookie. Then he said, "I ran those prints."

"And?" I asked. I hate it when I have to drag stuff out

232

of people. To hell with the drama, just tell me what it is you're going to tell me anyway.

"They don't match anybody's in the boardinghouse. Yours and Edwin's are on file," he said. "Everybody else we printed."

"Yes, I was arrested once," I said. To my amazement, I actually blushed. I was the only person in the boardinghouse who had prints on file except Edwin. M-o-r-t-i-f-i-c-a-t-i-o-n.

"Ah," he said.

"I'm sorry, Deputy, but you look as though you've got the weight of the world on your shoulders. What is it you want to say?"

"I decided to take a look at the case file," he said. "There's no way Norville Gross was killed by a panther. The autopsy report clearly shows that his death was caused by a modern weapon. And the autopsy was mistaken, I can tell that the weight and the angle of the entry wounds were definitely delivered by a human being."

"But—"

The shrill of the phone ringing made Deputy Russell and me both jump as if we had been shot. He looked a little embarrassed as his grey eyes met mine. Well, we were even. We'd both been embarrassed in front of each other tonight. "I'll get it."

I disappeared into the front room and answered the phone. "Hello?"

"It's Elliott," he said. "Thank God you're there."

"What?"

"The twins."

"The twin whats?"

"I called Louanne Hill back, just to see if there was anything else she could remember. While I was on the

233

phone, I thought to ask her about the girl twin that her adopted brother had. Remember, he had twins. The boy is still alive up in Morgantown and he's the father of Norville Gross," he said.

"Yeah, okay. We knew that."

"And remember Louanne said that the girl twin had died in a car accident a few years back?"

"Yeah . . . for God's sake, Elliott, just tell me!"

"Her last name was Justice. She married a Justice," Elliott said.

I looked over my shoulder at Deputy Russell, who had just come out of the dining room. The sheriff had lied about Norville Gross being killed by a panther. He'd put off running those prints. He had been married to Sherise Tyler. He had pinned me as the A number one suspect.

"Elliott . . ."

"I think Sheriff Justice is her son," he said. "I can't prove it right yet. Maybe by tomorrow."

The goose bumps lay across my skin, causing the hair on my arms to stand up. Quick, irregular breaths came faster than I wanted them to, and I found myself a little dizzy. "Right, Elliott, I'll talk to you later."

I hung up the phone and looked at Deputy Russell, who was desperately trying to figure out what was wrong with me. I think my body was actually shaking.

"Deputy," I ventured. "Whose prints did you find on the window upstairs in the attic?"

He looked down at his feet and shuffled them a few times. "I've got a call in to the state police."

"They were the sheriff's, weren't they? He never thought to wear gloves because he knew he'd be the one in charge of everything."

"Now, Mrs. O'Shea, I don't want you to go getting all upset."

234

"She didn't really die of an allergic reaction to penicillin, did she?"

He said nothing.

"Is there any reason that I am suspected of killing Clarissa other than Sheriff justice having deemed it so?"

His face answered that one for me. Pastor Breedlove had been correct in his suspicions about the sheriff. He'd said that things tended to end the way the sheriff wanted them to end.

"What else?" I asked. "What else were you going to tell me?"

Deputy Russell, with his large thick arms and his tall, tall frame, seemed suddenly afraid to talk to me. He'd lost his nerve. Maybe he just couldn't say out loud what he was really wanting to say. What he really suspected.

"Sheriff Justice used to be married to Sherise Tyler. Were they working together?" I asked.

"Look, Mrs. O'Shea, I don't know anything about that. I assure you that I have called the state police on this. You are free to go anytime you want to. What happens from here on out has nothing to do with you, really. I'll see to it that—"

Deputy Russell did not finish his sentence.

I only had time to gasp. I could not warn the deputy. A baseball bat conked him in the head, and he landed with a thud on the floor of the great room. The person on the other end of that baseball bat was none other than Sheriff Thomas Justice. "Deputy Russell always had this damn-fool sense of right and wrong. Couldn't get him to look the other way even for a parking ticket"

"Sheriff," I said. "What a surprise to see you."

"I'll bet it is," he said. "Now, don't try and convince me that you two weren't just talking about how I killed Clarissa Hart. You can't play that 'I don't know what you're talking about' game with me. If there's one thing you are not, Victory O'Shea, it is in the dark. You must be a bitch to live with."

I opened my mouth to say something but the sheriff just went right on.

"Always poking and prodding and asking questions about things that are *none of your business*!" he yelled. "I try and persuade you to go to the left, but no, you go to the right anyway. You're infuriating."

"I've heard that before," I said as I looked over to the clock on the mantel. Six-fifty. *Come on, Dexter. Come home.*

"Aldrich Gainsborough," he said, following my gaze to the mantel. I was looking at the clock, but he thought I was looking at the photograph of Aldrich Gainsborough in his casket. "He was responsible for all of this."

"I can see how you would feel that way," I said as I inched my way back toward the front door.

"Ah-ah-ah," he said, crooking his finger. "Come this way."

I looked at his baseball bat and then looked back at the front door. I could make it to the door before he made it across the room. What was he going to do? Throw the bat at me? But what were the chances that I would make it to my car without him catching up to me? In my present condition, there was no way that I could outrun him. No possible way.

In my present condition.

My God, my baby. Fear nearly paralyzed me as I thought about the unborn child cradled inside of me. If something happened to me, it happened to the baby, too. If I died, so did the baby. I tried to push that thought out of my mind, knowing that otherwise I would never be

236

able to have a clear thought long enough to save myself.

Danette. She was in the house. Did I really want her to come out here, though? What if she surprised him and he somehow hurt her?

"What are you going to do? Are you going to say that I, the pregnant lady, attacked your deputy?" I asked.

"No," he said. "I'll simply drag him outside and throw him in the river and then I'll dispose of his car and put out a missing persons."

He said that so coolly. So calculatingly. It made my skin crawl.

"Why?" I asked. I saw Deputy Russell moving behind the sheriff, but I tried not to let my eyes wander. "Was it the will?"

"Oh, now, why should I tell you?"

"If you're going to kill me, you can at least let me know if I was halfway close," I said.

"Why do you care?" he asked with a smirk. "Try living in this century, woman. You might find that you like it."

The door behind me opened, and in walked Sherise Tyler. I jumped three feet and scuttled farther into the great room. Great. Both of my exits were no longer options. The steps were my only choice.

"Torie," she said. "I'm not going to hurt you."

"Which one of you killed her?" I asked, taking my first step up the long stairway.

"I didn't kill Clarissa," she said. "I could never do that."

"Oh, but your ex-husband did, and you were going to let him get away with it, weren't you?" I asked and took another couple of stairs.

"It's not like that," she said. "I swear. Tom and I were getting back together."

237

Sheriff Justice moved a few steps into the great room. Sherise looked at him nervously. "Tom, don't. You can't kill her."

"Why did Clarissa cut you out of the will?" I asked. As long as Sherise was willing to talk, I was going to ask questions. Anything to buy time until Dexter arrived.

"When Tom found out that he was Clarissa's great-grandson he tried to blackmail her," she said. "He had all of my notes and my research. I was pretty sure that Clarissa had killed my great-grandfather and MacLean. Thomas took that and went to Clarissa. He told her that he knew everything. He knew that he was the descendant of Gainsborough and that he wanted what he deserved."

"Shut up!" Sheriff Justice said. He threw the bat onto the floor, and pulled his gun out of his holster and leveled it at Sherise.

"Shut up, Sherise. Do as he says," I said. I liked him much better with the baseball bat.

"Clarissa bluffed him. Said if he did go to the police or to the newspapers, she would see to it he didn't get a dime. The old broad bluffed him and won," she said with a smile.

I took a few more steps up the stairs. "I don't know if you noticed or not, Sherise. But that really isn't the type of man you want to be intimate with."

"We sought therapy. He admitted he was wrong and that it was just years of living in poverty that drove him to blackmail her. I believed him," she said with a slight tremble in her voice. "Come down off the stairs, Torie. I'm not going to let him hurt you."

"Sorry. Don't believe you."

"He can shoot you from down here," she said.

"Well, at least he'll shoot me as I'm trying to get away," I said.

"Thomas, put that stupid gun away. What is wrong with you?" Sherise's eyes left mine to enforce what she was saying to her ex-husband but he had gone over to the deputy, who was waking up. "I swear, Torie, I didn't know he was going to kill Clarissa. We started seeing each other again. Somehow he found out, probably through Ollie, that I was set to inherit fifty thousand dollars. That's the only reason he tried to get back together with me. I didn't know that then."

"I feel for you, Sherise, really I do, but I sort of feel for myself right now a little bit more."

I peeked over the railing to see Sheriff Justice cuffing the deputy.

Sherise walked over to where the telephone was on the corner table and picked up the receiver. "When Clarissa found out that we were seeing each other again, she cut me out of the will. After what Tom had done, I don't blame her one bit. Thomas became enraged," she said as she dialed a number. "I guess he thought if Clarissa was dead and it looked like somebody else had done it, I wouldn't be the wiser and I'd still inherit my fifty grand if the new will disappeared."

She stopped a moment as she listened to whoever answered the phone on the other end. I took a few more steps up the stairs.

"Yes, could you send a squad car to the Panther Run Boardinghouse? There's been an accident. Officer down."

She hung up the phone without giving any of the information that I knew the 911 lady would want. Like who she was, et cetera. Sherise started to walk over to the stairs. I wasn't so sure I trusted her, since I hadn't

239

heard the other part of her 911 conversation. It didn't matter.

As she got three feet from the bottom of the stairs, her body was flung back with the force of the bullet that had just left the sheriff's gun. I turned and ran the rest of the way up the stairs. As I turned and looked down, I saw Sherise's bloody hand reach up and grab Sheriff Justice by the pants leg and drag him down. Somehow she grabbed his gun and they wrestled back and forth for it.

Sherise was smart, though. While the sheriff had her hand with the gun in it pinned over her head, she squeezed the trigger and shot the entire round into the baseboards. Then she threw the gun across the room. Sheriff Justice kicked her in the face, and she cried out in agony.

Then he headed up the stairs for me. Two at a time. In a matter of seconds I had to make a decision. Go toward the end of the hall and end up where? In one of the rooms with doors that he could kick in. Or I could go into the elevator, take it downstairs, and maybe get to Deputy Russell's gun before Sheriff Justice could make it down the stairs and through the great room.

I chose the elevator.

FORTY-ONE

THE COLD METAL DOORS OF THE ELEVATOR SHUT WITH a bang that echoed off the upstairs hallway. I hadn't intended to shut it that hard, but I did. I pushed the down button and pressed myself up against the inner wall trying to catch my breath. *Be calm. Be calm.*

The problem with this plan was now that I had actually committed to something, I had to go through with it. The elevator landed with a jerk and I reached out to open the inner door. Just as I opened the inner door, Sheriff Justice appeared from what seemed like thin air, and grabbed my left hand. I tried to twist and pull away, but it did no good. A tendon popped somewhere in my lower arm, shooting pain all the way back to my elbow.

He smiled a wicked smile at me and then I saw him reach down ever so slowly, almost in slow motion, and turn the lock on the outside elevator door. It was a sliding lock, not the dead bolt that you needed a key for. I was locked inside the elevator. *I was locked inside the elevator!*

This was not good.

Breathe. Breathe.

Sheriff Justice slowly walked away and disappeared out of sight. Where had he gone? Where was Dexter? I peered down the hallway and realized that I could no longer hear Danette's music. She had most likely heard the gunshots and turned off the stereo to see if indeed gunfire was what she had heard.

Stay in your room, girl. Stay in there.

I paced back and forth along the elevator floor, working my lower lip between my thumb and finger. Where had he gone? Where was the sheriff?

Deputy Russell's gun.

Oh, Jesus. I ran over to the Control Panel and punched the up button just as Sheriff Justice came around the corner, took aim, and fired his gun. The bullet ricocheted off the lower part of the elevator as it left the first floor. I cannot express how distressing the sound of a bullet ricocheting is. You're just going to have to trust me on this one.

Seconds crept by like minutes as I huddled in the

241

inside corner of the elevator waiting for the inevitable. He was going to come upstairs. Of course he would. I was crouched right beneath the control panel so that I could just reach up with my hand and push the down button. One time was all I'd get at this, and then he'd get smart and figure out where I was crouched. I had no choice. Anywhere else and I wouldn't be able to reach the panels.

Ticktock, ticktock. More time elapsed and still no sheriff. Then, as if I'd asked for it, I heard the swish of his uniform and I slammed the down button. Again, the bullet ricocheted, and this time it lodged in the wooden panel behind me. Oh, that was just way too close.

Now what? How long could I keep this up? How long could I stay one step ahead of him? He had the upper hand. He knew when the elevator was up or down. I had no idea where he was until he fired the gun.

Suddenly I reached up and pushed the up button, thinking that he'd be halfway down the stairs by now and I'd throw him off. As soon as the elevator clicked into the top floor, I started counting to ten and then bam! I hit the down button. I could only hope that he'd just reached the top step.

My heart pounded in my chest, and the blood rushed through my head like a freight train. *Just calm down and breathe*. That should be easy. All of the Lamaze lessons that I've taken? Why the hell couldn't I breathe?

My blood wouldn't stop rushing long enough for me to be able to listen. Hearing his uniform swoosh was what had saved me last time. I *had* to be able to hear. I took a few deep cleansing breaths and then closed my eyes and listened.

Nothing.

Nothing.

Then I heard the cock of the gun and I slammed the up button. God, I couldn't keep doing this.

I didn't have to do this forever, I reminded myself. Just until Dexter got here. Or until the sheriff ran out of bullets, but knowing him he had extras somewhere. Maybe Deputy Russell would wake up. But even if he did wake up, he was handcuffed, I reminded myself.

The elevator and I waited on the second floor for a very long time. The sheriff had to be getting wise to the fact that I could hear him. I was calculating his moves because he was making noise. He wouldn't keep making that mistake. He would eventually catch on and stop making noise.

Maybe he already had.

What to do? If I stayed here and he made no noise, he'd have me. I wished I had my purse with me. It was sitting on the dining room table. I had a compact in there. I might be able to see him if I had that with me. I had to do something. I couldn't just sit here. He was going to come after me and I had no way out of this blasted elevator!

I pushed the down button.

I pushed the down button and Sheriff Thomas Justice stood waiting for me as the elevator hit the floor. There was no way I could get the elevator to go back up before he could fire off a round or two. He had me.

Instead of a gunshot, the most peculiar sound came from the sheriff. A thud and then a moan, and then he fell to the floor. The gun made a very light double thump as it hit the floor and bounced.

"Torie?"

It was Danette.

I stood up, tears running down my face. "Oh, my God. Danette. Get me out of here."

Danette stood there with the baseball bat in her hand, tears streaming down her face, as well. I don't know which of us had more tears.

"Oh, Torie. I . . . I . . ." she said and hiccupped. "I watched him going up and down and the elevator going up and down and up and down. When he ran upstairs . . . that last time . . ." Hiccup. "I ran to go for help and saw the other deputy in there with the baseball"—hiccup—"bat."

"That's great. Tell me about it later, Danette. Please get me out of here. If you don't get me out of here I'm going to scream!"

I screamed that last part of the sentence and it got her attention. I was like a crazy woman with my hand wrapped around the bars on the elevator, shaking it. No, rather, I looked more like a chimpanzee. And I was going to start climbing the damn doors, pregnant and all, if she didn't get me out of here.

"Uh . . . where's the key?" she asked, and wiped her nose on the back of her hand.

"My purse. In the dining room."

I stood there and watched the sheriff as he lay unconscious the whole time it took Danette to get my key ring and get me out of the elevator. It was at that moment that Dexter Calloway came in, followed by the police and an ambulance. I would have only had to hold on three, four, five more minutes at the most, if Danette hadn't conked the sheriff on the head. I'm not sure I could have. I'd played all of my trump cards.

Three cheers for hormone-pumped teenagers who can't face reality.

FORTY-TWO

ELLIOTT STOOD ON THE STAIRS OF THE PANTHER RUN Boardinghouse waiting to see me off. I couldn't leave without seeing it again. I had to see it, with its rusted screens and cracked paint. I had to look out upon the lynching tree, the Gauley River running slowly behind it.

I loved West Virginia. It was the land of my forefathers, and their blood ran in me so deep that I knew this was home the minute I'd seen it for the first time as a child. It's peculiar the way things work. Southeast Missouri is my home, too. The home of my paternal ancestors. The place where I grew up. I am that plateau of high country on the edge of the Ozarks in Middle America. And yet, I am Appalachia, too.

I suppose it works the same way genetics work. You get your nose from your father and your eyes from your mother. An equal partnership. It's what makes us who we are.

I would miss this place. I knew that I wouldn't make it back here for another five or so years. And that left a big old ache inside of me.

"Elliott," I said. "It was a pleasure."

He reached down and gave me a big hug, careful not to squeeze my arm that was in a sling. "Next time you come to West Virginia, call first. I'll go on vacation and up my life insurance policy."

"Ha-ha," I said. "You weren't the one trapped inside the elevator."

Gert stepped out of the boardinghouse onto the front porch with Lafayette following close behind. She wore

245

a yellow flower in her hair that I'd seen Lafayette pick earlier in the morning. The bump on her head was almost gone.

My stuff was packed, even the things I had decided to keep from inside the boardinghouse. Dexter had packed them all up, safe and sound. Speaking of Dexter, he also made his appearance on the front porch.

"Nice meeting you, Mrs. O'Shea," he said and held out his hand. I shook it and smiled.

"Nice to meet you, too," I said.

"You sure you're not due for another six weeks or so? You look awfully big and you're carrying awfully low."

"Well, I suppose there is always the possibility that something somewhere got screwed up. I think I look so big because I'm short," I said.

"Well, have a safe trip. We'll see you again."

I nodded to him, although I wasn't sure if or when I'd ever see him again.

"So, we really did it, didn't we?" Elliott asked. "We really figured it out."

"Yes, we did. I can tell you that I couldn't have done it without you. You were awesome. You, the man," I said.

"Oh, yeah?" he asked. His chest puffed out about five inches and he smiled from ear to ear. After a moment of thought he spoke again. "What do you think will happen to Sherise Tyler?"

"You mean after she gets out of the hospital and finishes the umpteen reconstructive surgeries she's going to have to have done on her elbow? I'm not sure. She wasn't really an accomplice to the murder. She only suspected it was the sheriff, and what could she do? Go to the sheriff? I think she'll be all right," I said. "At least the deputy is okay. I mean, what's a concussion when he could have been floating in the river?"

I looked around, again. I tried to soak it all up to take home with me.

"Well, Gert, are you ready?" I asked.

"Yes," she said. "Get me the hell out of here."

I couldn't help but laugh at her, as did Dexter and Elliott. Lafayette didn't think it was very funny. Oh, and Lafayette had come forward and said that Edwin was the one who had conked my grandmother over the head. Lafayette had apologized profusely. Maribelle would barely look at us all morning. And Edwin? Well, Edwin was long gone. Who knew where he was?

We stepped down into the yard and had made it all the way to the car when Danette ran out of the house and ran over to the car. Of course she ran. The whole time I was here I don't think I saw her walk anywhere. She was always running.

She held her hand out and offered me something brightly colored. I took it and said, "What's this?"

"I just want you to know that you've given me faith that just because you're over thirty you don't have to be a big dork. You're the coolest," she said and hugged me.

I unfolded the brightly colored fabric and held it up. It was a tie-dyed maternity shirt.

"I made it myself," she said.

"Oh, Danette. I will cherish it always. I'll even wear it when I'm not pregnant," I said. And that was no lie, because with all of the weight that I was gaining, I probably wouldn't fit back into my normal clothes for another two years.

"Get in the car," Gert said. "I am never going anywhere with you again. Dragging me all over God's creation and getting me hit over the head. I coulda had a heart attack. And there's panthers and everything."

247

"See ya, everybody," I said and waved. Just as I was about to get in the car, I stopped and took a piece of paper out of my purse. I walked back to Elliott and handed it to him.

"What's this?"

"The boardinghouse. I'm signing it over to you."

"What?" he asked. "No . . . I can't—"

"Take it. Make me proud," I said. "Restore it. Besides, you may not thank me for it if turns out to be really cursed."

"I don't know what to say," he choked.

"That I'm welcome anytime?"

"You are welcome anytime," he said and hugged me again.

I was happy with that decision, I thought as I got in the car. Elliott had the same relationship to Bridie that I had, and he already lived in West Virginia. He was a family historian, too. He knew what he had and he'd take care of it. If I kept it, I would feel as though I had to be here, and I couldn't do that. I belonged in New Kassel. And I couldn't live with myself if I sold it and two years from now they built those cheap pop-up houses in some stupid subdivision named River's Bend Luxury Homes, or something. No, it was where it should be.

Twelve hours later, Gert and I had not sung one song, nor had we played a single round of I'm Hiding Behind the Color . . . The trip home had been quiet. Reflective. I'd learned so much during my visit. So much about coal mining and life in the coal towns. I'd always known my family members were miners, but I never really *knew,* if you know what I mean. I'd learned a lot about desperation. Desperate people in desperate situations will do very desperate things.

I let out a huge sigh as the Gateway Arch and the St. Louis skyline came into view from the east side of the Mississippi. The Clarion Hotel the only round building sitting to the left, the riverboat casinos, all parallel-parked along the riverfront. New Kassel was just thirty or so minutes away. My home. My family. I was never leaving it again.

"Smooth sailing from here on, Gert," I said.

"Yup," she answered.

"Oh, my God."

"What?" she asked.

"I think my water just broke."

AUTHOR'S NOTE

I decided it was time to address the most popular question I get asked: Where is New Kassel? I thought long and hard when I started to write the first book in this series, *Family Skeletons*, about where the series should take place and decided it would be better if the setting was fictitious. New Kassel and Granite County do not exist. Nor do Wisteria, Partut County, or Progress. My inspiration for New Kassel can be found in Missouri's historic river towns, like Hannibal, Herman, Ste. Genevieve, Kimmswick, and St. Charles. Part of the reason I made this a fictitious place is because I can do so much more with it. I can place an ice cream shop anywhere I want. I don't have to be concerned if I accidentally pick a name that belonged to a real person from an actual place. Which brings me to the town in this book, Panther Run, West Virginia. For the same reason, the town and the town's coal company are both fictitious as well. The boardinghouse is architecturally based on the old Beech Glen boardinghouse located in Beech Glen, West Virginia, which was falling down and in disrepair when I saw it in the mid-1980's. The area along the Gauley and New River is real, however, and is, in fact, the land covered during Mary Draper Ingles's infamous escape from the Shawnee in the 1750s.

A note on the issue of coal mining: The miners of the early twentieth century led a very hard life, working sunup to sundown with no hope of a better life. I was humbled when I realized my great-grandfather, a slew of great uncles, my great-great-grandfather, and a

250

plethora of other male and female relatives lived in those conditions during hard times. Some of the anecdotes in this book come from my family. If you are interested in learning further about the life of the coal miner, you might rent the movie *Matewan,* a John Sayles film that accurately depicts the coal miner's predicament in southern West Virginia. Also, see the following books: *Images of Appalachian Coalfields* by Builder Levy; *Where the Sun Never Shines: A History of America's Bloody Coal Industry* by Priscilla Long; *Lament for the Molly Maguires* by Arthur H. Lewis; *Hillbilly Women* by Kathy Kahn; and *Life, Work, Rebellion in the Coal Fields* by David Corbin.

I hope you will all forgive me for venturing out of New Kassel and join me for Torie's next adventure, which will have her back home with the whole cast of characters you all have come to know.

—Rett MacPherson

Dear Reader:

I hope you enjoyed reading this Large Print mystery. If you are interested in reading other Beeler Large Print Mystery titles or any other Beeler Large Print titles, ask your librarian or write to me at

Thomas T. Beeler, *Publisher*
Post Office Box 659
Hampton Falls, New Hampshire 03844

You can also call me at 1-800-818-7574 and I will send you my latest catalogue.

Audrey Lesko chooses the titles I publish in Large Print. Our aim is to provide good books by outstanding authors—books we both enjoyed reading and liked well enough to want to share. We warmly welcome any suggestions for new titles and authors.

Sincerely,